Praise for Th

"A novel so real I kept expecting one of the characters to text me. A poignant, honest look at a single cataclysmic event and the changes, the growth, and the recoveries that follow. You will think about *The Last Birthday Party* long after the final page."

- W. Bruce Cameron, #1 *New York Times* bestselling author of *A Dog's Purpose*

"Gary Goldstein is a consummate storyteller, a master at combining humor with depth. In this delightful book, we really care about his characters as we try to anticipate what's coming next. It's a page turner with surprises around every corner. I highly recommend this book to anyone who wants to read a story that is warm, uplifting, and rewarding."

- Andrea Cagan, author of *Diana Ross: Secrets of a Sparrow* and *A Friendly Guide to Writing and Ghostwriting*

"Goldstein's crackling wit makes his debut novel an absolute joy. His characters are wonderfully drawn; by the end they feel like old friends. Come for the frothy plot and zippy writing, stay for the heartfelt storytelling and deliciously satisfying ending. A refreshing and uplifting read, highly recommend!"

- Susan Walter, author of *Good as Dead*

"A wonderful read: fun, insightful, and surprising right up to the last page. I found the inner life of our protagonist not only entertaining but thought provoking. Do not miss this party!"

- Robin Riker, author of *A Survivor's Guide to Hollywood*

"The adjectives 'hilarious' and 'painful' have never been so seamlessly married as they are in the pages of Gary Goldstein's new novel, *The Last Birthday Party*, an achingly funny love letter to 'midlife' in all its anxiety, anguish, and awe. I loved it."

- David Dean Bottrell, author of *Working Actor*

THE
LAST
Birthday
PARTY

a novel

GARY GOLDSTEIN

HADLEIGH HOUSE
PUBLISHING

Hadleigh House Publishing
Minneapolis, MN
www.hadleighhouse.com

Cover design by Alisha Perkins

ISBN-978-1-7357738-1-0
ISBN-978-1-7357738-2-7 (ebook)
LCCN: 2021903652

For Bill,

who never threw me a birthday party I didn't want.

So if you're tired of the same old story
Oh, turn some pages ...

- REO Speedwagon

CHAPTER
1

JEREMY KNEW THE birthday party was a bad idea. He just didn't know how bad.

First of all, fifty did not seem like something to celebrate. Endure, maybe. Elude, definitely. Lie about, well, Jeremy wasn't big on lying. "It's easier just to tell the truth," he'd contend whenever Cassie wanted to concoct some excuse for, say, begging off dinner with the neighbors. But lie about this? Maybe, yeah. Either way, throwing a party and inviting most everyone they knew seemed like asking for trouble.

"Did anyone ever tell you you're a stick-in-the-mud?" Cassie asked when he swatted away her notion of a "Jeremy's turning the big five-o" bash, well-meaning as it may have been. (It wasn't, actually, it was something completely else—which he would soon find out.)

"No, babe, only you," Jeremy responded, attempting to sound light and unbothered, which, it may go without saying, he did not.

But really, what did his wife expect? She was the one who liked being the center of attention, not him. She was the one who was always first to sing karaoke at any party while he'd rather hide behind the drapes or under a table. She was the one who would wave into the TV cameras if they were walking past a movie premiere (this was L.A., after all), while he would suddenly have to tie his shoe. She was the one who would talk in her outside voice when she wanted to prove a point indoors (like restaurant or movie theater indoors),

9

while Jeremy would have used ASL to argue if he only knew how to sign. He was also the first to admit Cassie was who you wanted on your side in a fight.

Maybe *she* wanted a birthday party. Maybe *she* wanted to celebrate the smack-dab middle of her own life; middle, that is, if one were going to live to be a hundred, which, at that moment, just sounded exhausting. The only problem: Cassie was going to be forty-nine, and who throws a birthday party with all the trimmings for turning forty-nine? In truth, Cassie would have—would have every year—if Jeremy would've let her. Also in truth, he *was* a bit of a stick-in-the-mud.

But not enough, apparently, because Cassie convinced him to have a party, convinced him fifty was a milestone to be commemorated, not ignored. And, much as he may want to let the day come and go without anyone knowing how old he was—and was it really that old in the scheme of things?—Cassie reminded him that no one's age was a secret anymore.

Cassie also promised she wouldn't go overboard, just close friends and family, their backyard, a Sunday afternoon if Saturday night felt too serious. Hell, she'd even cook instead of cater so Jeremy wouldn't worry about the money. To which Jeremy thought, as he always did, *well, somebody has to worry.* But he didn't say it because, y'know, stick, mud.

Still, something felt off about the whole thing. And if Jeremy learned anything in his, yikes, forty-nine years and forty-seven weeks, it was to trust his instincts. First thought that flies into your head about something: Pay attention. Listen. Act. He was rarely wrong about those pesky red flags, those instant warning signs that went right to his stomach. But he was also happy to admit if he was wrong, relieved when the shit didn't hit the fan—or at least didn't hit it as hard as he expected.

This was not one of those times.

First of all, Saturday night won out, with Cassie deeming the event "too special for a Sunday," steamrollering her original selling points and boxing in Jeremy, who decided not to put on the gloves for that one.

Second, "close friends and family" somehow morphed into everyone Jeremy and Cassie had ever met, or at least that's how it felt to someone (like Jeremy) who didn't want a party to begin with. Who was there? Joyce, Jeremy's mom (dad: dead, more later), still a force of nature at eighty-four; his and Cassie's son, Matty, and Matty's new boyfriend, Sven (or was it Lars?); Cassie's parents, the cranky Rhea and contrary Henry (Cassie's adjectives, not Jeremy's, he rather liked them. "*You* didn't grow up with them," Cassie would counter); Jeremy's editor, Lucien, and Lucien's third wife, Bonita; Cassie's lawyer buddies Ella and Sunil and Ella's wife, Jasmine; Cassie's best friend since high school, Valeria, and her husband Norm, who was, one could say, Jeremy's best friend by marriage—or default—though, strangely, the four rarely did anything together; and Cassie and Jeremy's new next-door neighbors, Katie and Crash (real name: Cyrus. Wouldn't you change it, too?), who were young enough to be their children (well, if Cassie got pregnant in high school).

Oh, and about fifty other people, which was around forty-five more than Jeremy would have liked—and forty-five fewer than Cassie would have liked, so, in her mind, she had compromised. "Is everyone's marriage such a tug-of-war?" wondered the rope-burned Jeremy. Cassie never had to ask; she knew the answer was an unequivocal yes and so be it.

Without Jeremy's knowledge (Cassie knew he'd balk and she was right), invites went out to second-tier friends and neighbors, random cousins and coworkers, and assorted acquaintances (yoga classmates for Cassie, fellow film critics for Jeremy). Looking around the party, Jeremy could swear he didn't know—or didn't want to know—three-quarters of them.

Needless to say, Cassie didn't cook that night. Bristol Farms did. And delivered, set up, served, and bartended. (Maybe the bartender, a tattooed hunk with a heavy hand, was a separate line item. Jeremy never got to ask.) And the gathering, which nominally began in their backyard, soon swelled, spread, and snaked throughout the house.

11

There was music—a deejay friend of Matty's did the honors and appropriately played a lot of early MTV hits—but, to Jeremy and, it should be said, only Jeremy, it all seemed ridiculously over the top. That night, he felt way older than his fifty years, especially when he realized his mother spent about quadruple the time on the make-shift dance floor as he did. The good news: there was no karaoke.

Jeremy, despite the two-drink limit he'd self-imposed ages ago following an incident involving mescal shooters and a reunion of his writing students, kept topping off his wine glass all night. This, Jeremy later learned, did not make him the most amenable host, even if he did manage to banter with lots of people, most of whom wanted to know if he'd seen any good movies lately, perhaps his least favorite question: he'd instantly blank on every recent film title as if his reviews had been written in disappearing ink.

The other prevailing question that night was, "Are you okay?" which any remotely self-conscious person can tell you is a surefire road to feeling not okay. Somewhere along the way it also occurred to the birthday boy that he and his wife had not spoken to each other the entire night and, when they finally did interact, it didn't go well. Something about Jeremy seeming ungrateful, which, he'd be the first to tell you—and not proudly, mind you—he was.

What kind of asshole doesn't appreciate the kind of effort put out on his behalf whether he wanted a party or not? That might have remained an existential—and, let's face it, totally fair—question had Cassie not verbalized it just so the second the last guest exited their backyard. By then, it was also a contest as to which of the lovebirds had drunk more that night, with Cassie, as usual, holding her liquor better than Jeremy by a tipsy mile. This didn't make for the most coherent or effective arguing, which may be why Jeremy, to this day, remains kinda hazy about their fight.

Had he known how pivotal it would be, he might have struggled to pay more attention to her words, instead of stumbling back into the house, locking the den door behind him, dropping onto the couch, and passing out into a dead man's sleep.

The next morning, Cassie was gone.

CHAPTER
2

NOT LIKE GONE to the store or to yoga or to the office for a Sunday emergency, but clothes gone, jewelry gone, photos gone, and French press and milk frother (really?) gone. This, of course, took Jeremy awhile to realize, much less process, arising as he did at an ungodly late 10 a.m. and frankly surprised to find he was still in his party clothes. His body felt like he'd been hit by a truck, but, it turned out, that truck was idling beyond the den door, waiting to finish him off altogether.

The kitchen looked exceptionally clean, given the mountain of celebration-centric pots, pans, dishes, glasses, serving trays, and utensils that, if Jeremy remembered correctly, needed washing the night before. He didn't immediately spot the missing coffee maker and milk frother. Though he did peek into the refrigerator and thought there wasn't much food left given how much there seemed to be last night and that he needed to ask Cassie what the final Bristol Farms bill was, and weren't those sushi platters, which had been polished off before he ever got to them, a little extravagant?

Padding down the narrow rear hallway of the Laurel Canyon bungalow he and Cassie had bought in their third year of marriage using the proceeds from the one screenplay Jeremy ever sold as a down payment, it struck him how quiet it was, not even the usual hardwood floor creaks heralding his arrival into the master bedroom.

"Cassie? Cas-sie?" He knocked on the closed bathroom door, called for her again, but there was silence. Jeremy gently opened the door. Nothing to see but his electric shaver still recharging where he'd plugged it in the afternoon before. It didn't yet hit him that a circle of water on the shower shelf remained where Cassie's bottle of tea tree oil shampoo normally stood.

He walked back into the bedroom and that's where he saw it, taped to the full-length mirror on the walk-in closet door: a note in Cassie's loopy, slightly exaggerated script:

I love you but I can't live with you. We are not good for each other anymore. Do not call or text or try to find me. I'm sorry and I hope you are too.

Jeremy peered at the message as if its words might rearrange themselves to say something far more innocuous. But they stubbornly hung there like little stick pins ready to gouge out his eyes should he get any closer.

I'm sorry and I hope you are too. Tug-of-war. He reflexively backed away and let this terrible and not so entirely shocking news wash over him.

The party.

Shards of their argument began to ricochet around his cobwebby head, adjectives like "selfish" and "dismissive" and "impossible" echoing about, though Jeremy couldn't be sure who said what. They were, after all, words that could apply to either one of them. Still, given that he was the one left sitting there alone, it was a good bet he was the recipient of said invectives. Deservedly so, he might add. But enough to drive Cassie to simply up and leave?

Jeremy fell back onto the pillows, the pillows he and Cassie shared on the bed they'd shared for years and years, he on the right side, she on the left, never once switching sides, seemingly happy in their prescribed spaces. Happy? More like habitually content, how's that? Not good enough, clearly. He stretched his legs, threw the down comforter, that heavy-ass monster, over his chilled body and huddled into its warmth. His teeth chattered like he'd been dipped in ice and, for a flash, Jeremy felt like his heart might actually stop.

But the feeling passed as quickly as it appeared and, as he tried to conjure up more of his dreamlike battle with Cassie, he once again gave in to sleep.

"Dad, what's going on? Did I wake you?" It was Matty calling, waking his father, who had grabbed his phone off his bedside table.

Jeremy focused. "What time is it?"

"I don't know, eleven something. Dad, I got this weird text from Mom. Is she okay?"

Jeremy glanced at the note still dangling from the closet door mirror, unreadable from the bed, but its meaning as clear and confusing as ever.

"What did it say?" asked Jeremy.

"Don't worry about me, just call your father. I'll be in touch."

"That's it?" Jeremy sat up, swallowed hard, his mouth tasting like a melted spoon. He got out of bed and started walking in circles.

"Dad, is she there? Would you put her on?"

"She is decidedly not here." Circle, circle, breath. "Honey, I think your mother left me."

Jeremy still called his adult son "honey," a holdover from when Matty was a little boy, the most beautiful and magical child one could imagine, at least to his adoring parents. There was a "honey" moratorium right after Matty's bar mitzvah, at the thirteen-year-old's request ("Dad, it's weird!"), but it slipped back into Jeremy's patter a few years later without comment or incident.

"Are you fucking kidding me?" asked Matty, voice rising with each word.

"No, son, I don't believe I am."

"Fuck. Are you okay? Dad, you *were* kinda hammered last night, you know that?"

"I do know. I know a lot of things now."

"And Mom's really not there?"

"Want me to text you a copy of the note she left me?"

"No, I want to see it in person. See *you* in person. I'll be right over." Matty hung up before Jeremy could protest.

"**Mom seemed so** happy at the party," Matty recalled when he arrived an hour later. "She danced with me twice, Sven once, and then the two of us together."

So his name *was* Sven. Jeremy couldn't keep up. His son was, to be charitable, a serial dater, which, at twenty-three, wasn't the worst thing. But like so much else with Matty, he had a little fol-low-through problem with relationships. Fortunately, he was so charismatic, confident, and effortlessly handsome that his boy-friends seemed to overlook his lack of romantic longevity just to be in his sphere for as long as it lasted. Still, as Jeremy took no pleasure in predicting, the tables might one day turn on Matty, and it'd be quite the rude awakening.

"I didn't want the party, you know."

"Well, that kinda sucks, doesn't it? I mean, it was a lot of work for her, right?" Matty shook two Equals into the coffee Jeremy brewed up in their drip coffeemaker in lieu of the French press that had taken its leave along with his wife of twenty-five years.

"Talk to me when *you* turn fifty, kiddo." Jeremy sat across from Matty at the glass kitchen table he and Cassie had had since their first apartment, a cramped if sunny love nest in Silver Lake. Look at all those scratches, he thought. Why had they never replaced it? Did it have some sentimental value Jeremy had no memory of? Were they just too lazy to change it? Maybe *he* might have been, but not Cassie. She was the least lazy person Jeremy had ever known. "No grass grows under that one's feet," his mother noted after just one lunch with her future daughter-in-law. It stood to reason, then, that Cassie would be the one to exit their marriage, but why did it take so long?

"Dad, are you freaked out? I mean, Mom's just fucking with you, isn't she?"

"Fucking with me?"

Jeremy and Cassie rarely censored their son, let him be and say and do what came to mind. But it still jarred Jeremy when Matty talked to him like one of his buddies, even if Matty considered his father—and his mother, only slightly less so—as much a friend as a parent.

"You read her note. You know as much as I do." Jeremy sipped some coffee. It was surprisingly smooth. He never liked that French press, so why did he continue to use it?

"Yeah, I doubt that," said Matty, eyeballing his coffee cup. "Is there any almond milk? I'm done with dairy."

"We have almonds and we have milk. That's it." Jeremy knew Matty, ice cream maven that he was, would be back on dairy before next weekend. The kid was lucky he worked out like a fiend, the one thing he *was* consistent about. "And what do you mean you 'doubt that?'"

"I mean, these things don't just happen overnight. Not really, right?" Matty swallowed his black coffee and grimaced. He glanced at his father. "Dad, I lived with the two of you for twenty-one years. I saw stuff, so I have my opinions but ... well, only you and Mom can really know."

Jeremy gazed into his cup, not sure he really knew much of anything at the moment, his thoughts a maze of good times and bum times (hat tip to Sondheim) with the woman who he once couldn't properly breathe without, the extroverted yin to his more circumspect yang, a force long the conduit to all things good and meaningful. And just like that: a ghost.

"Every couple goes through ... things, it doesn't mean they have to split up over it," said Jeremy, more to himself than to his son. He sounded detached and unconvincing.

"Dad, did you even try to call her?"

"She told me not to." Jeremy looked away from Matty's penetrating gaze: flummoxed, judgmental, sympathetic. Jeremy hated disappointing anyone, especially his boy, but he did so anyway.

"This would seem like a good time not to follow instructions," Matty told his father, pushing away his cup.

"Did *you* call her?" Jeremy asked in a challenge as he studied his son. Matty was a perfect cross between his parents: Jeremy's rangy height, Roman nose, floppy carob-brown hair (getting grayer on Jeremy by the month); Cassie's blue-green eyes, olive skin, full lips. Matty's toothy smile was all his own doing.

"A text like that? Of course I called her," Matty answered. "I got voicemail."

"We had a fight. After the party," said Jeremy. "I don't remember a lot about it, I was—"

"Shitfaced, I know. You were pounding that Pinot like crazy. What was up with that, Mr. Two-Drink Maximum?" Matty grabbed his coffee cup off the table, splashed some cow milk into it, and took a more satisfying swallow.

"It seemed like the best way to get through the night," Jeremy admitted. And, apparently, end a marriage.

"Well, I thought it was a really fun party. And so did Sven, who's not a big party guy." Matty took a seat again, glanced at his cell, slipped it in a pocket. "You must have some idea why she took off. And isn't the *guy* supposed to move out? I mean, in a hetero marriage?" Matty snuck another look at his phone, smiled this time, tapped a few keys. Jeremy watched his son, envious; he was so much less complicated, more guileless than either of his parents. Was it generational or … accidental?

"I guess it depends how much the woman wants out," answered Jeremy, realizing the thought, like so many others, hadn't yet crossed his mind.

"But you *are* gonna call Mom, yes?"

Jeremy was silent, had absolutely no immediate idea.

"No, Dad, seriously, you two have to talk. I mean, like, this is major."

"Gee, ya think?" Jeremy was instantly sorry for the sarcasm; his son was just trying to help a helpless situation. "Sorry, honey, I'm really at a loss right now." Jeremy rose, poured himself a second cup of coffee, his hands shaking—and not imperceptibly.

Matty studied his father. "You're in shock, Pop, I get it. Just let it sink in and, you know, figure out what to do, because you can't do nothing."

"I don't know, nothing sounds pretty good right now."

Matty drained his coffee cup. "I gotta go. Meeting Sven at the gym. It's leg day." He struck a mock pained expression, which made

Jeremy laugh in spite of himself. "Unless you need me to stay, for moral support or, I don't know, to make sure you don't do something stupid."

"Looks like you're too late for that, kiddo."

Matty grabbed his dad in a bear hug. Jeremy pulled the kid in close, held onto him for dear life, then kissed his forehead and sent him on his way.

Whatever Jeremy and Cassie may have done wrong, they did one thing right.

CHAPTER
3

JEREMY THOUGHT ABOUT what Matty had said, about this not being the time to follow instructions, specifically Cassie's. So after bits of lunch cobbled together from the Bristol Farms leftovers—Jeremy had to admit the Cajun shrimp was pretty great (Was it wrong that he even had an appetite?)—he decided to call Cassie. What was she going to do, just disappear off the face of the earth? She had a son, parents, a younger sister (okay, living in Santa Fe with her sculpturing spouse, but still), a job, coworkers, friends and, much as she might like to think otherwise, a husband, soon-to-be-ex though he may be. She had to resurface and, one would guess, soon. Then again, if Cassie wanted attention—and the lady liked her share—this was a good way to get it.

Jeremy had no idea what he was going to say if she answered, though he figured he was entitled to pretty much any civil question given her uncivil departure. But, like Matty, Jeremy got Cassie's voicemail, on which she sounded far too bubbly given the turn of events. (What, did he expect she'd swap out her greeting for something glum and remorseful?) He was about to leave a message, say *something*, for God's sake, but got weirdly self-conscious and tongue-tied and hung up. *Fuck*, Jeremy thought, *she'll see my number under Missed Calls anyway.* That was stupid.

No, Jeremy realized, what was stupid was that he had spent half his life with this woman—more than half, they were together two years before the wedding—knew a million little things about her, things he was certain he and only he knew, and he was standing there frozen with the phone still in his unsteady hand. Fuck that, he thought, and started to dial Cassie again—until he stopped midway and put down the phone altogether. Matty was right: Jeremy was in shock. He didn't know what the hell he was doing.

Still, he thought, he should probably call someone else, *tell* someone else. Like his mother? She'd have something smart and fair to say, as usual. No, he didn't want to involve her just yet. Though maybe he'd feel better—or at least feel something. It helped to talk to Matty, didn't it? He should've told Matty to stick around, forgo the gym, keep his old man company. But that wasn't Jeremy's style. He hated asking people for things, even those closest to him, always preferring to do for himself, never wanting to put others out. It's how he became so handy with a toolbox: Why bug someone else when you could do it yourself?

Cassie, who certainly had her own self-sufficient streak, said people sometimes thought Jeremy was a little detached, a little cool—and not in a laidback or hip way either. But it didn't seem to bother her. She'd even flagged it as a plus soon after they first met that unusually balmy October night outside the New Beverly Cinema, a storied revival theater on a busy stretch of L.A.'s Beverly Boulevard. Jeremy had gone by himself to see a double bill of *Risky Business* and *Fast Times at Ridgemont High*, two of his favorite movies from childhood that he'd never actually seen in a theater. Cassie was just walking past on her way, he'd later learn, to a yoga class being held at a nearby studio.

Jeremy was about to buy his ticket when he saw this attractive, lissome woman moving toward him. She didn't look like a moviegoer; maybe it was her athletic wear or the purposeful way she bounded up the block with barely a glance at the film nerds and hipsters swirling around the box office. Their eyes met and she stopped short in front of Jeremy, gave him a once-over and asked, "What's playing?"

"*Risky Business* and *Fast Times at Ridgemont High*," Jeremy said, pointing at the display posters.

"You're paying to see *those*?" she asked with no small amount of incredulity. "How old are they now, anyway?"

"1982 and 1983," Jeremy answered, checking out her honey blonde ponytail and glowing skin, but caught himself before his gaze made its way any further south. "Ever seen them?"

"I think so, somewhere along the line. *Risky Business* is the one with the Porsche, right?"

"Accept no substitutes," Jeremy said with a sly grin. She smiled back, maybe got the reference, maybe not. "Do you like movies?" he asked, just to keep things going, though anyone who wasn't totally sure they saw a movie as memorable as *Risky Business* couldn't be much of a film fan.

She studied Jeremy, with his thick, longish hair; three-day growth, soulful eyes, and USC film school sweatshirt. "Not as much as you, I'm guessing."

"Yeah, I'm kind of a die-hard."

"I should probably see more movies. Y'know, new movies. Just to … keep up." Glancing at the movie posters, the shrinking ticket line, then back at Jeremy, she moved in a step closer.

"I wholeheartedly recommend it." Even Jeremy, self-effacer that he was, could tell she was dawdling. Okay, he had his opening. Did he want to take it? My God, look at her—did he even have to ask? He could feel the window closing. Don't think, man, act! As his pulse raced and his breath shortened he made his move. "We should go some time."

"When?" she asked, with a slight challenge in her voice Jeremy found both startling and startlingly sexy.

He took a stab. "This Sunday?"

"What do you want to see?" Another challenge?

Jeremy scanned the living movie guide permanently lodged in his head.

"Have you seen *The Joy Luck Club*?"

As she considered the title, Jeremy wondered if she'd even heard of it. Should he have picked something more fun, more mindless?

"No, have you?" she asked.

"I did, yeah. But I'd see it again. It was great." It *was* worth a second viewing. But what she didn't need to know was that Jeremy never took a first date to a film he hadn't already seen; he didn't want any on-screen surprises to spoil the mood. In high school, he'd taken a girl he wanted to impress to see the teen-vampire flick *The Lost Boys*—it sounded cool, everyone was going to see it. But the movie was kinda icky in parts (who knew his date had an aversion to worms?) and she asked to go home immediately afterward. He never made *that* mistake again.

"It was that good, huh?"

Jeremy nodded a categorical yes. "You should definitely see it."

A knowing smile crossed the woman's lovely, heart-shaped face, her eyes glinting in the marquee's shimmery lights.

"Let me rephrase that," Jeremy said, with an uncharacteristic charge of confidence. "You should definitely see it with me."

"It might help if I knew your name. Just in case I need to call you something."

"I'm Jeremy." He extended a hand. It hung there as the woman in the athletic wear considered it as if sensing at some primal level that what happened next might inform the rest of her life.

She grasped Jeremy's hand, shaking it with firm self-assurance. "Cassandra. Cassie."

Cassie pulled a pen and a register tape from her shoulder bag and handed them over. "Give me your number, I'll call you," she said.

Jeremy, slightly dazed, wondered if he shouldn't have been taking *her* number or if that even mattered. He scribbled his digits on the back of the Rite Aid receipt.

She studied his phone number as if memorizing it, then looked up. "I'm late for yoga," she realized, indicating a spot up the street, "but I'll call you tomorrow."

"Yeah, that's what they all say," joked Jeremy.

"I don't," Cassie answered, dead serious. She brightened and took off down the block.

Jeremy turned to the box office, took out his wallet to buy his ticket, but went home instead. Suddenly real life felt far more relevant.

CASSIE DID CALL Jeremy the following day. They made plans to see *The Joy Luck Club* in Westwood Village near UCLA. "I read up on it," she said, "it sounds good." He offered to pick her up at her West Hollywood apartment, but Cassie said no, she'd just meet him at the theater.

"Nothing personal," she assured him.

"How can it be personal when you don't even know me?" Jeremy retorted.

"Exactly," she said.

It was a good thing Jeremy *had* already seen the film since he couldn't concentrate all that well. He spent as much time watching Cassie in cagey side glances as he did the movie, fascinated by how she sat in her seat, held her head, gazed at the screen, or expelled little sighs at the film's more touching moments. To Jeremy, just observing Cassie was worth the price of admission. Jesus, what was happening to him?

After, Jeremy suggested they get a drink, but Cassie asked if they couldn't just take a walk around Westwood Village; she hadn't had any exercise that day and was feeling guilty.

"If that's the case, I should feel guilty every day of my life," he joked.

Cassie didn't laugh, just eyeballed Jeremy, who certainly looked fit enough, at least to the naked eye.

"Like what you see, or are you thinking about what gym I should join?" he asked, wondering, perhaps for the first time, if he *should* join a gym.

"If I didn't like what I saw, we wouldn't be here to begin with," Cassie said, with that slight challenge in her voice that held far more charm than churl. She punctuated the comment with a sexy head tilt and fleeting smile. Jeremy was entranced. "Still," she continued, "I think everyone should join a gym. Or work out somewhere, some way. We won't be in our twenties forever, you know?" She got that right.

They walked and talked about the movie, how she loved it and now wanted to read the book. They discussed their work: he was a freelance film journalist writing a screenplay, she was training to become a paralegal (which wouldn't have been Jeremy's first guess). They chatted about their politics: both had high hopes for Bill Clinton's first term, though she was a bit wary; and their romantic histories: he hadn't dated anyone seriously since college, she happily ended a long-term thing six months ago and hadn't been looking (which felt "mixed signals-ish" to Jeremy). As for astrological signs, Jeremy was a Taurus, Cassie was a Gemini; they were born exactly one year and one month apart. He'd turned twenty-three that year; she was twenty-two. God, they were young. Maybe too young for the journey they were about to take.

Three dates and one sleepover later, Cassie revealed to Jeremy what had kept her coming back. "You're a little mysterious," she said. "A little reserved, but not in a geeky way. You're not one of those men who has to tell you everything about himself from the jump. You have no idea how many of those guys I've met—they're exhausting."

Jeremy went with it, figured "reserved" was okay with him, if it was okay with her. He purposely failed to explain that he was basically shy and self-conscious, which, frankly, is not as sexy as "mysterious."

"Oh," she added, "and you don't seem needy, which, let me tell you, is *such* a relief. You're not, are you?"

"A relief?" He knew what she was asking but needed a second to figure out a truthful answer.

"Needy."

"Are *you*?" He was still stalling.

"A little. But not in typical girly ways, if you know what I mean."

He didn't really—and didn't want to touch the comment with a ten-foot pole. All Jeremy knew was that Cassie seemed refreshingly independent and confident but also a tad elusive. Who was he try-ing to fool? He was nuts about her.

"I have needs but I'm not needy," Jeremy finally answered. "Does that make sense?"

It apparently did. They were inseparable from that moment on.

CHAPTER
4

SITTING ALONE IN the dark, pondering his predicament, it hit Jeremy that he had a review to file the next morning, a Monday, for a film oddly opening on a Tuesday (instead of the usual Friday or occasional Wednesday). Worse, it was the umpteenth Holocaust documentary he'd covered since he'd started writing for the *Times*—the *Los Angeles Times*, not the *New York Times*, as some of his snobbier East Coast film friends would have preferred.

Since he was one of two *Times'* reviewers of the Jewish persuasion, Jeremy was often assigned movies involving the travails of his religious brethren, the State of Israel (and by extension Palestinian issues), the Holocaust (pre-, during, post-, post-post-) and most any indie comedy or dramedy (it's a real word, look it up) about a wacky, dysfunctional Jewish family because, really, is there any other kind? In fact, there was and, for better and worse, Jeremy got to review lots of those cuckoo-clan films, too.

Anyway, the Holocaust. Not exactly what Jeremy felt like dipping back into at this very moment; he didn't feel like watching any movie, much less writing about it. He just wanted to sit in the shadowy living room and break his two-drink limit for the second time in as many days.

Jeremy never blew a review deadline, and he wasn't starting now. But he needed some kind of brain-numbing to force himself in front of his laptop to watch the viewing link sent by the film's publicist.

And since he didn't have any weed (he rarely did, was never really a fan), alcohol it was.

He rooted around for a bottle of red but could only find two rosés and a half-empty, uncorked chardonnay. Not unlike the left-over food, there was a curious lack of surplus wine. Who knows, maybe he'd polished it all off the night before. Not interested in the available grape choices, Jeremy considered a belt of the hard stuff. Hmm ... When was the last time he'd had scotch? Maybe with his Dewar's-drinking dad who'd been gone six years (attacked by his own heart, imagine that).

Jeremy flashed on his old man, Larry, a blustery, impatient guy who ran hot and cold about people and things but could also be funny and sentimental and would have walked through fire for his wife and son. Jeremy felt a weird pang for his father, wondered how *he* would have handled what just happened with Cassie (not that Joyce would have ever left Larry—she worshipped him, may-be more than she should have). His dad always loved Cassie, their big personalities enlivening rather than embattling each other. She called him "Lar-dog," he called her "Cat's Meow." They had their own language. Jeremy always thought she gravitated toward his spirited father because she didn't have the closest relationship with her own stodgier dad; Cassie was like the daughter Larry never had and maybe always wanted, though he'd never admit that.

Okay, a drink to Dad. Jeremy tried to reach the scotch, which lived on the tippy-top shelf of a kitchen cabinet with the other booze that Cassie stashed up there and out of the way. In reality, they were the only shelves tall enough to accommodate liquor bottles. But as Jeremy climbed their old stepladder and grabbed the Dewar's, he lost his balance and took a tumble, landing on the floor with his right arm splayed out over his head.

The bottle landed with a thud and, miraculously, didn't break. Jeremy, on the other hand, felt shortness of breath and instant pain. He laid on the cold tile for a minute until he was able to get up, his breathing returning to normal. Jeremy's shoulder throbbing, he took a seat at the kitchen table and rested. Finally, he rose again, picked the bottle off the floor, poured himself a few fingers over ice, and took a gulp.

As the amber liquid did its little burning act, Jeremy thought again of his father and how they never got to say goodbye. By the time Jeremy and Cassie made it to the hospital (his mother called him frantically in the middle of the night), Larry was gone. What would their last words have been? What pearls of wisdom would his departing dad have left him with? What did Jeremy wish he could have said? What would he say now if he had the chance?

He felt like such a giant fuckup: not because he hadn't made it to Cedars-Sinai fast enough to bid a final farewell to his dad, but because Cassie couldn't live with him anymore, didn't want him in her life. How could he have let that happen? How *did* it happen? They were good people, weren't they? A little self-absorbed and thoughtless sometimes, yes, but also responsible, reliable, and well-meaning. And good parents—no, very good parents. Jeremy took another slug of Dewar's and considered this, his head getting fuzzy from the booze.

He composed himself and imagined his father's voice: "You think women like Cassie grow on trees, son? Don't let her get away, you'll regret it for the rest of your life."

Jeremy didn't "let" Cassie do anything, she did it all by herself, but Jeremy got his dead father's point. He grabbed his phone; this time, he'd leave a message. Or maybe she'd actually answer and they could talk things out. Civilly, like adults.

Jeremy finished his drink in one stiff, piercing swig and rubbed his aching shoulder. He hit redial and clenched his teeth as the phone rang. Shit, voicemail.

"Cassie, it's me, are you there?" he asked, realizing that even if she was, she couldn't hear him. It wasn't like the old answering machines. What was wrong with him?

"Anyway," he continued, "it's me ... Jeremy. Look, I know you're upset, I know I was kind of a jerk last night about the party, but you can't just walk out. This is ridiculous. We need to talk, okay? I'm here, call me, would you? Please?"

Jeremy gazed into the bits of melted ice left in his highball glass, wondering if he should have another. He also wondered when he'd hear back from Cassie, *if* he'd hear back from her. And where was she staying? At Ella's? Sunil's? Valeria's? With her parents? No, that was doubtful. Jeremy couldn't imagine they'd ever be her first choice for comfort, though they did have a nice place, still living in the Mid-Wilshire house Cassie grew up in. (They'd make a killing if they sold it, but wouldn't consider it.) Or was she just crashing in her office? She did have a couch there, more of a loveseat, really, but she could make do if she was desperate. Nah, she'd probably want to be around people; she liked an audience, and would want to tell her side of the story.

Of course, there was no shortage of hotels in L.A., but would she want to spend the money? Even the most mediocre place was expensive these days. What was he talking about? Of course she'd spend the money, if only because she figured he *wouldn't*. Order up room service, eat ten-dollar macadamia nuts, soak in a hot bubble bath, burrow into one of those plush hotel beds with the feathery mattress pads. Forget your troubles, c'mon get happy.

It was all too much for Jeremy to think about so he got up, poured another glass of scotch, and screamed in agony as he moved his shoulder just so. Okay, this was not good. That fall, the splayed arm, the shooting pain: Did he break something? No, he could move his shoulder *and* his arm, stiff and tender as they were. Maybe it was just a sprain—no, a *strain*! Put one of those flexible ice pack thingies on it, take away any swelling. It'd be fine by morning, right?

Shit, the movie! He had to sit down and watch it, couldn't go to sleep till he wrote the damn review. At least it was what they called a capsule, 200 or so words that wouldn't take forever to bang out. Okay, get on with it, Jeremy thought, so he pulled the cold pack out of the freezer, swiped his cocktail glass off the counter, and head-ed off to his home office, formerly Matty's bedroom. Now Matty stayed in the tiny guest room every once in a blue moon when he happened to sleep over, mostly so Cassie would make him her famous blueberry waffles in the morning.

Wait, was Cassie staying with Matty in his apartment? No, he would have said something, mentioned it in that last text. Unless it was too awkward or embarrassing for him, their son not wanting to take sides.

On a more pressing note, where the heck did Cassie keep the Advil?

ONE THING ABOUT revisiting the Holocaust—it can make you feel better about your own problems. What's a little marital abandonment and shoulder ache compared to the systematic horrors of Nazi Germany? Still, watching this documentary, which looked at the last day of World War II through the eyes of a group of concentration camp survivors, was grueling: almost two hours of wrenching testimony from an array of ancient, deeply haunted men and women backed by acres of unbearable archival footage from Treblinka and Auschwitz and Bergen-Belsen. It all caused Jeremy to pause for a third and fourth pour of Dewar's, which got him through the stressful journey unfolding on his laptop screen, not to mention help muffle the shoulder pain that announced itself with every move.

He checked his watch: 11:45 p.m. How the hell did it get so late? He was usually in bed by eleven. Had he fallen asleep somewhere between Auschwitz and Treblinka without realizing it? God, he was such a fucking disaster. And he still had to write that review. He sat at his desk trying to decide what he really thought of the film aside from how tragic it was, how tragic they always were, and realized he had formed no real critical opinion of what he'd just watched, couldn't really remember much of the past two hours if he was being perfectly honest. And there was that awful shoulder throb again. He wondered: How many Advil *could* you take at a time?

Jeremy opened a new document and typed atop the blank page *The Last Worst Day by Jeremy Lerner*. No, it wasn't a recap of his own horrible, terrible, no-good Sunday but the sadly appropriate title of the documentary he had yet to critique.

Maybe he should just lie down for a minute, settle his head, and then get back in front of his laptop and bang out the review. He'd figure out what to write, he always did. And was Cassie asleep already—wherever she was?

CHAPTER
5

"JEREMY, DID I wake you?" It was Cassie, on Jeremy's cell, in fact waking him from a dead sleep. He was under a tangle of covers, barely awake, momentarily forgetting why his wife was calling him and not occupying her usual spot to his left.

"Jeremy? It's me, are you there?"

See, now those words made sense, unlike the message he left her yesterday. It also made him realize, in a sudden flood of gloom, why it was so crucial that Cassie was finally making contact. Had she changed her mind? He sat up.

"Cassie! Yeah, I'm here, sorry. Didn't you get my message to call me?" asked Jeremy. Sunlight was peeking in through the edges of the blackout blinds. What time was it, anyway?

"Didn't you get *my* message that said *not* to call me?"

There was that old challenge in her voice. But without the sexy twist that used to make it alright.

Jeremy glanced at his bedside clock: 10:08 a.m. "Oh, fuck!" His film review was due eight minutes ago, and he hadn't written a single word.

"Really? That's the best you've got right now?" Cassie was evidently loaded for bear.

"What? No, I wasn't talking to you! I was … I way overslept and—it doesn't matter. Look, when are you going to come home and end this ridiculous protest?" Jeremy threw his legs over the side of the bed, staring at the phone in his hand like it was a grenade. He felt a sudden stab in his shoulder—fuck, that again?

"Protest? Is *that* what you think this is? My God, Jeremy, where have you *been* for the last five years?"

"Right here. In this house. With you. Where have *you* been? Wait, more importantly, where are you now?" Jeremy could mount his own challenge to Cassie. She deserved at least that, didn't she?

"I'm ... away. That's all I'll say. And ... I'm not coming home." Cassie's voice had a slight quaver to it.

"Like, right now or like ... ever?" His shoulders had a visible droop.

"Like now," Cassie answered. "But I will be moving out." She sounded both wistful and deliberate. As if she'd thought about it for a long time.

Jeremy began to pace around their bedroom, evidence of his wife, his marriage, their world, in every square inch. He was at a loss for words. He really did think maybe it was some kind of protest, a passing marital thunderstorm, a ... thing. Where *had* he been? What should he say? What could he say?

"I don't know what to say," Jeremy sighed into his phone.

"You don't have to say anything. Just respect my decision and my need to detach," she answered. Jeremy could hear traffic sounds in the background.

"I have a million questions for you, Cassie."

"I thought you didn't know what to say?" A car door slammed. She had either gotten in or out of her car, Jeremy guessed, realizing he had never even looked to see if her red convertible MINI Cooper was still parked in their garage next to his silver Prius. He was a really shitty detective.

"I didn't mean it literally," though he kind of did. But he also did have a ton of questions for her, with *why* being atop the list. He started out for the garage, massaging his shoulder with his free hand. "You can't just decide you're leaving and not even have a conversation with me."

"Whether you realize it or not, we've been having 'the conversation' for a long time," Cassie said.

"No, not in so many words we haven't." As Jeremy unlocked the front door, he glanced in the foyer mirror and was startled by how wrecked he looked. Watch, he'd run into Katie or Crash or another neighbor and have to explain his ghastly appearance. Fuck it—he was out the door.

"Please," Cassie simmered, "you're a writer. I think you know subtext when you hear it." Jeremy could hear a car engine start, definitely the MINI.

"Yes, I'm very familiar with subtext, Cassie. I just don't think I need to be playing guessing games with my own wife." He reached their attached garage. "Are you in your car?"

"I am, and that's the last question for now."

He punched in the keypad code. The garage door groaned open revealing an empty space to the left of Jeremy's car. He gazed at the vacant spot, noticed dark patches of oil on the cement beneath where Cassie's MINI should have been parked.

"You have an oil leak, by the way," he said with an unexpected air of superiority.

"How do *you* know?" Cassie replied.

"If you were still at home, standing with me in our garage, you'd know too. So I guess you'll have to take my word for it. Get yourself to a gas station or something."

"I will … thanks."

There was silence, which Jeremy was not going to fill. Not this time.

"Okay, well," Cassie finally said, "I'll be in touch, but really, Jeremy, please don't try to reach me." Another awkward beat and then: "This is the only way I can do this."

"What about your job? Your things?" Jeremy asked. "What about Matty?" There was a catch in his voice.

"I said no more questions," Cassie answered, her quaver returning. "I'll talk to Matty, I promise."

Jeremy tapped the single keypad button that closed the garage door. He watched blankly as it made its noisy descent. "Final question, Cass: Just tell me, was this about the party?"

"All I'll say is, you failed the test, J. I've gotta go. Take care of yourself, okay?" And before Jeremy could respond, Cassie hung up.

Test? What test? What the hell was she talking about? Jeremy felt more confused, more at sea, *after* his conversation with Cassie than during all those hours of radio silence. Had he failed, what, the husband test? The lover test? The companion test? The breadwinner test? Maybe they shouldn't have talked altogether. This was feeling like a bad dream, but he was pretty sure he was awake. Was this what his fifties were going to look like?

"Hey, Jeremy." He turned around. It was Crash, walking his and Katie's loopy yellow Labrador, Lola, who leaped upon Jeremy, her huge paws pressed against his chest like a pair of furry defibrillators. His heart could use a jump start, but not this kind. "Lola, down!" ordered Crash. She reluctantly obeyed, with a look in her eyes so contrite Jeremy almost invited her back up. "Sorry, Jeremy," said Crash. "As you can see, our training is really paying off."

"Don't worry about it." Jeremy looked at the hopeful dog, tongue flapping out the side of her mouth, big tail wagging like a metronome. Concealing the pain that had now spread from his shoulder to the entire right arm, he bent down to pet Lola, eager to make at least one being happy that morning. Crash studied his crouching, disheveled neighbor.

"Is, uh, everything good with you?" he asked.

Jeremy rose, hyper-aware of his bed-headed, barefoot self. "Yeah, just got a late start on the day." It hit Jeremy again: the review. Fuck. "In fact, I've gotta get back inside. Deadline debacle." Lola squatted and peed on a patch of weeds.

"Sure, sorry, go," said Crash. "Oh, and hey, we meant to stop by yesterday and tell you and Cassie what a great party that was. *So* much fun. Did you have fun?"

Jeremy stared at the kindly Crash as if to say, Do I look like someone who's had any fun in the last forty-eight hours?

"It would have been more fun if I were turning thirty," Jeremy joked. Crash gave a respectful nod to his elder, the kind that read: best not get into any age discussions considering I'm thirty-two. Jeremy relented for the sake of getting back inside: "It was a really good time. Glad you and Katie could make it. Hey, enjoy your walk, okay?"

Jeremy dashed back into the house, raced to his desk, and checked his email. The last four messages to arrive were from Lucien, each in increasing levels of urgency culminating in the final note's subject line: "Are you dead?" As Jeremy contemplated how to answer and what exactly he could do to rectify this one-off truancy—and let's be real, it's not like Jeremy was a surgeon who had blown off a lung transplant—his phone rang. The screen read: "Lucien."

Jeremy considered not answering but knew that was not an option. Just man up and tell the truth. Well, maybe not the whole truth. What even *was* the whole truth? Anyway, Lucien was his friend, not his enemy. He'd understand and probably even have a quick solution; editors were nothing if not resourceful. Without, as they say, further ado, Jeremy took the call.

"Hello?"

"What the fuck happened, man? Where is it?"

Okay, sounding more enemy than friend, and not particularly resourceful.

Jeremy steeled himself and blurted out, "Cassie left me."

"What? Seriously?"

"Yeah, apparently it's official." Jeremy switched to a document screen, gazed at the blank page of his would-be review.

"Oh, my God, dude, I'm so sorry. I mean, she just threw you that rockin' party and then, what, dumped your ass?" Jeremy's normally erudite editor suddenly sounded like Matty.

"Yeah, I'm pretty wrecked," Jeremy admitted.

"Shit. Okay, look, I want to hear more about this, I do, but first— where's the review? Please tell me you already sent it and that it just did one of those email disappearing acts?" Lucien sounded a bit hyper-desperate; Jeremy's empty stomach churned.

"I'm really sorry, Lucien, I watched the film last night and was going to stay up and write, but it was late and I guess I fell asleep and I didn't wake up till—"

"So you never sent it?" Lucien interrupted.

"No, but if I start now, you can have it in an hour, tops." Jeremy spoke completely out of his ass. "I mean, it's just a capsule."

"No, it's not—it's full length!"

Okay, that surprised Jeremy. Before he could check last week's email assigning him the review, Lucien continued, his voice escalating: "Besides, you know noon is my drop-dead to get copy to the desk for next day's section. Which is why I need my reviewers to file no later than 10 a.m. How many years have you been doing this?"

"Twelve, give or take," said Jeremy, the pain starting up in his shoulder and arm. He was greeted by a loaded silence. "Look, Lucien, I fucked up, I know. I'm really sorry but, truly, give me a couple of hours, and I'll get you something you can at least post online today, maybe get it into print Wednesday?" But even as Jeremy was tossing this Hail Mary pass he knew better, knew this was not how things worked.

"We planned a big opening day spread for the movie—your review, interview with the filmmaker, the works. You know why?"

Jeremy had no idea. To him, it was just another obscure, if meaningful documentary that too few people would see.

"I'll tell you why: the producer is Geneva's cousin and she promised him great opening day coverage in print, which, as I think you know, is where most of the audience for a movie like this still gets their information." Geneva Harcourt was Lucien's erratic boss.

Oh, shit on toast. Why didn't Lucien tell him this sooner? Would it have mattered?

"Well, Geneva runs the whole section, right? Can't she push the schedule? Pull some 'stop the presses' move?" What was it, the 1940s? If Jeremy were a car he'd have been running on fumes.

"You're joking, right? She's an editor, Jeremy, not fucking Moses!"

"I know, Lucien, I'm just grasping here. I feel awful. Is there anything I can do?"

"Yeah, you can let me off the phone so I can give Geneva the good news."

"Okay, this might be a stupid question," said Jeremy, "but should I still write the review?" It took Jeremy a few seconds to realize Lucien had already hung up. *Might* be a stupid question?

Jeremy stared at his unwritten review page, blinking cursor taunting him. *Damn, he was starving.* The review, if he even had to write it at this point, could wait a few minutes, certainly until he heard back from Lucien with the verdict from above. Besides, he'd really need to zip through the documentary again, try to recall more of the key moments than he could right now, before digging into his critique. Christ, 750 words on this thing! Capsule length he might have been able to power through, but a longer piece he couldn't fudge.

It was all so unlike Jeremy. He approached every review he wrote, not to mention the various entertainment features and interviews he was often assigned, with the utmost care. He took his work, his responsibility—to the reader, to the artist, to Lucien, to himself—super seriously. Jeremy took most things super seriously. Too seriously sometimes, at least so said Cassie, who, for so much of their life together, brought a welcome lightness—a kind of enviable blitheness—to Jeremy's and, later, Matty's world. She didn't think ten steps ahead the way Jeremy did. "If it sucks, you can stop, or you can start over, babe," Cassie would say. "But not trying is unacceptable."

Had she just taken her own advice? She thought their marriage sucked, so she stopped, wanted to start over (without him, apparently), had to at least try to make a change? How could the words that had so often been his engine, the proverbial wind beneath his wings, turn around to bite him in the ass with such unexpected force and irony?

And, really, what test *did* he fail?

Jeremy returned to the kitchen and checked the fridge for lunch potential. He decided to throw out the remains of the party leftovers. Just seeing them made him angry and sad—even if he *was* able to stomach some yesterday. Another day, another mindset. When they were safely stashed in the garbage bin, Jeremy peered back into the fridge, spotted an egg carton and decided an omelet was in order. He took out three eggs, milk, a bag of grated cheddar, placed it all on the counter, then hunted around for a tall mixing bowl to whisk it all up in.

There it was, in the same cabinet as the scotch bottle that had wreaked so much havoc the day before, perched just one shelf below. It was a bit high, but no way was he getting out that wicked stepladder again. Without thinking (something Jeremy had gotten ridiculously good at lately), he stood on his toes, shot his right arm up toward the mixing bowl, and let out an anguished scream. Everything went black.

CHAPTER
6

THE NEXT THING Jeremy knew he was lying on a stretcher in the back of a lurching ambulance as a burly, bearded EMT worked a blood pressure machine at his side.

"Don't worry, Mr. Lerner, you're going to be okay," said EMT guy as he read the blood pressure gauge.

"What happened?" asked "Mr. Lerner." He eyeballed his stalwart attendant ("Kyle" was stitched on his steel gray polo shirt), then scanned the oxygen tanks and monitors and straps and hooks and piles of bandages and medical whatnot that lined the cramped van's walls. "I'm sorry, I don't remember anything since ... I think I was in my kitchen and I—"

"Thank God I found you, is all I can say!" chirped a familiar voice from the front of the van. It couldn't be ...

"Wait—Mom?" He'd never been so confused in his life.

"Honey, I'll tell you all about it later, okay?" said Joyce, whose melodious voice could make even the worst news sound less dire.

Jeremy turned to Kyle. "Why is my mother here?"

The long and the short of it, as Kyle and Joyce eventually explained, was that Jeremy had blacked out a few hours ago reaching for that mixing bowl, maybe from the piercing pain in his shoulder, or maybe because he hadn't eaten in nearly a day. Then again, Kyle speculated, it may have been from a severe form of stress. No one had mentioned a brain tumor, so Jeremy certainly wasn't going to bring it up.

"Have you been under unusual stress?" the EMT asked.

"His wife just left him, so the answer would be yes," Joyce called from the front seat, with a bit less lilt than usual. His mom had clearly taken sides in the short time she'd been aware of Cassie's departure.

It turned out that when Jeremy hadn't returned Joyce's many calls since the party—though he wanted to answer, he'd let her messages go to voicemail, still not wanting to enmesh her in the mess of it all until he had a better handle on things—she got hold of her grandson who broke the news about the split in, no doubt, a rather burning and dramatic fashion.

Joyce then hopped in her ancient BMW (it was his dad's car, she wouldn't give it up), tore away from her Encino condo and high-tailed it down Ventura Boulevard and up into Laurel Canyon. Without knocking or ringing his bell—a mother knows when there's a crisis unfolding—Joyce entered Jeremy's house with the key he'd given her years ago just in case (of what, he didn't know back then, but it sure wasn't this) and found her son conked out on the kitchen floor. An egg had rolled off the counter and lay splattered at his side. Without skipping a beat, or even trying to wake him, she called 911.

Matty met Jeremy and Joyce—and yes, Kyle, who by then had been convinced by Joyce to learn to play canasta, don't ask how or why—at the Cedars-Sinai emergency room. The place was packed to the gills, and all Jeremy wanted was to get out of the ER bed and back into his own. His wishes were nobody's command.

"Dad, you're a mess. You're not going anywhere except for an X-ray. And maybe a shower," ordered Matty, who, as usual, called it as he saw it—or in this case, smelled it.

"Sweetie, you don't want to end up passed out on your kitchen floor again, do you?" asked his mother. "I may not be there to rescue you again."

"Thanks, Ma, but I don't need rescuing. It was a little accident, I'm fine," said Jeremy.

"I've known you for fifty years and two days, baby doll, and this ain't fine," Joyce said, sounding like a Prohibition-era song lyric as she wiggled her index finger at her son.

Matty checked his phone, tapped a few keys. He started out. "Be right back, got a work thing." He'd started working recently for an event-planning company as an assistant. ("I'm really a 'coordinator,' but they cheaped out on the title," Matty had grumbled when he was hired, one foot already out the door.) Jeremy was sorry he'd screwed up his kid's workday but was secretly happy he'd shown up.

"Shouldn't Cassie know you're in the hospital, dear?" asked Joyce as soon as Matty had left the emergency room.

"I'm not really 'in' the hospital and no, she doesn't need to know. Right now, she doesn't need to *know* anything. Or, trust me, even wants to." Jeremy was suddenly parched. "Think I could get some water?"

Joyce, prepared as ever, pulled a bottle of Fiji from her oversized purse. "Honey, what in the world happened with you and Cassie? And, by the way, I wish I'd heard about it from you and not my grandson."

Jeremy scanned the emergency room for whatever doctor might be headed his way. God, his shoulder hurt. "I don't know, Ma, apparently I failed some test."

"What kind of test?" She leaned in, swept Jeremy's lank hair off his forehead, and eyed him with deep concern.

"I have no idea, but whatever it was, it's the biggest test I've ever failed in my life." He gulped some Fiji and felt the electrolytes seep into his brain. He met Joyce's questioning gaze and could tell she was formulating her words to be as gentle and direct as possible. It was one of her specialties.

"Honey, I was married to your father for a long time. It wasn't all a bed of roses, as you are well aware. But I always knew one thing— if I wanted to know what was causing a rough patch I just had to look in the mirror."

"He was the one who should've been looking in a mirror," Jeremy said. Joyce looked wistful. "I mean, you know how he could be," he added apologetically. He should have known better than to dump on Saint Larry.

"All I'm saying, sweetheart, is that it takes two to foxtrot." She brought the thin blanket up over Jeremy's shoulders. They kept the place like a meat locker.

"I believe it's tango."

"Any dance will do," Joyce said with a knowing smile.

"Except maybe the conga," he managed to joke. Jeremy realized he'd misread his mother's earlier disdain for Cassie. Or maybe she'd just had some time to think it through. Either way, Jeremy knew that whatever sent his wife packing was as much his doing as hers. He just wasn't ready to dissect it yet. Some critic he was.

Speaking of critics: "Oh, *fuck*, I completely forgot!" A few people glanced over at Jeremy, then returned to their own troubles. "Where's my phone?" he asked, eyes darting.

"I've got it, honey. What's wrong?" she asked, fishing it out of her bottomless purse.

"I'll tell you in a second." Jeremy took his cell from Joyce and steeled himself as he found a text Lucien had sent a few hours earlier. His face fell as he read: "Geneva livid. Tried to convince her not to fire you, but failed. Sorry, J. Call me." He looked up at his mother, sighed.

"Is it from Cassie?" Joyce asked. Jeremy shook his head in defeat and showed her the phone. She read the text, confused. "Who's Geneva?"

"She runs the Calendar section," Jeremy answered, flashing back over twelve years and some 2000 reviews he'd written. "I blew a deadline," he explained. It felt as much like a death as Cassie's exit, but one that, perhaps unlike what went down with his wife, had been completely avoidable. The connection between the two events was hardly lost on Jeremy and, from the look on her face, Joyce as well. He felt angry and miserable and, most of all, ashamed.

"Oh, Jeremy," his mom said. She thought for a second. "But can they really 'fire' you? You're not officially an employee, right?"

"They can just not hire me, how's that?"

There was a commotion somewhere in the vast waiting area. Jeremy couldn't tell what was going on but the gruesome sounds made his shoulder pain seem minor.

"But you're the best reviewer they have!" Joyce said, staying adorably on message despite the outer fracas.

"Spoken like a true mother," Jeremy responded with a sideways grin.

"Not just me, *all* my friends think so," she said as if she and her circle of eighty-year-old Valley gals ran the joint. Jeremy wanted to get up from the wheeled bed and hug Joyce for her unwavering cheerleading skill but plopped his head back on the squishy pillow instead.

They were silent for a moment. The tumult had died down. Someone, maybe someone else's devoted mother, quietly wept from afar.

"Well," reasoned Joyce, adjusting herself in the plastic chair, "maybe now you'll have the time to work on your new screenplay."

Jeremy had been working on his "new" screenplay for six years, almost finishing it several times, then starting all over again. He was never quite happy enough with what he'd created, much less why he created it—guilt over his aborted screenwriting career more than any great desire to write a new script. Whenever Jeremy returned to the pages of that convoluted political thriller, it felt as if he were merely catching up instead of progressing.

Before starting that script, it'd been years—thirteen to be exact—since Jeremy had written his last screenplay, discouraged by selling a grand total of zero scripts after *Parting Gifts*, the romantic comedy he'd managed to set up at Universal for a shockingly tidy sum when he was a wee twenty-seven, in what now seemed like the fluke of all flukes. (After about four years in development hell, people stopped asking Jeremy when "his movie" was going to get made. It wasn't.) The script doctoring gigs open to Jeremy in the wake of his *Parting Gifts* success were also short-lived.

Needing to make some kind of steady living again, he'd applied for the film reviewer position at the *Times* that he'd heard about from a publicist friend. And, though it turned out to only be free-lance, he grabbed it, eventually parlaying the gig into all kinds of other print and internet writing assignments, and cobbling together a new career.

"Good idea, Ma, maybe I *will* get back into it," Jeremy finally said, with no intention of diving into that script again.

"You know what they say, honey, one door closes and another one opens," Joyce reminded Jeremy, as if that said it all about his situation.

Who knows, he thought, maybe it kind of did.

Matty, a Coke Zero in hand, reappeared with a doctor in tow, a thirtyish fellow with a metal clipboard, oversized white coat and a genial smile. "Dad, this is Dr. Bhattasali. We met in the hall. He's going to take care of you."

"Ready to take a little ride, Mr. Lerner?" the doc asked cheerfully. Before Jeremy could answer—as if there was any response but yes—an orderly took hold of the bed and wheeled him away.

CHAPTER
7

IT WAS WELL past nine by the time Jeremy returned from the hospital to his dark, eerily quiet house. Matty had driven him and Joyce back, stopping at Panera for soup and sandwiches to go. Jeremy was so beyond hungry at this point, he wondered if he could even eat. Joyce laid the food out for them on the kitchen table. That splattered egg still lay on the floor but now, congealed, looked like a rubber prank toy. Strangely, no one moved to clean it up.

"So when will you have the surgery, Dad?" Matty asked as Jeremy took a seat and began to unwrap a chicken pesto club.

"I don't know. I don't even know that I will," said Jeremy, examining the neatly assembled sandwich, its heavy basil-garlic waft giving him pause.

"A torn rotator cuff doesn't heal itself, darling," noted Joyce as she sat across from him.

"Actually, Grandma, it can," Matty said as he took the lid off a bowl of curry lentil soup. "A guy I know from the gym—two guys, actually—tore their rotator cuffs, did nothing about it, decided to just lay off lifting for a while."

"How are they now?" asked Jeremy, hopeful.

"I don't know, they don't go to my gym anymore," Matty said, clearly not realizing how ominous that sounded. He eyed Jeremy's chicken club. "That looks awesome. Want to trade halves? I got the Tuscan tuna." The kid couldn't even commit to a sandwich.

"Gladly," answered Jeremy, making the switch.

A battery of tests, X-rays, and scans found nothing irregular in Jeremy (busted marriages being undetectable) except for one big thing: an apparently torn rotator cuff in his right shoulder. "Apparently" because, as an orthopedist on call who swept in to read the CT results said, "They won't know for sure till they go in there," sounding like something someone would warn in a horror movie. The tear, it didn't take a medical degree to surmise, was the result of that death-defying fall off the rickety stepladder, which, in reality, deserved the blame for all this. Then again, Jeremy thought, maybe it was *really* the fault of that unreachable bottle of scotch, the need for which would never have arisen had Cassie not packed up and left. Aha, so Cassie *was* to blame!

With that conclusion out of the way (for now, anyhow), and the ER-administered tramadol managing his shoulder pain (for now, anyhow), Jeremy bit into his savory sandwich, his first real food in what seemed like forever. He got it down and, after a dicey moment, felt pretty sure it would stay there.

"You should see Richard Hockstein immediately," Joyce announced between spoonfuls of cauliflower parmesan soup, an unlikely choice that looked better than it sounded.

"Who's Richard Hockstein?" asked Jeremy, glancing at the telltale egg mess on the floor.

"Only the best orthopedic surgeon in L.A.," said Joyce. "All my friends have gone to him."

"Are these the same friends who think I'm the *Times'* best film reviewer?" He didn't mean it to sound snarky but it did.

"You know they're right," Joyce said, focused more on her soup than his sarcasm.

"Oh, shit, Dad, that's such a bummer," said Matty, who'd already inhaled his half of Jeremy's sandwich, "about you and the paper. But if it's any consolation, I don't know anyone who reads it anymore."

"You're twenty-three. Did you *ever* know anyone who reads it?" asked Jeremy. "And, honey, that's ridiculously beside the point."

"I'm just trying to make you feel better." Matty eyed his gloomy dad. "And I can see it's working like a charm."

"I lost my wife, my job, and all shoulder mobility in one stinking day. Sorry if I'm not seeing the bright side of things just yet."

"You don't *really* know if you lost your wife," said Joyce, attempting, as usual, to see the bright side of things.

Jeremy indicated around the room with his sandwich. "Do you see her anywhere, because I don't." He remembered he also had soup—vegetable barley—and tried a spoonful. He could feel its warmth mellowing his fraught insides. Jeremy looked up at his mother and son. "I don't think she's coming back, certainly not to me," Jeremy added. "But I'm just going by what she told me."

"Okay, but, honey, did she say those words exactly?" Joyce asked. "Because you know, people say a lot of things they don't mean when they're angry or upset."

"I don't know, Ma," said Jeremy. "It's what she implied. It's what I inferred."

"Wait, which one is which again?" Matty wondered aloud. "I always get them confused." He was now making quick work of his Tuscan tuna. "And Grandma, I gotta say, Mom sounded pretty harsh when we talked."

"She called you? When?" Jeremy put down his soupspoon. Cassie had said she would talk to their son, so why was Jeremy so surprised? Still, after all this, why wouldn't he be?

"This morning, at work," Matty answered. "And don't ask me what she said, because I don't really know."

"Matty, darling, did you talk to her or not?" Joyce asked gently, confused.

"She was weird and intense," said Matty. "And kinda vague. So I just listened. She told me she loved me, and that I shouldn't worry, and that whatever happened was for the best. Then I had to jump into a meeting, so." He dipped a spoon into Jeremy's soup, made a face. "Celery, eek." Then: "Anyway, Dad, I wouldn't wait up for her, if you know what I mean."

"I wasn't planning to, kiddo." Jeremy lost what little appetite he'd had, and left the table to sop up the splotched egg from the floor.

"I can do that, honey," Joyce offered, getting up to help him.

"No, Mom, I need to clean up my own mess," said Jeremy as he grabbed a sponge and some paper towels. In its way, it felt like the first moment of the rest of his life.

AFTER DINNER, JEREMY and Joyce hugged Matty goodbye, and he left to meet up with Sven, mumbling something that sounded like "booty call" and probably was. Jeremy went to clear the table of the remains of their meal, but Joyce bumped him aside. "I'll do this," she said. "You go sit down, you look terrible."

"Gee, thanks, Ma," Jeremy shot back, knowing she was absolutely right. He plopped back into a kitchen chair as his mom scurried about, tidying up. For a moment, he was a kid again, his father lounging in the den recliner after dinner with a Montecristo like the grand pooh-bah that he was while Joyce efficiently washed and stacked the dishes, never asking for Larry's help (like he'd ever have given it) or even his company (c'mon, he had a cigar to smoke), while Jeremy did his homework at the now spotless (Joyce, again) kitchen table. Back then, it just seemed like that was the drill—women do this, men do that—but Jeremy, watchful and inquisitive boy that he was, sensed at some level there was an imbalance that needed fixing, even if his parents didn't. That's why, from day one of their marriage, when Cassie cooked, he cleaned; when *he* cooked, they cleaned together, mostly because he made much more of a mess of things than she did. Still, they practiced teamwork, in raising Matty as well, everything shared right down the middle. They were good together, so happy together—me for you and you for me, isn't that how the old song went?—for such a long time. Then Matty left for San Diego State and something slow and steady and unnamable started creeping into their relationship—imperceptible at first, like a drop or two of drizzle. But even drizzle, if it continues long enough, can add up to something murky and slick and precarious.

"Promise me you'll call this Dr. Hockstein first thing tomorrow, would you, dear?" Joyce called from the sink, startling Jeremy out of his reverie. He glanced at the wall clock: 10:17. He was tired. So tired. How did she still have so much energy? "He's in one of those office towers at Cedars, I think," said Joyce. "What is that, Beverly? Third?"

"I'll find him. I'll call him, promise," Jeremy said, wondering how much health insurance would cover, wondering what he was going to do for income in general without the regular *Times* gig. And it wasn't just the reviews, he realized, it meant no entertainment features either; Geneva ran the whole shebang and he was, for the first time in his work life, persona non grata. Oh, how the nowhere-near-mighty have fallen! He still had his other jobs: he occasionally reviewed for some decent websites (though not in a while), taught writing classes and one-off seminars (but those had dried up the last few years), moderated post-screening Q and As with actors or filmmakers (mostly during awards season, which this wasn't), and wrote publicity kits and bios (which were fewer and farther between). Maybe he *would* dust off that screenplay.

Joyce finished up at the sink and joined Jeremy back at the table. She looked at him a moment, then took his hand. "How's my little boy?"

"Fifty and hating it. How are *you*?" he asked, hoping to change the subject. Fat chance.

"Worried about *you*, that's how I am."

"A parent's work is never done, is it?"

Joyce studied her son, still so badly in need of a shower, shave, and attitude adjustment. "Honey, you can tell me. Was there someone else?"

Jeremy paused to think, really think about that. Sure, the notion had crossed his mind, as it would have anyone whose better half began to seem only half there the better part of the time. Still, he would end up dismissing the possibility, convinced he would know—just know—like a sixth sense if betrayal was in process. What Jeremy didn't take into account, however, was that not every marital perfidy had to involve sex—or even another person, for that matter.

"I don't think Cassie would've cheated on me," Jeremy said,

though it came out more like a question than a statement.

"I didn't mean Cassie, darling, I meant you," Joyce said softly. Jeremy stared at her, uncomprehending. She gazed back. "Do *you* have someone else?"

The question truly caught Jeremy off guard, not because what his mother asked was so out of the realm of life's general possibility, but because it had never been on his own personal wish list these past years. If he *had* been so inclined, the opportunity to step out on Cassie had reared its sordid head more than a few times during their marriage. Jeremy was considered an attractive guy in his own increasingly bookish, distracted, lean-bodied way, made perhaps even more appealing by the fact that he didn't seem much aware of—or driven by—his looks. (Matty once commented that if Jeremy were gay he'd know how "hot" he was; Jeremy didn't get his son's line of reasoning and left it there.) As a result, friends, friends' wives, neighbors, colleagues, students, strangers at the car wash had all, at one time or another, left a door open for Jeremy that other husbands might have eagerly walked through but had left Jeremy cold. It was not that he was such a paragon of virtue, but he loved his wife and didn't want to be "one of those guys." Maybe it had been enough to know he'd had the opportunities.

"No, Ma, there was no one else," Jeremy answered Joyce.

"I wouldn't judge you if there were," his mother said. "Either of you. Marriages are complicated—at best. And, well, shit happens."

Jeremy couldn't help but smile at that. And, of course, she was right. Though he got the sense she was secretly happy that he was in the clear on the infidelity thing. No mother wants her son to be a scumbag.

JEREMY AWOKE WITH a jolt the next morning with little memory of actually falling asleep, his still-lit bedside lamp a clue that he must've conked out before his head touched the pillow. No matter, he was glad to see that this time he'd at least taken off his clothes before getting into bed—they sat in a dingy pile on the adjacent area rug—though was less pleased to realize that he still hadn't showered.

His shoulder smarted as he reached across the nightstand to grab his cell. He glanced at the phone: no messages. Cassie remained enigmatically O.O.T.: out of town and out of touch. True, she'd spoken to Matty yesterday morning *before* the hospital visit, but even if she did somehow know what happened to Jeremy, would she have checked in on him? Or was anything less than the brink of death ineligible for Cassie's concern under her baffling new rules?

Before he rolled over and went back to sleep, Jeremy pulled himself out of bed, popped a tramadol, and took the longest, hottest, soapiest shower he could remember. It was glorious—and desperately required.

He toweled off, feeling like a new (okay, new*ish*) man, until he wiped the steam from the mirror and his face slowly came into focus. Jeremy leaned in and gazed at his half-century-old self and, even without his glasses, was struck by the lines and crinkles and crevices that had seemingly multiplied across his face overnight. What was *that* about? Turn fifty and age in exponential leaps? Or had he just not noticed them until now, more mindful of his graying hair (everywhere, he might add) and retreating hairline than this insidious collagen collapse?

Had it never occurred to him to take even the slightest hint from Cassie's near-religious devotion to skincare, a regimen that involved a seemingly arcane, ever-expanding and pricey collection of tubes and vials and jars? Did Jeremy think her youthful air and the lovely, unblemished skin he admired even during their more disconnected moments was luck? No, she worked at it, worked at her body, too. Still did yoga, added Pilates and power walking and planks and so many things Jeremy found boring so Cassie never forced him to join but did them anyway. Just like Jeremy never forced Cassie to sit and watch the grim documentaries and austere foreign dramas and those navel-gazing, coming-of-age-at-any-age indie comedies that he had to write about each week. (Being married to Jeremy, she'd learned to like movies more, but not *that* much more.)

Awhile back, Cassie had stopped reading his reviews in their entirety, if at all, once commenting that she didn't need to read everything he writes to know he's a good writer—but don't take it personally, okay? He didn't, but he did. But he also let it go because it wasn't worth getting into with her, even though it was a given that those little articles were like mirrors into his heart and soul, but whatever. And these issues were all symptomatic of that fatal disease in which married people—some, many, too many—take each other for granted and start going through their days like zombies who share a bathroom and a refrigerator and a mortgage but not a whole lot more.

Before Jeremy depressed the complete shit out of himself he started to shave, at which point he considered growing a beard, but then realized that (a) his beard would come in really gray and might make him look older, and that (b) if he did grow it but decided, say, years later, to shave it off, it might be super-shocking to see how many hundreds of lines he'd have accumulated. In the end, he left bad enough alone and put his electric razor to work.

He was interrupted by the plunk of an arriving text. It was his mother, offering Dr. Hockstein's phone number: "How are you feeling? Call him, honey." Jeremy, his shoulder opioidally lulled into submission, didn't feel any great urgency to deal with that right then—and by right then he meant ever. But he finished shaving and called for an appointment, figuring if this Hockstein was that great he'd probably be booked for months, and Jeremy could deal with it then.

"You're in luck," announced Hockstein's peppy scheduler, "the doctor just had a cancellation! Can you be here at 9:15?"

It was already 8:30, but Jeremy did something spontaneous for a change and said "I'll be there," grabbing the *Times* that sat plastic-wrapped on his front stoop and tearing open the Calendar section to see how Lucien and Geneva solved the problem that got him fired.

And there it was, the simple solution that should have been the go-to fix. They ran a review of *The Last Worst Day* off one of the newswires, a move they sometimes made when there was no *Times* writer available to cover some random local release.

It was an excellent review, better than Jeremy might have given the film considering his state of mind, and it looked great next to a lengthy phone interview with the documentary's Toronto-based director. From where Jeremy stood (in his garage now), it was all happily ever after—except, of course, for him.

Did no one believe in second chances? That was a question not only for Lucien but, Jeremy realized, for Cassie as well.

He shot Lucien an email pleading for that second chance, then drove off to see the wonderful wizard of orthopedics.

CHAPTER
8

"SO WHAT DO you do, Jeremy, aside from wrecking your rotator cuff falling off a kitchen stepladder?" asked Dr. Richard Hockstein, a big, bald, jovial guy with a honking New York accent and signed pictures of pro athletes and TV stars grinning from the walls of his examining room. (Subsequent visits would reveal different celebrity photos in different examining rooms, lest anyone think Hockstein hadn't treated an impressive enough range of the rich and famous.)

"I'm a writer," Jeremy answered, straining to make out the actors in those photos; from afar, they all looked like John Stamos—from the first *Full House,* not the second. Clearly, Hockstein had been setting bones for a while.

"What do you write?" he asked loudly as he studied Jeremy's CAT scan results on a laptop.

"I'm a journalist, mostly," said Jeremy. "I review movies for the *L.A. Times.*" Who knows, maybe it *could* still be true ... he hadn't heard back yet from Lucien.

The doctor, eyes never leaving his computer screen, asked the inevitable question: "Seen any good movies lately?"

"Yeah, but most of what I review is kind of on the obscure side, things you probably haven't heard of."

"Try me." Hockstein's gaze shifted from the CAT scan to a paper printout.

He didn't want to be rude so he did a quick mental scan. "Well, I really liked this Peruvian film called *Dreams of Light*," said Jeremy, trying not to sound too hoity-toity but knowing he did. Hazard of the profession.

"Never heard of it," Hockstein replied, turning away from his laptop. He gazed at Jeremy as if awaiting more movie recommendations. Jeremy fidgeted, his shoulder throbbing again, as if on cue.

"Do you read the *Times*?" asked Jeremy, stalling whatever Hockstein had to say about his rotator cuff, which, from the grim look on his face, was not going to be "Go home, you're fine."

"I used to, but who has the time? I read it online now and then, but not the movie reviews—no offense."

Jeremy shrugged: none taken.

"We still get the Sunday paper delivered, though. Force of habit."

"Do you read that?" asked Jeremy.

"No, not really." Chitchat over, Hockstein broke back into a buoyant grin, gave a "play ball" clap and delivered his verdict: "My friend, you need surgery. Pronto."

Jeremy sank. At some level he was hoping the doctor would say the ER staff misread the CAT scan—hey, it happens—and not only had he not injured himself but that he was a perfect physical specimen and the pain he was feeling was all in his head, not his shoulder. Dream on. "How ... 'pronto?'" Jeremy asked.

"Sooner we reattach that bad boy, the better. Looks like you really did a number on it." He checked his laptop again. "How's tomorrow morning?"

"Tomorrow *morning*?" Jeremy asked, incredulous.

"Or nine weeks from tomorrow morning. That's all I've got. You lucked out, bubby."

"Doesn't feel that way." Jeremy forced out a smile to match Hockstein's self-satisfied beam, but it didn't take. He tried to recall his schedule. That took about a nanosecond. Right now he *had* no schedule unless his wife should suddenly return to take up residency on her side of the bed, which seemed as unlikely as Jeremy getting his job back.

"Is it that bad?" Jeremy had to ask, finally identifying one of the actors smiling down on him from the wall: David Hasselhoff, maybe from his *Baywatch* days.

"Looks that way, though I won't know for sure till I go in there," said Hockstein, apparently reading from the same horror movie script as the ER doctor.

"What happens if I wait nine weeks?"

"Could go from bad to worse. If I can't do it arthroscopically, it could be a big freakin' megillah. You don't want that, do you, young man?"

What kind of doctor says "big freakin' megillah?" The same kind who calls a fifty-year-old guy "young man." This was all feeling kind of nightmarish.

"Can I think about it?"

"Sure, think all you want," Hockstein said, rising from his swivel stool. "I'll be back in five minutes." He went to clap Jeremy on his bad shoulder, then stopped midway, broke into another broad grin. "Sorry, kid, orthopedist humor."

LUCIEN CALLED JEREMY soon after he returned from Hockstein's office. Bottom line: Jeremy was still fired. Geneva was pissed, didn't care that Jeremy was a well-respected reviewer (by folks other than Joyce's friends, it should be noted), that he'd been a diligent employee for a dozen years and, not a small thing, that he really needed the gig.

"When she gets this way, there's just no fighting it," said Lucien with an audible sigh. "But look, anything I can do to help you—uh, elsewhere—you know I will." The editor lowered his voice: "Don't tell anyone, but I think you're our best freelancer."

Jeremy said nothing. What did it matter? Lucien, aware of the awkward silence, added, "Did you know that I edit your reviews last because they always need the least work? Trust me, that's not nothing."

"And I'm assuming I'm boxed out of feature pieces, too?"

"Sorry, man. I know it's the shits," said Lucien, again sounding more like Matty than the intellect Jeremy always considered him to be.

Lucien shifted gears: "Okay, look, I've just got a minute here but … are you and Cassie still … I mean, what the hell happened? Was it, like, mutual, or …?" Lucien trailed off, likely checking an email, or maybe he didn't know what to say. Neither did Jeremy.

"Hey, thanks for trying with Geneva," said Jeremy finally. "Sorry I fucked up. You've been a good boss."

"I appreciate that, Jeremy, really, because, y'know, I've always felt that—"

But Jeremy hung up. If he was going to cry, it wasn't going to be in front of that spineless twerp. It wasn't going to *be* in front of anyone. In fact, you know what, he thought, it wasn't going to be at all. He had surgery to prepare for and had to figure out how he would navigate things if, as Hockstein told him, he'd have to keep his arm immobilized to help the healing process.

"Don't be surprised if you wake up with your arm in a sling," the doc had advised. "Though, I won't know till I go in there." Again with the horror-show talk. *The calls are coming from inside the house!*

"Any chance I won't need one?" Jeremy asked, wondering if it was too late to back out of the procedure.

"It happens. Mario Lopez didn't need one," boasted Hockstein, pointing to a photo of the TV celeb on the wall.

Ah, thought Jeremy, *that's* who that was.

"Though *he's* fit as a rock, so that helped," added the doctor, the emphasis on "he" connoting that Jeremy was no A. C. Slater in the musculature department.

"Your wife will need to drop you off and pick you up after the surgery," Dr. Hockstein's scheduler, Lorena, cheerfully reminded Jeremy as she handed him a printed sheet with a long list of pre-procedure instructions.

How did Lorena know he had a wife? *He* didn't even know if he had a wife. "I'll just take an Uber," he said.

"Oh, no, it has to be an actual person," said Lorena, with a little "tsk-tsk" in her voice. "They should also be there when you wake up from the surgery. You probably won't remember a lot of what

Dr. Hockstein tells you until the anesthesia completely wears off, so you'll need your wife to take notes."

Jeremy wanted to say that his wife had obviously been "taking notes" a lot these last few years, which may be why she was no longer in his life. "I'll have an actual person with me, promise," Jeremy told Lorena, who smiled back, satisfied she'd done her job.

Matty was shocked to hear Jeremy was having the surgery so soon and, without skipping a beat, agreed to be his "actual person" at the hospital the next day. Jeremy hated asking him, knowing it would interfere with his son's work schedule. But Matty wouldn't hear of it.

"As long as I have my phone with me, I'm cool," Matty said. "I'm happy to represent."

"Thanks, honey," said Jeremy. "I really, really appreciate it." He glanced at his office bookshelf and caught sight of his favorite photo of them. It had been taken at some local film festival Jeremy had dragged him to as a teenager: Matty looked so casually handsome and adult, access badge hanging from his neck; Jeremy remembered being so proud of him that day.

"No biggie, you'd do it for me, right?" Matty responded, realizing: "Duh, you *have* done it for me about a million times. Uh, you and Mom, so ..."

That was Matty, remembering to be an equal opportunity supporter, and why not? Cassie was exiting Jeremy's life, not their son's; Jeremy wanted them to be close no matter what and he hoped—no, this he *knew*—Cassie felt the same.

Matty even offered to sleep over in his childhood home that night so he could drive Jeremy to the hospital in the morning.

"Are you scared, Dad?" Matty asked.

"Not scared, exactly. Maybe a little apprehensive. The doctor wasn't real specific about what to expect."

"I meant scared about doing this without Mom around."

Jeremy considered that a moment. He and Cassie had gone through every big and little thing together for so long that doing something this major without her—her strength, her insistence, her protectiveness—seemed vast in ways he couldn't have predicted. He still hadn't grasped the extent of the entire situation, kept seesawing between acceptance and disbelief, was operating on automatic pilot. He didn't know what he wanted, but it wasn't this.

"Yes," Jeremy admitted, "I wish your mother were here. I wish she hadn't left. I wish I had more answers. But I'm glad I have you."

Lying in bed that night, trying but failing to fall asleep (counting backward from one hundred only kept getting him to zero, not zzzs), the minutes inexorably ticking down to his 6 a.m. wake-up alarm, 7 a.m. hospital arrival, and 9 a.m. surgery, Jeremy found himself again trying to resurrect the argument with Cassie that followed his birthday party. More came back to him now, individual words adding up to phrases, then sentences, full thoughts and reactions, the more of which he remembered, the worse he felt. And the less he could sleep.

It may not have been a fair fight per se, Jeremy unnerved and spent and still a bit drunk, Cassie out on a limb and ready to pounce, her mind maybe made up before the night even began. They both said things they had to be sorry for: Jeremy accused Cassie of having no interest anymore in anything but herself, Cassie railed at Jeremy for caring more about his "beloved movies" than their relationship. Each condemned the other for giving up on what they once had together, neither accepting any blame for how they got there.

Had they fought instead in the light of day, cooler heads prevailing and all that, could they have worked through the anger and disappointment and recriminations, found a path forward together? Did they even want to?

That was the question that haunted Jeremy as he finally drifted off to sleep, remembering what it had been like to fall in love with Cassie, to be in love with her, to be a part of her—then to lose the part that had made it all work.

CHAPTER
9

JEREMY HEARD A familiar female voice in muffled conversation with a less familiar but not unrecognizable male voice. It sounded like they were talking from miles away, but it was Jeremy who was not quite there. At least not yet. Their voices were slowly becoming louder and clearer.

She: "How could you not know this?"

He: "The CAT scans only show so much. There are always surprises. Trust me, young lady, he'll be fine."

Young lady. And a Brooklyn or ... yes, Queens accent. Dr. Holstein—no, Hockstein. (Holstein's the cow, right?) Jeremy sensed his thoughts gelling as he swam to the surface of a watery pool, his right arm resting on something that felt both dependably firm and soothingly soft.

She: "I understand, but was there no way to prepare him?"

He: "Who's ever really prepared for anything? Am I right?" A warm chuckle followed his words.

Yep, definitely Hockstein, but who was he talking to?

She: "Well, he's gonna shit a brick when he wakes up. I know I would."

Jeremy, unsettled by words he still didn't comprehend, opened his eyes to nearly shit that brick. But not because he was strapped into this giant pillow contraption that immobilized his right arm at a 90-degree angle—Jesus, what the fuck?—but because his previously vanished wife sat next to a beatific Dr. Hockstein. And where was Matty? He was definitely there before the surgery, said he'd be there afterward. Jeremy figured he must not have woken up yet from the anesthesia and was still in dreamland, even though things were beginning to seem pretty damn real.

"There he is!" announced Hockstein, as if he'd been looking for Jeremy all along. "How are you feeling, bubby?"

"Uh ... I don't know. A little ..." Jeremy's gaze drifted back to Cassie who, he finally decided, was real—as real as whatever the hell the top half of his body was currently attached to. "Where's Matty?" Jeremy asked Cassie, his mouth sandpapery, his back sore. He tried to sit up, but the strap-and-pillow thing weighed him down.

Hockstein jumped in before Cassie could answer: "So, Jeremy, as I was telling your lovely wife, Casey—"

"Cassie," corrected not-Casey.

"*Cassie*, the procedure went perfectly. You'll be like new in no time. But yours was the biggest rotator cuff tear I ever repaired arthroscopically. We both deserve medals!" Dr. H chuckled again, then sobered. "Frankly, my friend, you were in worse shape than I thought. The upside: We avoided open surgery. I *told* you that you were lucky!"

"The downside?" asked Jeremy, glancing at the massive pillow brace.

"You're going to be in that monster for six weeks," answered Cassie. "And Matty had a work emergency. So you got me."

Jeremy stared at her, still couldn't believe his eyes. She looked more beautiful than he even remembered. Her hair, only slightly less honey-blonde these days, was pulled back in the same lush ponytail as that first night they met; her makeup-free face still radiating the flush of youth, her eyes crinkling with wry detachment. He wanted to hold her, feel protected by her once again. But he couldn't move.

Then it hit Jeremy: "Six weeks?" He gazed at his outstretched, strap-and-Velcro-bound arm and the massive pillow it rested on. "In *this* thing?"

Hockstein looked antsy, ready to roll off to his next joint repair or bone fusion. "It's called an abduction pillow sling. But don't you worry, Jeremy," he assured his patient, with another wide-eyed smile, "the time will go by like a shot."

"Maybe for you," jabbed Cassie.

"Sadly, for all of us," said the doc, with sudden gravity. "Seems like yesterday I graduated from med school." A pause, then: "And that was forty freakin' years ago!"

"Wait, so you're saying I have to keep this thing on, like, what, *every day* for six weeks?" Jeremy asked. The diagonal torso strap was already digging into his neck; the brace felt like it weighed a ton.

"Every day, all day," said Hockstein, with a bit of Joyce's musicality (which was far more annoying coming from a medical professional). "You've gotta keep that arm in place 24/7 if you want to heal like the champ that I know you are!" Those last four words were accompanied by jaunty index-finger stabs at Jeremy. If Jeremy was supposed to smile in response, he didn't.

Cassie piped up: "Jeremy, you have to work in it, eat in it, sleep in it." Indicating a printed page of directives she'd apparently been given before Jeremy woke up, she added, "Says here you can take the brace off to shower, though frankly I have no idea how you do that, much less get it back on." Reading on she noted, "Oh, and when you do shower, you have to keep your arm level at the same 90-degree angle, so good luck with that."

"So," Hockstein clapped his hands again. "Any questions before I go?"

"Did Mario Lopez have to wear this ridiculous thing?" asked Jeremy. He couldn't resist. Cassie looked utterly confused.

The doc belly laughed. "Okay, wise guy. Anything else you need, do not hesitate to call Lorena in my office. She's my right arm—no pun intended!" A salute to Jeremy and Cassie and he was gone.

Jeremy rolled his eyes. "He's a better surgeon than comedian, though I'll admit the lines blur."

"Mario Lopez?"

Jeremy's mood shifted. "Where *were* you?" he asked Cassie.

"And when did you get back?"

Cassie hesitated as if she'd made no plan on how to proceed, what to say, how to act. Maybe she hadn't. "Sorry to hear about your job. That really sucks."

Jeremy looked at her: How did she know?

"Matty filled me in on the … well, the last few days."

"Yes, it does suck," said Jeremy, about to remind Cassie that if it wasn't for her he would still have his job, but he hoped that was already evident. He indicated the abduction pillow. "Almost as much as this."

She folded the instruction sheet in half, and then in half once more. Jeremy studied her. He knew every square inch of this woman yet also knew nothing. He could tell Cassie felt his eyes on her as she unfolded the instruction sheet—once, twice—smoothed it out and then passed it to Jeremy.

"You'll need this," she said, avoiding his gaze.

Jeremy took the page with his free hand. "What are we doing, Cassie?"

"You know what we're doing. We're separating."

Jeremy was silent.

"And for the record, I drove out to Palm Springs, stayed with a friend."

"Yeah? What was his name?" Jeremy didn't mean to ask that, but too late. Maybe he hadn't really dismissed the possibility after all.

"I'm not going to dignify that with an answer." Cassie held herself back, stood. "Look, I don't know exactly how you're going to handle your life for the next six weeks stuck in that thing, but I can't move back in to help you. It's shitty timing, I know, and I'm sorry, but … I can't."

"Did I ask you to move back in? Or help me in any way whatsoever?" Then again, thought Jeremy, how was he going to manage by himself in that mammoth brace? He didn't even know how he was going to get off the hospital bed. Cassie stayed remarkably composed.

"If you're ready to go, I'll drive you back to the house," she said.

"Your mother's going to meet us there."

"My mother? When did you talk to her?" Jeremy went to swing his legs over the side of the bed but tipped backward from the weight of the unwieldy abduction pillow. Cassie jumped in to help him up.

"Matty spoke to her. He took care of everything. He said to tell you he'll come by after work," she explained as she used both hands to get Jeremy upright and balanced. His hospital gown—that joke of sartorial indignity—became untied from the back, a breeze swooping up over his jockey-shorted ass. Cassie went to cover him up but Jeremy pulled away.

"Let me help you get dressed, and then I'll bring the car around," she offered evenly, seemingly trying to move through this with the least amount of drama. It was unlike her and, for Jeremy, made this awkward reunion even more unnerving. It's not that he didn't want to see her, he just didn't want her to see *him*. Not like this.

"Could you just ask one of the nurses to help me get dressed?" he asked tightly.

If that took Cassie by surprise she didn't show it. "Sure," she said calmly and pushed past the wraparound curtain, leaving Jeremy standing there alone.

He took a good look at the pillow sling that hung against him like a ghastly new appendage. It reminded him of those trays vendors used to sell drinks at stadiums. Hey, Jeremy thought darkly, I need a job—maybe I could kill two birds with one stone!

Forget Hockstein's "time flies" baloney. Jeremy knew it was going to be the longest six weeks of his life.

CHAPTER
10

AND HE WASN'T wrong. But not necessarily for the reasons he may have first thought.

What he had no way of knowing at the start, since he was completely unprepared for his shotgun marriage to the abduction pillow he would soon name "Big Bertha," was how difficult, if not impossible, most everything would be with this fucking thing slung over his tender shoulder. Though Jeremy was furious that neither Hockstein nor the indispensable Lorena warned him there was even the slightest chance he could be stuck in such a humongous sling, he quickly realized that if they *had* told him—and explained everything that might entail—he may have thought a whole lot harder about having the procedure to begin with. And, he guessed, most people would have—or did and bailed—which was why details were doled out on a need-to-know basis.

The trouble started right off as Jeremy had to remain in the hospital gown, with the brace strapped over it, because getting dressed, even with the nurse's practiced help, was proving far too complicated. He told her to forget it and just let her wheel him out to Cassie's car with his clothes in his lap instead of on his back. Fortunately, it was mild May and not chilly December.

The next hurdle was trying to wedge himself and his abduction sling into the passenger seat of Cassie's MINI Cooper, which was not called a MAXI Cooper for good reason. As if Jeremy wasn't self-conscious enough being around his future ex-wife in his current state, he had to enlist whatever math, engineering, and logic skills she possessed to help him fit into the little car. It was looking like they would have to call an Uber (a big one) to take Jeremy home until Cassie rolled down the top and he was able to squeeze into the seat.

There was nothing to say about their ride home, as nothing was said between them. As in, literally nothing. (Oh, Cassie did ask if Jeremy needed to stop for anything, but he declined; he didn't want to prolong the trip.)

Jeremy's mom was waiting as Cassie pulled up in front of the house. She was talking with Crash, who stood there with Lola in tow. Joyce and Crash both went wide-eyed as they got a load of Jeremy in his hospital duds, attached to the mega-sling and wedged into the MINI. Although Joyce clearly had filled Crash in on Jeremy's surgery (did she mention his neighbors' split?), neither was prepared for what they saw. Lola barked at Jeremy and leaped at the car; Crash yanked her down. The dog whimpered and sat on her haunches.

Crash hung back respectfully, but Joyce went full-on mother. "Sweetheart, are you alright? Where are your clothes? What's with that pillow? My God, it's as big as you are! Let me help you out."

Lola barked again, though stayed seated, as Joyce opened the car door and thrust two helping hands at her son. Jeremy nodded at Crash, who was a bit speechless (unlike his dog). Cassie joined Joyce and together they got Jeremy fully on his feet. He felt like an idiot.

"Geez, sorry, man," said Crash, finding his voice. "Your mom told me what happened to you but, well ... wow."

"Quite the fashion statement, huh?" joked Jeremy, though no one laughed. Without warning, Lola sprang up again, but Crash pulled her back before she could topple Jeremy. Joyce, animal lover though she was, shot the pup a harsh look and reflexively pulled her son aside. It wasn't lost on Crash.

"I better get this wild thing inside before you're wearing two of those contraptions," he said. "Let me or Katie know if there's anything you need, okay, dude?" Crash turned to Cassie as if seeing her there for the first time. "I mean if you're not around." He studied the subdued Cassie in a way that made Jeremy suspect he knew the entirety of recent events; who knows how long Joyce and he were out there talking.

There was silence among the remaining three until Cassie broke the spell. "Joyce, you can take it from here, yes?"

"You're not coming in?" Joyce's eyes locked on her daughter-in-law as if to say, Why don't you two just kiss and make up? But even she knew that was not to be.

"I'm just going to grab a few things, but then I have to go," said Cassie.

"You already took one coffee pot, don't take the other, alright?" It was the first thing Jeremy could think of and at least it showed he was paying attention. Cassie nodded tightly and made her way into the house.

"I'm so sad for you two," said Joyce when Cassie was out of earshot.

"Thanks for being here, Mom," Jeremy said, bypassing whatever other feelings he was having just then.

Joyce took her son's free arm and guided him up the weathered brick path.

CHAPTER
11

MATTY AND JOYCE both offered to stay over to help Jeremy deal with his first night in the clunky abduction sling. But he stubbornly declined, said he'd figure it all out even though he had little to go by. (Was it okay to stretch his right arm at all? Could he loosen that brace strap jabbing into his neck?) He had an expanding list of things to call Lorena about in the morning.

The truth was, he wasn't sure how he was going to handle his life on his own for the next six weeks, left-handed eating—left-handed everything—being among the many tests he'd be up against. Fortunately, he was not supposed to shower for four or five days so he didn't have to worry just yet about that mind-boggling adventure. Still, how the hell was he going to get the fucking sling off and then back on much less not kill himself on the slippery shower tile?

And he couldn't stay in that stupid hospital gown forever. But, as changing into clothes still seemed like such an unfathomable feat of engineering under the circumstances, it was simply too exhausting to ponder.

The list of challenges currently facing Jeremy was so daunting that he decided to calm his brain and just go to sleep. Easier said than done, he'd discover, although at least left-handed electric tooth-brushing wasn't that hard once you figured out how to get toothpaste on the brush with one hand. (Think about it.)

But he was in for yet another unwanted surprise when he tried to get into bed: there was no way to even remotely lie flat on the mattress with the gigantic brace, which, in doing so, thrust his attached arm up in the air and painfully over his head. And forget about assuming his usual sleeping position on his side. The sling's bulk prevented him from rolling over on his right; rolling to the left brought the abduction pillow back up into the air and, of course, his arm with it, straining his troubled limb at an impossible angle.

After much anguished negotiation, Jeremy settled into the only seemingly workable position, if not for sleep then at least for some measure of physical comfort: sitting up against his two bed pillows with the brace at his side, Velcroed arm resting flat and straight atop it. Oh, and scratch the physical comfort part: in a matter of minutes, Jeremy developed pain in his arm and shoulder from the unnatural sleeping position and had to constantly adjust himself by degrees until he found relief, temporary though it was.

Twenty minutes and an OxyContin later ...

Sleep remained a ridiculous expectation as Jeremy's mind raced, replaying the day's crazy hodgepodge of events. Though he tried to keep thoughts of Cassie at bay, they refused to stay submerged, bubbling to the surface with a stubborn, needling intensity. She wanted out of his life but was still demanding his attention. He wanted her *in* his life—at least he thought he did—but had seemed unable to give her the attention she needed.

Then again, how much attention had Cassie shown Jeremy these last years? Real attention: spontaneous, probing, loyal, passionate (and not just physically but emotionally). Sure, no longer reading his film reviews—or much else he wrote—was an indicator of her pulling away, not even trying to make the effort to connect with Jeremy on one of his most essential levels. But wasn't it Jeremy who had gradually stopped enlisting his smart, objective, forthright wife as a creative sounding board, one that he once so wholly depended upon for inspiration and validation? Had he stopped respecting her opinion, or had he started better respecting his own? And if it was the latter, was it because Cassie had made him more confident—as a writer, a creative force, a man? Was her work here done? Was that her plan all along? Get her husband to a higher level of independence and then give him complete independence? Was that what he'd wanted without really knowing it? A self-fulfilling prophecy?

How was it, exactly, that Jeremy started needing less and less from the people around him? Yes, he and Matty were really close, and Jeremy depended on his mom in ways that were such carry-overs from his youth that it felt a bit embarrassing when he thought about it, which is why he tried not to. But he'd slipped away from so many others who'd been constants in his life for so long. Friends like Norm, and Joshua who he'd known since third grade, and old college pal Cliff who was Jeremy's best man as he was Cliff's, and Zoë from the first screenwriting class he ever took who soon went pro, and wickedly funny fellow film reviewer and inveterate gossip Candace, and his cousin Amie with whom he shared photographic memories of their grandparents. They were all at his birthday party and, while it was good to see them (even if he didn't really want anyone there to begin with), he could also feel a kind of remove, maybe a result of their less frequent calls and emails and texts and lunches and drop-bys.

It was not as if Jeremy could blame Cassie for any of that. On the contrary, she encouraged him to see his friends, ask them over, invite them to screenings rather than go alone. In general, she liked people more than Jeremy, liked having others around more than he did. Jeremy could go either way and, of late, that way seemed to be more solo than not. Meanwhile, Cassie expanded her friend network, often spending more time out and about with them than in with Jeremy. The fact that Jeremy had become just as happy if she was with him or not was not lost on either of them. And it had gone largely if entirely undiscussed.

JEREMY PUT IN an SOS call to Lorena as soon as Hockstein's office opened at 8 a.m. He'd gotten through a rough night, dropping in and out of sleep—mostly out—finally getting out of bed around six when he could no longer sit in that dreadful upright position. He managed to make one-armed, left-handed coffee and some rye toast but for all the effort it took he might as well have been trying to paint the *Mona Lisa*. And, for the record, the hospital gown wasn't smelling so hot.

"You know what you need?" asked Lorena after offering Jeremy a few answers to his first wave of how-the-hell-do-I questions.

"A time machine so I can jump ahead six weeks?" He was sitting at his desk (don't even ask how he fit into his ergonomic chair with the pillow brace), about to turn on his laptop, which, unlike Jeremy, had been in sleep mode for the last two days.

"That's funny! Good you can keep a sense of humor," Lorena said with a little laugh. While she'd completely missed the point, Jeremy had to admit she had a pleasant voice. "No, an occupational therapist," she explained.

"I thought I had to wait until the brace was off for that." He watched the Apple logo materialize on his computer screen.

"That's a physical therapist. This is different."

Jeremy slowly typed in his password with his left index finger. "How different?"

"Why don't I just read you what we have?" she asked, the tap of computer keys echoing through the phone. "Okay, here we go: 'Occupational therapists treat patients post-surgery to improve the skills they need for everyday activities such as living and working. They provide therapeutic interventions such as strengthening programs, modalities, home and workplace modifications, manual therapy techniques, pain management, and more.'" Lorena clucked her tongue and said, "Really, who wouldn't want one of those miracle workers?"

"Well, when you put it that way," Jeremy said, gazing at his screensaver: a photo of him and Cassie and Matty standing at the Tower of London from Matty's post-bar mitzvah trip. Jeremy had thought about changing the picture for years, but kept it from laptop to laptop, so sentimental about Matty's first trip to Europe, which, the kid announced on the flight home, in his usual dramatic flair, had "changed his life."

"We can set you up with one, Mr. Lerner," bubbled Lorena.

"One what?" Jeremy asked, still lost in London.

"An occupational therapist!" she exclaimed. "Would you like a man or a woman?"

That felt like a trick question, so Jeremy took a guess and answered "a woman," then asked if his insurance would cover it. Lorena checked and confirmed it would, which made Jeremy sink a bit, remembering that he was on Cassie's coverage and wondered how, all things being equal, that would work from now on.

"I'll make you a referral, and she'll call you this morning, how's that?"

"Feeling better already," Jeremy lied.

"Wonderful. Dr. Hockstein will be very happy to hear that," Lorena brightly signed off.

Then it'll all be worthwhile, thought Jeremy dryly as he tried typing hunt-and-peck with just his left hand. Maybe it was a good thing he didn't have any writing deadlines right now.

CHAPTER
12

JEREMY STOOD IN front of his bathroom mirror assessing the damage, before greeting his occupational therapist, who was momentarily due for her first home visit. All he knew was that her name was Annabelle (coincidentally—or not—the name of a deadly doll in a successful series of horror movies) and that she was one of Dr. Hockstein's go-to referrals. Oh, and that Lorena must have deemed his case urgent, or at least sufficiently desperate for Annabelle to schedule Jeremy for the very next day.

He tried getting his matted hair into some kind of passable shape using a one-handed, left-handed brushing technique that completely did not work and possibly made him look even worse. Shaving was a nonstarter; Annabelle, not to mention the rest of the world, would simply have to put up with his salt-and-pepper scraggle. Ever try washing your face with one hand—with a two-ton pillow blocking the sink? Not fun. Nothing to be done with his stinky hospital gown, though hopefully his "miracle worker" could teach him how to change into his real clothes and then help him set fire to said gown.

Still, he *had* to change his underwear before getting in breathing distance to another human being. Joyce and Matty didn't count, or at least so they said the previous night when they brought him dinner again, and he complained of feeling gross. "We're used to it," his mother said, and Jeremy left it there.

With his single arm working in concert with his two feet, he shimmied out of his briefs and into a new pair, which took far more stretching, sliding, and bending than he ever imagined in the service of that simple everyday act.

Doing so, it struck Jeremy how dingy and shapeless his skivvies looked. Maybe it was time for an undergear overhaul if only for his self-esteem and not, as Matty had so randomly floated, for any new potential viewers.

Finally, given that a dose of deodorant was about the best he could do to mask the telltale signs of his current hygienic state, Jeremy had quite the task ahead to apply his Mennen Speed Stick. And under the hospital gown no less. Although it seemed as if reaching his right pit with his left hand could work, he didn't count on the pain it would cause to tilt up his affixed right arm ever so slightly to make way for the roll-on. Let's just say there was a howl, and not from one of the many coyotes that haunted Laurel Canyon. Meantime, he had to twist his left arm all the way out and up so he could reach into his left pit with the deodorant stick. But that required more acrobatic skill than Jeremy possessed, and he gave up. Maybe Annabelle would have a hack for him—if she could stand getting close enough to demonstrate. He suspected, or at least hoped, she'd had her share of grungy patients.

"Well, aren't you a sorry sight?" was the first thing out of Annabelle's mouth when Jeremy greeted her at the front door. It might have seemed brash if it wasn't completely true.

"This is good. You should have seen me before I tried to clean myself up," joked Jeremy, partly to relieve the anxiety he'd been feeling about this stranger who'd be coming into his home to help and partly because there was something so instantly disarming about Annabelle, with her loose, wavy locks, petite frame and crinkly eyes. She wore olive green capri pants, a stretchy, long-sleeved T-shirt with a koala bear on it, and a pair of stylish memory-foam sneakers. She was, in a word, adorable.

"Well, don't you worry. My line of work, I see it all," Annabelle said, confirming Jeremy's suspicions. She looked beyond him and into the house. "Though it'd be much more effective if we did this inside and not in the doorway." There went those crinkly eyes again.

Jeremy moved away from the door and made an "entrée" gesture with his free hand. Annabelle gave his abduction sling the once over as she walked in.

"You must've torn the shit out of your rotator cuff to end up in a brace that size," Annabelle said. "Only the second one of those I've ever seen."

"Think you can handle it?" Jeremy asked, and then realized how double-entendre flirty it must've sounded. He cleared his throat, swallowed. "I mean, yeah, it's huge." Okay, that didn't sound right either. He quickly switched gears before she could respond. "Can I get you some water? A coffee?"

"Thanks, but I come prepared," she answered, pulling a metal water bottle from her oversized shoulder bag. Annabelle looked around the living room with its beamed ceiling, curved archways, and nubby, overstuffed couch. She pronounced the room "cozy" and then proceeded to take a seat on the Mission-style armchair.

She gave Jeremy no directions but, since it was his house and all, he figured it was okay to sit on the couch. He settled in as best he could. Annabelle opened an iPad and made some notes, then looked up at Jeremy.

"So," she said.

"So," Jeremy echoed.

"How are you doing?"

"Honestly?"

"No, lie to me, because that's *really* going to help me help you," she quipped. That got an unexpected laugh out of Jeremy; Annabelle grinned in return. She took a few more notes, and then fixed her gaze back on the patient.

Jeremy fidgeted and then said the first thing that came to mind: "My wife left me less than a week ago, and, frankly, I don't know what the fuck I'm going to do."

Annabelle was not expecting that, nor was Jeremy.

"Was that honest enough?"

Annabelle tapped at her iPad, then took a slug of water from her bottle, which Jeremy now realized had a decal on it that read: "Fuck Cancer." "Yeah, that was super honest," the therapist said. "I'm really sorry." When Jeremy offered no rejoinder, she asked, "Should I be?"

"In general, probably. But in the specific, hard to say," he answered, unsure why he was being so open to this person he just met. Maybe it was his way of expressing his disappointment that, except for a four-word text ("Hope you're adjusting OK"), Cassie hadn't been in touch since she dropped him off the other day. Her absence spoke volumes, and he needed to hear that, loud and clear.

"So then you're dealing with your injury all by yourself?" Annabelle asked, looking around the room as if a caregiver might pop out of the wall.

"Well, my son and my mother have been in and out to help, but, yeah, I'm pretty much flying solo." He flexed the fingers of his stiff right hand, trying to work back some circulation.

Annabelle noticed. She rose and went to Jeremy and, without a word, tore off the Velcro straps that fastened his arm to the abduction pillow. He looked up at her confused.

"Guess what? You can take your arm out for a spin now and then, loosen it up a bit. Go ahead—give it a little stretch."

"But I thought—"

"I know what you thought," she said patiently. "But as long as you keep your arm straight out at that 90-degree angle and just gently move it, you'll be fine. I promise." Annabelle put her hand over her heart (that's when Jeremy noticed her wedding band, wondered what *her* marriage was like) and gave her head an endearing tilt. "Ready?" she asked.

Jeremy nodded, entranced, and slowly lifted his arm up out of the open straps and carefully stretched it out. He gave a little groan of pleasure. "Oh, my God, this feels so good." If he wasn't already so self-conscious, he would have shed a tear of joy.

"Right?" Annabelle held her hand above his untethered arm to make sure Jeremy didn't accidentally jerk it up. "You don't have to completely baby yourself, y'know."

"I know—I mean, I guess I do *now*, but I'm really afraid of doing anything wrong." He considered that and added, "You could say that's pretty much my life's MO."

Wait, did he actually believe that? Especially after he clearly did something so wrong, maybe many things wrong, to make Cassie leave. Did he just *think* he was so careful about things when, in fact, he was sloppy and irresponsible? Look at what happened with that film review. Jeremy rested his arm back atop the brace.

"Being afraid of doing the wrong thing and actually doing the wrong thing are two different things, wouldn't you say?" asked Annabelle.

She re-strapped his arm into the Velcro. Jeremy looked spooked by her prescience. She sat next to him on the couch awaiting an answer.

"In my case, they're not mutually exclusive," he realized. "Or at least I don't think they are."

Annabelle snapped a photo of Jeremy's sling set-up with her iPad. "Want to hear my life's MO?"

He couldn't begin to guess what his spritely guest would come up with.

"Life can be a bitch," she said flatly, "and sometimes, you just have to get out of the fucking way." She checked herself. "Sorry, that was unprofessional. But you get my drift." Annabelle, who maybe realized sitting so close to her patient could also seem a tad unprofessional, rose and returned to her original chair.

"Not unprofessional and probably a good way to look at it," Jeremy surmised. "Anyway, you don't need to hear about my problems."

"No, I don't need to. But something tells me they're connected to all this." She made a triangular finger sketch of his arm, shoulder, and the brace.

Jeremy looked at her hands with their neat, unpainted nails; they were dainty, as was the rest of her. Yet there was a solidity to her as well, a kind of deceptive strength. Jeremy didn't know how he knew this, but he believed in first impressions. Maybe it was her profession, the knowledge she had yet to impart that he seemed to so desperately need.

Jeremy realized she was waiting for a response. "Yeah, it is all connected." He wanted to tell her all about it, start to finish, get her take. Instead, he said, "It's complicated, I guess."

"For another day, then," Annabelle declared. She leaped up and gestured for Jeremy to do the same. So he did. "Okay, who wants to learn how to shower with that ridiculous brace?" she asked as if it was going to be the most fun lesson ever.

Jeremy would've enthusiastically raised his right hand—if he could have.

CHAPTER
13

ANNABELLE CONFIRMED WHAT Jeremy already knew from Hockstein's instruction sheet: The abduction pillow had to come off before he got into the shower; she'd show him how to remove it next time. What he'd been trying not to think about, however, but the therapist forced him to decide (the big event was now two days away), was who would help him in and out of the brace for said body cleanse and generally stand guard while he was washing up. She didn't equivocate: "Jeremy, no way in hell can you do it yourself. Period, full stop."

He had a few choices, all of whom made him uneasy. Had Cassie not chosen this particular time to take her leave, his wife would have been his aide throughout this ordeal. He could bite the bullet and ask her to stop by every few days. The way things were going, Jeremy could probably go four days at a crack without showering. It's not like he'd be playing pickup basketball or digging ditches in that damn sling. Besides, he'd gotten used to being a little gamy. It wasn't *that* terrible, was it?

Jeremy was, at least in theory, a lot less uncomfortable with the thought of being bare-assed around Cassie than, say, around his mother or son. Even though, yes, they'd both seen him naked: Joyce when he was a child, Matty when *he* was a child. Now, though, it was a nonstarter. And who's to say Joyce or Matty would be cool with that scenario either? They were an open-minded group but not exactly commune dwellers.

And what if he needed help and someone had to get into the shower *with* him? Cassie was the one who'd done that most recently (if, what was it, seven or eight years, was recently). But what made him think Cassie would now agree to assist him in any way? He could picture her terse response: "I'll hire you a nurse." Click. Would she be wrong?

Annabelle was coming back in two days for more OT (that's what the pros called it, apparently) at which time she was expecting the name—and who knows: birthday, shoe size, social security number?—of Jeremy's shower buddy. He could tell, when it came to his well-being, she meant business. He wouldn't disappoint her.

Jeremy considered all this as he and Big Bertha sat in a chaise lounge in his backyard, the first time he'd been back to the scene of the crime—that is, his fiftieth birthday party—since the crime itself. Maybe he *should* just hire a nurse or caregiver a few hours a week to help with his more … intimate needs. It was more in line with Jeremy's comfort zone anyway, not having to ask too much of others or put anyone out.

He tried to lean back as best he could in the padded chair, tilting his face up to the late afternoon sun. It felt good to marinate in the warmth a bit, truly relax, not a feeling he'd experienced these past days. Jeremy nursed a cup of coffee—he'd finally mastered one-handed coffee making that morning, no small triumph—and thought about the last time he'd found himself alone, physically compromised, and unexpectedly needing help.

Jeremy and Cassie had been dating for about a month, together most every night, doing the getting-to-know-you dance with increasing ease and familiarity. There was a level of depth and propulsion to their pairing unlike anything he'd experienced with other women and, though she didn't exactly come out and say it, he sensed it was unlike what Cassie had been used to as well.

He was essentially right, though what he didn't know back then—how could he?—was that a small, imperceptible, but key disparity in their attachment to each other, even throughout the best of their years, would inform their future. It was a simple imbalance, really, and not that uncommon among even the happiest of couples. Except that, in the case of Cassie and Jeremy, it was the hairline crack that would slowly, but steadily, grow and spread and eventually fracture the foundation of what they had built together.

The difference was this: Jeremy loved Cassie more unequivocally, more completely than she loved him. It was that way from the start, from the moment when he saw her in her ponytail and yoga pants walking toward the New Beverly Cinema. He was instantly smitten; she was coy and challenging, and, of course, enticing.

That Jeremy was the more reserved of the two may have created a misperception, if not quite a deception, in the who-loved-whom-more contest. Although Cassie, for so many years, more outwardly displayed her awareness and affection—not just for Jeremy, but for everyone she cared about—it didn't necessarily have the focus and gravity of Jeremy's quieter attentions. Until maybe it got a bit too quiet.

In any case, at the ripe old age of twenty-three, Jeremy had begun to have some mild, but unprecedented, back pain, more likely due to the weights he'd started lifting to impress the athletic Cassie (he'd joined a gym for the first and last time) than the sexual gymnastics the new couple had been avidly engaging in. He didn't think much of the increasing stiffness in his lower back—wasn't paying attention to much of anything at the time except his infatuation with Cassie—and continued to carelessly overdo his crash course in body sculpting.

One night, toward the end of their amazing first month, Jeremy and Cassie were exploring each other's nether regions on the kitchen floor of the dowdy—but affordable—Valley Village apartment Jeremy had been renting since he graduated from Berkeley. Just as Jeremy landed beneath Cassie who was about to lower herself onto her outstretched boyfriend, he felt a seizing in the small of his back that made him cry out in agony, well before he might have otherwise cried out in pleasure. Suddenly, he couldn't move, frozen on the cold linoleum floor, arrows shooting up his spine.

"Baby, are you okay?" Cassie had asked, pulling away, her eyes going wide.

"Uh, I think you should call an ambulance," Jeremy had quietly suggested. He didn't know if he was overreacting but was willing to take the chance as those arrows tied themselves into a furious knot just above what he would later learn was his sacroiliac.

Cassie, who was naked but for Jeremy's unbuttoned flannel shirt (it had devilishly ended up on her instead of him), leaped into action. She called 911 and, in five minutes, a pair of paramedics arrived. They asked a bunch of questions, took Jeremy's vitals, and then transferred his immobile body onto a stretcher.

An ER visit and one well-placed shot of cortisone later, Jeremy was back home, semi-mobile, and assigned to three days of bed rest until his inflamed back fully settled down. Cassie packed a bag and moved in with Jeremy to take care of him. She even took a few sick days off from work so he wouldn't be stranded, ignoring his protests that his parents could stop by to spell her during the day.

As much as he hated to inconvenience her, Jeremy was secretly thrilled that Cassie would be with him 24/7, for once really relishing someone's undivided attention. That he wanted her around all the time, in a kind of impromptu trial run for cohabitation, only further confirmed what Jeremy already knew: he was madly in love with her and was the luckiest guy in the world to ever have his back go out on him.

Nothing was too much trouble for Cassie during those idyllic three days. She cooked, tidied up, organized his kitchen cabinets, did a little redecorating, watched bad movies on cable with him (she only fell asleep during one, *Ishtar*, and who could blame her, though Jeremy was a bit fascinated by the film's awfulness), gave him erotic sponge baths (making sure he never had to overexert himself at, er, peak moments), told him stories about her childhood, and was the all-around best caregiver, companion, lover, and friend he could have imagined. And he hoped one day he could do the same for her—in sickness and in health.

It was also the first time they said "I love you."

The memory of those few days so long ago was more than just bittersweet. It was like a knife to Jeremy's heart. It was also the first time since Cassie's untimely departure that he really and truly felt the seriousness, the permanence of his situation. He knew it for sure now in his bones and in his soul: Cassie was not coming back.

"**DAD, YOU'RE SUCH** a freak!" said Matty. "How could you think for even a second I wouldn't want to help you deal with the shower?"

"I could still hire someone," Jeremy answered with minimal conviction. He was relieved that Matty was so unequivocal in his response. "I think my insurance will cover at least part of it."

"They can pay me, how's that?" Matty shot Jeremy one of his trademark looks. It made Jeremy smile. That kid.

It was Saturday, the day before Annabelle was returning for round two of "let's help Jeremy feel more like a human being." Jeremy and Matty were at the kitchen table eating lunch. Matty had picked up, as he called it, "responsibly sourced" food from Tender Greens: Mediterranean Steak Salad for Jeremy, the Grilled Salmon Bowl (with extra salmon—muscle-building protein, you know) for himself. Jeremy didn't know how "responsible" his meal was, but it was pretty tasty.

"And let's just get the weirdness in the room *out* of the room, okay, Dad?" Matty met his father's eyes squarely as he chewed a hunk of salmon. "I won't be traumatized if I see your dick."

Jeremy could feel his face flush. "Honey, it has absolutely nothing to do with that," he white-lied unconvincingly. "You're a busy guy, I just don't want to put you out." Jeremy returned to his salad. He'd really made headway on his left-handed fork management—as long as he didn't have to cut anything.

"I mean, it's no secret I've seen a lot of dicks," Matty pressed on.

What could a father say to that but: "I'm proud of you, son." Matty laughed out loud. It was a jokey response by Jeremy, of course, but he *was* proud of Matty—not for the number of penises he'd encountered in his young life (honestly, Jeremy didn't need to know the specifics), but for his son's unselfconsciousness, his spontaneity, his offhand charisma. Jeremy didn't know how much of that Matty got from Cassie, but he sure didn't take after his father in that regard. Jeremy made a note to self: "Be more like my son."

"Besides, it's not like you've got anything to be shy about in that department, Pop." Matty popped up from his seat, stuck his head in the refrigerator, and returned with a bottle of soy sauce.

"What are you getting at?" Jeremy asked as he watched his son douse his fish in Kikkoman.

Matty suppressed a grin. "Nothing, ya big stud," he said, diving back into his salmon bowl.

The last thing Jeremy wanted to talk about with his son was schlong size—his own or anyone else's—though he had to admit, bringing up the so-called weirdness did relax him about it all. It also made Jeremy feel a little ridiculous.

"Matty, tell the truth. Do you think I'm too uptight about stuff? I mean, in general. Y'know, a stick-in-the-mud? That's what your mother called me, anyway."

Matty looked up and assessed his father. "Why, because you don't want to talk about your dick? Dad, most fathers don't want to talk about their dick with their sons beyond how they should protect it once they're old enough to figure out where they want to put it."

Jeremy mulled that. "Did we ever have that conversation?"

"Ha! Are you kidding? Old stick-in-the-mud like you?" Matty speared his last bite of salmon. His eyes twinkled at his dad, who looked a bit hurt. "Kidding! I'm kidding! Yes, you gave me a very responsible lecture about sex—well, safe sex—when I was, like, thirteen, and you and Mom realized I liked boys and you wanted to get ahead of the curve."

Jeremy now recalled that chat. Cassie had asked him to do it, thought it would be a nice bonding experience for father and son. Little did she know the real bonding over it wouldn't happen for another decade. "For the record, I would have had the exact same talk with you had you liked girls. Well, maybe not the *exact* same talk, but you know what I'm saying."

"I do," Matty confirmed. "And, believe me, it meant a whole lot to me back then." He took the last bite of his lunch. "I was lucky—*am* lucky—to have parents like you and Mom. Not sure I say that enough." Matty pushed aside his bowl, checked his phone.

Jeremy watched him, moved and appreciative. He thought back on that sex talk with Matty, the details taking shape. After Jeremy had laid out the basics for his son, in the clearest but least awkward way he could, he felt obligated to reassure Matty that his sexuality was a nonissue to both Cassie and him.

"But you'd be happier if I wasn't gay, wouldn't you?" Matty had asked, his eyes filling up.

"There's nothing you could be that would make us unhappy, honey," Jeremy had answered in all truthfulness. "Except maybe a Republican."

They'd laughed at that then, and Jeremy chuckled again now.

"What's so funny?" asked Matty, as he began to clear the table.

"You are," said Jeremy, and left it at that. He loosened the Velcro straps, keeping his arm in place and stretched it out a bit, flexing his fingers. Matty looked aghast.

"What are you doing? Are you supposed to do that?"

"Relax, it's fine. It's something Annabelle showed me. It really helps," Jeremy explained as the ache drained from his arm.

"Well, okay, she's the expert, I guess." Matty dumped the take-out containers in the trash pail under the sink, then rinsed off the silverware. (He was okay eating out of plastic but not *with* plastic.) "What kind of name is Annabelle, anyway? Is she, like, from the South?"

"I don't know, it's her name. She's very nice. I like her."

Matty turned to face his father with a Cheshire grin. "Do you *like* like her?"

"What? Why would you ask me that?"

"I just asked if you liked her. What's wrong with that?"

"It was the way you asked." Jeremy reattached the straps to his arm and resettled himself in the chair.

Matty dried his hands on a dishtowel, which he then folded into a square. "Well, maybe it's because of the way you answered. All defensive like."

"I was *not* defensive."

"Ah, doth the lady protest too much?"

It took a second for Jeremy to realize he was the lady. "Do you *want* me to '*like* like' her?"

"I want you to do whatever you feel like you want to do." Matty plopped down across from Jeremy, glanced at his phone, then back at his father, who looked unsettled. "What?"

"Would you tell your mother the same thing? To go for it—with some new guy she met? Like, right now?" asked Jeremy, perhaps unfairly.

"I wouldn't have to."

"What does that mean?" Jesus, was there somebody else after all? Had Jeremy completely misread that, overly trusted Cassie's loyalty, if not her commitment to him?

"Y'know what? Sorry I said anything—about anything. I'm glad you like this Annabelle, and I'm *really* glad she taught you how to put on something other than that ratty hospital gown. And you don't have to tell me how she did that if you don't want to." Matty waved a hand at Jeremy's new "ensemble": gray Adidas track pants, a black and scarlet San Diego State T-shirt (a gift from Matty's freshman year) with the right side scissor-cut open and closed back up with safety pins, gym socks, and some seen-better-days Nike slides. Dashing.

"There's not a lot to tell," Jeremy answered, trying hard not to sound defensive. "Annabelle cut the T-shirt so I could put it on without having to take the brace off, which, let me warn you, is a bear. She also pinned it back together. The rest I managed myself, with a couple of pain-saving tips she gave me." He felt obliged to add: "It's her job, it's what she does."

"Okay, cool," said Matty, whose interest, as it was wont to do, vanished as quickly as it had appeared. He rose from the table. "Anything else you need before I go?"

Jeremy steeled himself, then stood to face his son. "Just tell me: Have you heard from your mom?" Even though he was starting to come to terms with their break, Jeremy still had so many questions for Cassie, and it was driving him a little crazy. He truly didn't want to involve Matty any more than necessary, but, well … maybe just a little.

"We had a few texts this morning."

"Do you know where she's staying?" Jeremy caught himself. "You don't have to tell me if you don't want, or if she doesn't want you to, or whatever."

"Okay."

"Okay, what?"

"Okay, I won't tell you."

"Wait, did she ask you not to?"

"Dad, I've gotta go." He grabbed his retro-style Ray-Bans off the counter and slipped them on, looking like a 1980s movie star.

Jeremy and Matty stared at each other a moment, as if they both wanted to say something but were thinking better of it: Jeremy to press his son on what he knew; Matty, never the world's best secret keeper, to *tell* what he knew, but struggling to respect his mother's wishes—whatever they were.

"Hey, I didn't even ask, how are things with you and Sven?" Jeremy, rarely one to leave things on a sour note—except maybe with Cassie—tried to right the ship.

"Sven? Good, I think." Matty removed his sunglasses, wiped them clean with his T-shirt, and put them back on. In that moment, Jeremy saw a flash of concern in the boy's eyes.

"You 'think?'"

"Yeah, I don't know. He's been a little elusive lately. But he's also been busy with work, so maybe …"

Jeremy could tell Matty was realizing something may be up with his boyfriend. Jeremy also realized that Matty might be more into this guy than he'd been letting on, had moved beyond the "I like him, he's cool" phase.

"It's all good," Matty offhandedly concluded.

Yeah, thought Jeremy, *that's what we all say.*

CHAPTER
14

THE CALL FROM Lucien the next morning was, to say the least, a surprise. Jeremy had been trying not to stress about his job loss or his new work prospects, of which there were none—not that he'd exactly been burning up the world to find any. He had largely convinced himself that even if he could land another steady gig, he was too hamstrung by his current one-handed, one-fingered typing style to commit to writing anything longer than an email—and a short one at that.

Or was he being a wimp? Was he not going to write anything for another five weeks? Really? That seemed like a colossal waste of time, of his ability, and of the one thing he did best.

Then, of course, there was Jeremy's money situation, which he had also been avoiding thinking about, having no idea yet how things would shake out financially if—no, when—he and Cassie came to terms on their split. It was time to get real. He'd ask Annabelle for help at the keyboard today, see if she had a plan.

Jeremy's first thought upon seeing Lucien's name appear on his phone display was that he was being rehired. That hope was immediately dashed.

"I wish I had better news for you, sport," said Lucien, sounding once again like the Connecticut WASP he aspired to be.

"That's okay," Jeremy lied. "I've actually got a few new irons in the fire." Yeah, like learning how to shower without ending up back in surgery.

"That's outstanding, J, good to hear. I knew you'd land on your feet."

That made one of them, thought Jeremy as he paced the length of the kitchen.

"Though, to be honest, that's not what I was calling about—on a Sunday."

"Oh, okay, then. What's up?" Jeremy gazed out the window above the sink that looked out on their sunny backyard. A pair of hummingbirds frolicked in the ceramic birdbath, a housewarming present from his parents so many years ago.

"I ran into Cassie last night," said Lucien.

"You did?" Jeremy didn't even try to feign casual. A third hummingbird now joined the birdbathers.

"Yes. At Salt & Straw? On Larchmont?"

It was an artisan ice cream shop where for a mere six bucks you could get a scoop of bone marrow and smoked cherry ice cream, hold the attitude.

Jeremy's first thought was that Cassie didn't eat ice cream, avoided sugar when she could, and not just in Matty's passing-fancy way either. And what was she doing in that part of town? Was she staying somewhere in well-heeled Larchmont Village or maybe nearby in the even tonier Hancock Park? Was she at Salt & Straw alone, or …?

"What did she have to say?" asked Jeremy, dialing back his tone of alarm.

"That the two of you were taking a break."

"Oh, is that what she's calling it?" Jeremy simmered, turning away from the kitchen window. Fuck those happy hummingbirds.

"I pretended I didn't know, because, well, I really don't."

Jeremy studied his flip-flopped feet. "Yeah, well, it's a long story, one I can't even fully explain."

Lucien took that in, then: "Anyway, it's none of my business, and you can tell me to go stuff it if you want, but I consider you a friend and …"

He hesitated, as if he were suddenly sorry he'd started the whole thing. Jeremy certainly was. And "friend" was becoming debatable.

Lucien exhaled. "I think she was with someone."

For all of his ex-editor's attempts at propriety, he wasn't above a good bit of gossip, though it was usually consigned to the antics of his fellow newsroom staffers and the occasional off-the-wall film publicist.

"Well, was she or wasn't she?" asked Jeremy, taking a seat in the kitchen chair. He had a feeling this conversation was just beginning.

Lucien painted a vivid picture of what he saw at the upscale ice cream parlor. That is, after he got his order (a pint of black olive brittle and goat cheese) and said goodbye to Cassie, he glanced back and saw a younger, athletic-looking guy with short dark hair and a trimmed beard, someone who Lucien had assumed was just another customer in the long line behind Cassie, put his arm around her and snuggle in for a kiss—which she returned, as Lucien put it, "with enthusiasm."

Jeremy closed his eyes, felt a rock the size of a bowling ball settling in his stomach.

"Jeremy, are you there?" asked Lucien.

Jeremy still said nothing, and Lucien picked up the slack.

"I'm so sorry, Jeremy, but I thought you should know—if you didn't already. I mean, you didn't, did you?"

Jeremy shook his head no, then, realizing Lucien couldn't see it, said it out loud and hung up the phone.

Jeremy stared out the window again as the sun spread across the grass- and slate-covered yard. The hummingbirds were gone. A shadow fell over the ancient grapefruit tree that filled the far corner of the garden. He thought about the times in the first years after he and Cassie had bought the house, when they would put toddler Matty to bed, grab a bottle of anything red and relax in the teak Adirondack chairs that once sat beneath the drooping branches of that august citrus tree. They'd sip their wine, talk about the day's events, their future plans—Cassie wanted to get her law degree (she did); Jeremy wanted to write and sell another screenplay (he didn't);

as a family, they wanted to take wonderful trips (they took a few)—and hold hands while they'd sit back and wish upon the stars.

He felt a tear stream down his cheek, then another. He stood there, eyes glued out the window, weighed down by that nutty abduction pillow and the stunning realization that the train had left the station, and he was still standing on the platform.

THE SLING WAS off for the first time since the surgery, and it was positively terrifying. Annabelle showed Jeremy how to safely remove it—or rather, how someone else should safely remove it for him. As she said during her last visit, there was no non-injurious way he could physically do it himself. He was also warned that any sudden upward movements with the affected arm could damage the healing rotator cuff. By simple force of habit, patients would often reach for the soap or adjust the showerhead with their distressed arm. So, in effect, don't fucking move—unless you're paying complete attention.

Jeremy didn't realize how much, in a few short days, he had come to depend upon the brace, intrusive as it was, to protect him from potential discomfort or damage. Standing in the bathroom without the pillow was far more painful than wearing it. Paying complete attention or not, he had no idea how he would shower sans sling without accidentally screwing up his shoulder.

Enter the beach ball.

Annabelle, her dark waves bunched atop her head, a few stray gray strands peeking out at the hairline, watched Jeremy with an eagle eye as she held an inflatable rubber beach ball under his carefully tilted arm. Thank God he went extra heavy on the Mennen that morning; he'd even spritzed himself with an old bottle of Aramis he'd exhumed from the back of a bathroom cabinet.

She gently pushed the colorful ball up into his armpit. "Now slowly squeeze your arm and hold it," Annabelle ordered, gradually removing her hands from the ball. The waxy rubber against Jeremy's skin felt strange and cold. He tried to relax, if only to be a good boy for his earnest therapist who, he noted, had replaced her capris and koala shirt with snug black jeans and a print peasant blouse. Instead of sneakers, she wore a shiny pair of baby pink Crocs with short white socks. Again, adorable.

Distracted by Annabelle's sprightly Sunday wardrobe, Jeremy let the beach ball slip out from under his arm, which inadvertently jerked upwards, causing him to let out a high-pitched yelp. Annabelle reflexively reached out and steadied his arm as the beach ball rolled across the porcelain floor.

"Sorry," said Jeremy, his shoulder throbbing in time with his panicked heart.

"Gotta keep your eye on the ball, son," Annabelle joked. Her hands were still protectively on his arm. Jeremy eyed her, appreciative, trying not to seem too unnerved by the close call he'd just had.

Satisfied that he was okay, Annabelle let go of Jeremy. "Watch the arm," she reminded him. She picked the ball up off the floor and aimed it at her patient. "Beach ball, take two."

This time, more fully concentrating, Jeremy kept the slippery sphere lodged under his arm as Annabelle explained how he should "handle" himself in the shower (not that way, but they did get a laugh out of the phrase). She even took photos with her iPad that he could show Matty so he could duplicate her efforts when he arrived later that day. She emailed the pictures to Jeremy.

"Do you just have the one son?" asked Annabelle as Jeremy led her into his office. Next up was some occupational therapy at his laptop so he could continue with his own occupation.

"Yeah, Matty. Matthew, actually, but no one's ever called him that. Too formal. He's always been kind of a … jaunty kid, I guess you'd call it." Jeremy dragged an extra chair over to his desk so Annabelle could sit next to him.

She pointed to the old snapshot of Jeremy and Matty on his bookshelf. "Is that him?"

"Yeah, maybe eight years ago. Some film festival around town I took him to." Jeremy sat at his desk, turned on his computer, and gestured for Annabelle to join him.

"Good-looking boy," she said, studying the photo.

"Blame it on his mother," Jeremy answered with needless self-deprecation. He couldn't help but flash on an image of Cassie and some hot, younger guy feeding each other fancy ice cream off plastic spoons, and tried in vain to shake it off. Was Cassie's date someone new? Someone she met right after she left Jeremy? Someone she'd known for a while? A long time? A very long time? The reason she exited the marriage? None of the above?

Jeremy felt Annabelle's eyes on him as she took a seat. "Actually, I think he looks just like his father," she said without a hint of coyness.

Annabelle moved her chair in closer to better see Jeremy's screensaver: that decade-old family photo from their London trip. "Is that her?" she asked, pointing at Cassie, fresh faced and ponytailed like the day they met.

Jeremy nodded and, as quickly as his one finger would allow, opened a new document file, preferring to see a blank screen. But Annabelle wasn't done.

"She's pretty. And on the tall side, no? I've always wanted to be tall. You looked happy back then. Were you?"

Jeremy hesitated, had to think about it in light of recent developments. "I think so. But my head's apparently been up my ass about a lot of stuff, so, y'know, I can't swear to it."

"I don't mean to pry, but I'm always interested in what brings people together—and what splits them apart. I mean, one minute you're standing at the altar vowing to love, honor, and obey, next minute you want to kill the person. How does that happen?"

Annabelle had a way of cutting to it without being cutting; charmingly inquisitive, if Jeremy had to define it. She was without that inherent little challenge that would so often enter Cassie's voice—a note that had lost its appeal as time went on.

"What about your better half? Is he still 'better?'"

Why was there a part of Jeremy that was hoping the answer would be no?

"How do you know it's a 'he?'" asked Annabelle with a flat stare.

Oops, kneejerk alert. Jeremy felt like a dope, once again misreading a situation. How many times had strangers asked Matty if he had a wife or girlfriend? Why did people just assume these things? It was disrespectful. He really had to start doing better.

"In fact, I don't," Jeremy answered, a bit cowed.

Annabelle let loose one of her playful smiles. "I'm just messing with you," she said. "*He* is correct. But *he* is also, unfortunately, quite dead."

Fuck cancer. Jeremy recalled the phrase on Annabelle's water bottle. "Oh, I'm so sorry," he offered. Now he felt really dumb. "When did he ..."

"It was a year this past Monday," she said, gazing at Jeremy's blank laptop screen with resignation.

He wanted to know more, wanted to know everything, felt such sudden compassion for Annabelle that it was almost overwhelming. Jeremy's recent trifecta of trouble was tough, but it couldn't be anywhere near as bad as what she must have gone through. What she still must be going through.

Annabelle snapped to, sat up straight and pointed to his computer. "Wait, are you the same Jeremy Lerner who writes for the *L.A. Times*?" Jeremy was jarred by the sharp turn in the conversation, and realized Annabelle maybe needed to return to more neutral—read: less emotional—territory.

"That would be me," he answered. "Or should I say, used to be me."

She looked confused. "What do you mean 'used to?' Are you no longer Jeremy Lerner? Because if that's the case, I totally have the wrong house." She started to stand and stopped midway. "Should I go?" It made Jeremy laugh out loud.

"No, sadly, I'm still me. But I got shitcanned last week."

"Oh, fuck. Your wife left you *and* you got fired?"

"Don't forget: *and* I'm in this stupid sling." He remembered her dead husband and wished he could take that back. Though she had brought it up, so ...

"I can't vouch for your wife because, well, I don't know the whole story—or any of it, for that matter—so maybe she *should* have dumped you. But I love your movie reviews; you are such a good writer. There couldn't have been any logical reason in the world to fire you. Should I write a letter to the editor? Threaten to cancel my subscription? Picket headquarters?"

"You have a subscription? Like, a real one?" Jeremy was always surprised when he met someone who still read the physical paper, much less paid for it. Fair or unfair, it was one of his litmus tests.

"Call me old school, but I can't start my day without reading the *Times* cover to cover—on big ole messy sheets of ecologically dubious paper," said Annabelle. "But you—your reviews were always a Friday highlight. You know why?"

He couldn't begin to guess, but his heart was warming by the second. "Because the real news is always so depressing?" he joked.

"Because you're not one of those pretentious know-it-alls who jams in ten-dollar words I have to look up and never misses a chance to name-check some obscure Russian or German director from the 1920s to show how smart they are when all I really want to know is 'Should I waste my time on this thing or not?'"

If she was trying to make Jeremy feel good she was succeeding— in spades.

"Wow, thank you. Couldn't have said it better myself," he smiled, feeling a bit bashful but also quite sad that he was now, well, yesterday's news.

"You don't have to, I just did!" Annabelle exclaimed.

"So you like movies, I gather?"

"Who doesn't like movies?" Before he could answer her rhetorical question, she continued, "By the way, a couple of weeks ago? After reading your review? I saw that movie from Peru? *Dreams of Light*. Wow, you were so right. What a beautiful film."

Jeremy was startled and gratified that someone actually took his advice. He couldn't have gotten Cassie to see that movie with a cattle prod, much less read what he wrote about it.

"Well, I'm honored," Jeremy said. "Thank you."

"I could talk about movies for hours—and I seriously do want to know why you were fired, and I'm really sorry about that, by the way—but you and I have work to do, mister," she said, slipping on a pair of chunky, black-framed glasses that not every petite woman could pull off, but Annabelle did. "Let's get you writing again."

CHAPTER
15

ANNABELLE DID, IN fact, help to get Jeremy writing again, or at least typing again. She gave him the go-ahead to loosen the sling's Velcro straps just enough to still hold in his arm while allowing the fingers of his right hand to creep up to the keyboard. She warned that it may hurt a bit (it did) and he may not be able to type for extended periods (he couldn't), but it was an option.

"So what are you going to write?" Annabelle asked as if to say, "You got a lifeline back, Jack, so show some appreciation."

What *was* he going to write? "I don't know," he answered, "but at least now I can start to look for work again."

"Another film-reviewing job?"

"For starters. There are some good websites out there that pay okay," Jeremy considered, though it felt like small potatoes. "Maybe get back into teaching—once this brace is off."

Annabelle studied him as if there were more, as if someone like him should have a bigger plan.

"I may also jump back into this screenplay I'd been working on," he said, surprising himself. It felt more decisive than it sounded.

"Wow, you write movies *and* you write about them. I love that!"

When it was time for Annabelle to leave, Jeremy realized he didn't want her to go, grateful for the company—*her* company if he was being completely truthful—and not looking forward to an afternoon of solitude (though Matty would arrive at five for shower duties and Joyce would be over with a home-cooked dinner for them all around six).

"Don't take this the wrong way," he said, "but would you like a drink or something?" They were standing at the front door at this point, Annabelle fishing a car key from her mammoth shoulder bag.

"What's the wrong way to take that?" she asked, still unable to locate her key. "Unless you're talking about the 'or something' part?"

"No, I just ... I didn't know if it would sound weird or ... against some visiting therapist rules. Though, wait," he said, giving her a gracious out, "you probably have another client."

"Nope, you're it for the day." Annabelle whistled into her purse; there was a responsive beep. She pulled out a keychain and dangled it at Jeremy with a sly smile. "Electronic key finder. Cool, huh?"

He nodded, and she eyed him.

"Nothing alcoholic, okay? Because I *am* a professional." A wink told Jeremy she was kidding, but he fired up the coffeemaker just in case.

Minutes later, java mugs in hand, Jeremy gave Annabelle a tour of the backyard but not before mentioning that Cassie had pilfered the French press and milk frother before she split. He didn't know why he was compelled to share that bit of minutia but it's what he would have told a friend. Or maybe someone he wanted as a friend. Or, at that point, maybe anyone who would listen. Annabelle was amused.

"Definitely grounds for divorce," she punned, lifting her coffee mug in case he missed the connection. He didn't. He smiled.

After picking a few overripe grapefruits from the sagging tree for Annabelle (she asked), they sat in sling-back chairs at the patio dining table and traded a few life highlights, mostly of the more recent kind. Jeremy didn't exactly go chapter and verse about what happened with Cassie, but he did mention his ill-fated birthday party, how scarce she'd been since she jumped ship, and the ice cream shop sighting. The latter elicited an "Uh-*huh*" from Annabelle that read: "You've been had, pal." It reconfirmed his growing suspicions.

A woman knows.

She was incensed by the tale of how he got fired from the *Times* even if the image of him passed out drunk in front of a movie about the Holocaust made her eyes crinkle in amusement. Annabelle dubbed Geneva a "toadstool" and Lucien a "toady" (there was clearly a theme) and offered again to cancel her subscription in protest, but Jeremy said it wouldn't make any difference: the *Times'* customer service reps were overseas and the news wouldn't make it across the Pacific.

Annabelle talked a bit about her late husband, Gil; how they met (on JDate even though neither of them was "J"), their patient courtship but whirlwind city hall wedding, his tenured professorship in history at Cal State Northridge, his love of the Dodgers and the Clippers, the speed at which the lymphoma commandeered his body, and how—"and don't take this personally"—she would give anything to have been able to throw him a fiftieth birthday party (he died at forty-eight; she was forty-six). Jeremy felt lower than dirt.

Oh, and Gil was Annabelle's second husband. She married her first, Andy (yes, friends nicknamed them Raggedy Ann and Andy; they hated it), in their senior year of college. She called it her biggest mistake except for dying her hair blue when she was fourteen. It lasted four rocky years until Andy decided to drop out of veterinary school and move to Nova Scotia to start a wind farm. Annabelle, looking for an out anyway, declined to join her flighty hubby (dubbed him "gone with the wind") and went for her OT degree instead.

As for children, Annabelle said it was off the table with Andy—they were nearly children themselves—and seemed more likely with Gil, but they soon realized they were happy just the two of them and their resolve to parent faded.

Jeremy talked more about Matty and, when he mentioned he was gay, Annabelle said she had a "darling" nephew, Gabe (her brother Will's son), who Matty should meet if he was looking. Jeremy said he didn't know what Matty's deal was with his current boyfriend, but would tell him about Gabe if Sven went the way of all the others.

Two hours flew by, and Jeremy almost forgot that he was saddled with Big Bertha, had no new job prospects, and was on the verge of what could be a contentious divorce. Annabelle was easy to talk to and even easier to listen to.

He found himself disappointed when Matty showed up early for shower assistance, which put a pin in their cozy tête-à-tête. For his part, Matty seemed intrigued to meet his father's therapist, who immediately won him over when she commented on the fine state of his tank-topped torso. (Matty had come straight from, where else, the gym.) They chatted physiology a bit; Matty even asked her professional opinion on weightlifting's stress on the shoulders, perhaps spooked by Jeremy's injury and realizing he may not be as invincible as your average twenty-three-year-old may think. Annabelle gave him some protective exercise tips that Matty urgently typed into his Notes app.

"See you Tuesday?" Annabelle asked Jeremy, who didn't know they had made another appointment—and maybe they hadn't until now. "We'll do 'How to cook and clean with Big Bertha by your side,'" she informed him, with her usual disarming smile. Annabelle thanked Jeremy for the "caw-fee tawk" (doing a spot-on impression of Mike Myers' Long Island-inflected *SNL* character, Linda Richman), warmly shook Matty's hand goodbye, and made her exit.

"Well, isn't she a breath of fresh air?" said Jeremy's son with hiked eyebrows and an exaggerated grin. He looked like he was playing a game of charades.

"She's a really good OT, that's for sure." Jeremy felt self-conscious, as if he had to explain why he'd just spent two hours yakking with an attractive near-stranger over coffee and Trader Joe's Peanut Butter Cartwheel cookies (a "feel better" gift from Katie and Crash) in the backyard that, until a week ago, he'd shared with his wife of twenty-five years.

"I can see why you're defensive about her," Matty said. "She's definitely got something."

Jeremy let out an impatient sigh. "I'm not de-*fen*-sive," he said, meting out the syllables to underscore a lack of defensiveness, which only made it worse. He tightened his brace with its shoulder straps, which had loosened while sitting with Annabelle. Now they were digging into his neck again. Jesus, five more weeks to go in this fucking thing.

Matty didn't buy his dad's faux outrage. "Though she may want to rethink her choice of footwear. Crocs are so over." He checked his phone.

"That's your takeaway?" Jeremy didn't know if Crocs were over, under, sideways, or right on top—just that they worked on Annabelle.

"Only one of them! I *said* I liked her," Matty answered. *Now* who sounded defensive? "Oh, speaking of footwear," he brightened, "I almost forgot!" He made his way to the front door. "Be right back."

Jeremy stood in the living room awaiting Matty's return, startled by whatever it was he was feeling about his occupational therapist, trying to tamp it down like a chunk of pipe tobacco.

He was always hard on himself, too often feeling guilty until proven innocent (if only by himself). So it wasn't such a stretch that his "awareness" of Annabelle was a little unnerving, as if he was somehow cheating on the wife he no longer had, as if she hadn't already jumped back into the dating pool seemingly head first, hold the double entendre.

Matty returned bearing gifts from Nordstrom Rack: a shiny pair of bright blue Nike slides and some teal woven sweatpants by Puma. "How old are those flip-flops anyway?" he asked as Jeremy kicked them off and tried on the new ones.

"I stopped counting five years ago, which is my way of saying they could be older than you." The slides fit Jeremy perfectly and were comfier than they looked. "Nice," he told Matty, "thanks so much."

He gazed at the brightly colored gym pants, unsure.

"What?" asked Matty, already knowing his father's answer. "Too colorful?"

Jeremy shrugged.

"Dad, you've got to get past this black and gray and police

uniform blue thing that's the entirety of your wardrobe. I'm telling you, throw in a little color, it'll change your life."

"My life has changed enough, thank you. Ready to not watch me shower?" Jeremy, teal sweats dangling from his free hand, headed to his bedroom. Matty kept pace.

"Dad, I don't think you're taking in the enormity of things."

"Really? And I think that's all I've been doing." Jeremy sat on the edge of his bed and struggled to one-handedly remove his socks. One-fingeredly, actually: his left index.

Matty stood over him. "Can I help you?"

"In a minute. I'm saving you for the big stuff," he answered, working around the bulk of the brace to get completely barefoot.

Matty sat down next to Jeremy. "She's not coming back. I mean, like, definitely. You *do* know that, don't you?" He gazed at his father with a look so unusually measured and serious that it stopped Jeremy in his tracks.

"You apparently know something that I've only been assuming," Jeremy said as he shimmied out of his sweatpants, which was far easier to do while standing. He felt that bowling ball forming in his stomach again. He knew what was coming next.

"She rented an apartment. A one-bedroom off Doheny, not far from her office," said Matty. "She moves in this week." He kept his eyes fixed on Jeremy's, not allowing his father to look away, to interpret this update as anything but the facts.

"When was she planning to tell me?" asked Jeremy as he moved toward the bathroom.

"This isn't easy for her either, y'know," Matty said, trailing Jeremy.

There were many pithy things Jeremy wanted to say in return, but he held back. Cassie was Matty's mother, and Jeremy needed to respect that, respect her—or at least her wishes. Still, had Cassie given Matty permission to blab or had Jeremy just frustrated the info out of him? Either way, the news hurt, but definitive knowledge was better than the possibly-maybe-probably bullshit he'd been living with. Cassie's literal new lease was Jeremy's figurative one.

His stomach soothed.

"I'm sure it isn't, honey," Jeremy said. Matty looked relieved, the clouds moving off his face. "And by the way," added Jeremy, "I really do like the sweatpants you got me. I'm definitely ready for some new color in my life."

CHAPTER
16

JEREMY'S FIRST POST-SURGERY shower, despite Annabelle's advice and Matty's expert assistance, was a grueling, awkward, painful experience with more than its share of opportunities for disaster. From removing the abduction pillow and his clothes to keeping his right arm frozen with the help of that slippery-ass beach ball (it popped out from under him four terrifying times) to soaping up body and hair with his left hand, all while trying not to fall on the slick tile floor, it proved an Olympics-level test of physical and mental dexterity.

Matty, God bless him, jumped smack into the fray more than a few times, popping in and out of the shower to steady, guide, and protect his nervous, birthday-suited father, ending up as drenched as Jeremy before the whole ordeal was over. As for Jeremy, once he was in shower survival mode, he couldn't have cared less who saw whatever, a concern that seemed frankly idiotic in retrospect.

Matty also did a yeoman's job helping his father reassemble himself—clothes, sling, dignity—after the shower, then cleaned up the whole hot, wet mess of it all just before Joyce arrived with homemade roast garlic chicken, chunky Yukon gold potatoes, and her famous braised string beans as well as a chocolate babka from Gelson's.

They sat at the rustic, wood-plank dining room table for a change of scenery. Joyce carved up the still-warm chicken as Matty doled out the potatoes and beans onto the country Italian dinner plates that looked expensive—and may have been at some point—but that Cassie had bought years ago for like 90 percent off in a Macy's Cellar closeout. Jeremy wondered where these dishes would land in the detritus of divorce and decided right then and there that they were nice but not worth fighting over. He'd save that for stuff that actually meant something to him, though he couldn't think of what that would be at the moment.

Joyce placed a pile of breast meat plus a golden drumstick (his preferred chicken pieces since childhood) onto Jeremy's plate, took some dark meat and a wing for herself, and passed the platter on to Matty. He dithered over the chicken parts like he was making Sophie's choice, and then heaped healthy amounts of everything onto his plate.

Jeremy gazed helplessly at his chicken, then at Joyce. "Mom, sorry, but could you cut this for me?"

"Oh, of course, darling, what was I thinking?" She leaned over, diligently cutting his chicken into pieces the size of diced carrots.

"Mom, I'm wearing a pillow brace, not dentures."

"Oh, right," Joyce giggled, realizing. "Silly me." She gave Jeremy's remaining chicken a few quick slashes. "Now eat, before it gets cold. Both of you." She didn't need to include Matty, as he'd already polished off all his white meat and was halfway through his thigh. Joyce watched her grandson with pride, then turned her attention to Jeremy.

"So, honey, tell me about this new therapist of yours," said Joyce over bites of potato. "She sounds like a doll."

Jeremy glanced at Matty, the only possible source of that information. He shrugged at his father, vacuuming up his potatoes.

"I don't know about that, but I think she's a really good OT," Jeremy evaded as he speared some string beans. His left-handed eating skills had improved, though it still felt like he was doing it backward.

Joyce, she of the champion bullshit meter, studied her son, who seemed unnaturally focused on his dinner plate. "I hear she's a widow," Joyce said.

Jeremy didn't look up, partly because he didn't want to get into this—at all—and partly because he was so enjoying Joyce's roast chicken. He was swept back to his childhood when the garlicky bird made its weekly, highly anticipated appearance at the Lerner dinner table. Jeremy's dad was never more complimentary to Joyce than at those tasty times: "I'm giving you fair warning, my love, this is what I want for my last meal," he'd say.

"Great chicken, Mom, as always," said Jeremy between mouthfuls, bounding back to neutral territory.

"Oh. My. God," Matty emphasized in agreement as he refilled his plate.

Joyce soaked in the praise and returned to the business at hand: Jeremy's future. "All I'm saying, dear, is that maybe you need to start thinking about moving on with your life. It sounds like Cassie got way out in front of you there."

Jeremy shot his tell-all son another look.

"Sorry, I didn't know there was a cone of silence," said Matty, working through his seconds.

Jeremy gave in, clearly outnumbered. "I appreciate both of your concern and advice. I really do. Thank you," he said, sounding a bit like a hostage reading from his captor's script.

"How did her husband die?" asked Joyce, who was going to piece together this puzzle if it killed her.

"Cancer," Jeremy said with finality, and then turned to Matty. "What's happening at work? Any interesting new events?" He didn't mean to sound dismissive about Annabelle's late husband but he thought it best to shift focus.

"I don't know how *interesting* it is, but I'm helping coordinate a 'bark mitzvah,'" Matty answered, wielding a forkful of string beans. Jeremy and Joyce looked at him blankly. "Some TV executive's dachshund is turning thirteen," he explained, "and, well, I guess it's a thing. She's spending a ton."

"Oh, 'bark' *mitzvah*. For a dog! I get it!" Joyce exclaimed. "That's adorable!"

"Is a rabbi involved or does a schnauzer in a yarmulke preside?" Jeremy was thrilled for a new topic.

"It's not a real ceremony, it's … it's basically just a birthday party for old dogs," Matty answered, impatient, as if realizing how trivial his career choice must seem.

"What do you serve at a bark mitzvah?" Joyce asked like she was setting up a joke.

"Hot dogs?" Jeremy said with a smile, though a pet lover might have found it rude. From the sour looks on Matty and Joyce's faces, they did.

"All I know is there's going to be a grain-free cake shaped like a giant bone with 'Muzzle Tov' spelled out in kibble," Matty reported. He trained his fork over the uneaten chicken leg on Jeremy's plate. "You gonna eat that?"

"Knock yourself out," Jeremy said, though Matty had already speared the spare drumstick.

"Your work sounds so fun, Matty!" said Joyce, who may have known better but always erred on the side of support.

Matty chewed his chicken and considered. "There are worse jobs," he finally answered, sounding as if there were, in fact, no worse jobs. Jeremy sensed the boy wasn't long for the event-planning world.

"What about you, darling?" Joyce asked Jeremy as she got up to clear the table. "Any decent job prospects?"

"None, decent or indecent." He rose to help her with the dishes, but she shook her head and motioned for him to sit. He obeyed. "But Annabelle just showed me how to type with, like, one-and-a-half hands, so I should be able to start getting more done." Just saying that felt awfully proactive. A hint of optimism coursed through his veins.

"Your Annabelle sounds like a guardian angel," Joyce said, balancing plates in each hand.

My Annabelle? thought Jeremy. Strangely, he didn't hate the sound of that. Still: "What say we break out that babka?"

SHORTLY AFTER JOYCE and Matty left (babka: decimated, Matty: off to do an hour on the Peloton), Jeremy, wind in his sails, made an executive decision. Sick of hearing news about Cassie second-hand, he decided to just fucking call her. Her silence had been deafening, selfish, and, frankly, rude. There was much to discuss, and if Jeremy was going to move on with his life, as his mother and son so unequivocally kept urging him to do, several ducks needed to be put in their proverbial order.

Jeremy fortified himself with a slug of scotch (he was beginning to like the stuff), sat at the edge of the bed, and dialed her number. Amazingly, she answered after one ring.

"Hello," Cassie said without emotion, as if she were as resigned as he was to have to talk.

"Cassie." The scotch provided a nice buzz that made him dislike his estranged wife a bit less than he might have—or should have.

"How's your shoulder and the sling and all that?" She sounded a tad nervous, not her usual style.

"It sucks, if you really want to know. But Matty and my mom have been an incredible help."

Which was to say: You haven't been, so feel free to feel guilty for the historically bad timing of your removal from my life, though you probably don't feel anything, so go fuck yourself.

"Good, I'm glad." Silence, and then: "Matty said you're working with an occupational therapist?"

"I am," Jeremy said, followed by another swig of Dewar's. "She's pretty terrific, actually." That sounded far more enthusiastic than it needed to but what the hell. Let Cassie think what she wanted. He got up, started pacing. "Where are you, anyway?"

"Does it matter?"

He thought for a second. Did it matter? She wasn't here with him; in the end, that's all that really mattered. "Apparently not," Jeremy mumbled.

Wait, was that a TV on in the background? Sounded like the theme from *The Big Bang Theory*. Cassie never watched sitcoms, rarely watched TV at all except for cable news. Yep, *Big Bang*. Canned laughter swelled over the phone line. Who was she with? Maybe someone younger who liked that show? Maybe … ice cream guy? Jeremy went for it: "I heard you ran into Lucien. On Larchmont?"

Cassie went silent, which only increased the sound of the sitcom chatter. "Wow, news travels," she finally said.

Jeremy stopped pacing and gazed into the walk-in closet. So many of Cassie's things still hung from the racks and filled the shelves. When did she plan on collecting it all? Wouldn't it be funny if he donated all of Cassie's clothes to charity without telling her? A wicked grin crossed Jeremy's face, imagining the look on *her* face when she realized her stuff was gone. How weird. He'd never wished any ill on his beloved Cassie. If anything he'd wanted to protect her the way she'd protected him, defended him, supported him—at least for so much of their marriage. How does all that just disappear?

Jeremy put one foot into the quicksand: "Lucien said it looked like you were on a date. With a guy." No, with a giraffe.

More silence; Jim Parsons and Johnny Galecki traded barbs in the background.

"Well, isn't Lucien the little detective."

"I'll take that as a yes," said Jeremy, turning away from the closet.

"You can take it any way you want," Cassie said. "And you can *do* anything you want. You have my permission."

"Uh, one: I don't *need* your permission. And two: I can barely take a shower, I don't think I'll be hanging out on Tinder—or whatever people are meeting each other on."

"Matty meets people on Grindr. Says it's very effective."

"If you're gay," Jeremy reminded her.

"Or bi," she quibbled.

Was she getting at something or just being annoying? "I'm not that either."

"Well, maybe you should be. Double your chances."

"Okay, this conversation is going nowhere."

"You're the one who called."

"For fuck's sake, Cassie, don't you think we have a few important things to discuss?"

Jeremy heard the TV channel change on Cassie's end: the familiar CNN "breaking news" music. She paused, clearly diverted by the news flash.

"Yes," Cassie finally answered, "there *are* a few items, while I have you."

Jeremy took a seat on the bed, his right arm and shoulder throbbing as they did when he stood for too long. For the hundredth time that day, he pulled the brace strap away from the spot on his neck where it dug in like a mofo. There had to be some permanent adjustment; he'd have to ask Annabelle.

Speaking of permanent adjustments, Cassie relayed her list of "items" with businesslike velocity. "I'll be by in the next few days to pick up the rest of my things; I'd appreciate it if you weren't there. I have a lawyer. I suggest you find one; I can recommend a few if you'd like. I also know a few good realtors so I'd be happy to pick one and get them started on listing the house."

Jeremy felt like he was on the losing end of a game of dodgeball: *thwack, thwack, thwack!* And that last *thwack* almost knocked him to the ground. Lucky he was already seated. He gathered his thoughts—and cojones.

"Come by any time you'd like, but I'll be here, because not only do I have nowhere to go in this stupid fucking sling, but I couldn't drive there even if I did." He continued in Cassie's rat-tat-tat style: "Second, I was hoping we could avoid lawyers and work this out ourselves like adults and maybe just use a mediator if it came to that."

This was something that just occurred to Jeremy, and he wasn't sure he knew what he was talking about, especially to someone who was a lawyer herself. Still, this tack, at least in theory, appealed to his sense of fairness and lifelong disdain for drama and confrontation.

As for their house, no way was he moving—he'd just made that decision—so he'd have to figure out how to keep the place. Maybe he'd need a lawyer after all, or at least have to talk to one, but it sure wouldn't be one *she* recommended.

"What if I don't want to sell the house?" Jeremy asked, immediately realizing he should have more proactively said: "I don't want to sell the house." Too late.

"That's your choice," Cassie answered. "But just know it'll totally complicate matters. And more for you than me."

Jeremy didn't know what that meant per se, though assumed it had something to do with the fact that Cassie currently made more money than he did.

"We can think about a mediator but, in my experience, they're not all that effective," she continued.

Jeremy could still hear CNN droning on behind her; a door slammed on Cassie's end of the line. She was not alone.

"And can't you just go hang out with Katie and Crash for an hour when I stop by?"

"And do what?"

"I don't know! Sit and talk to them, watch TV, take a nap. I'm sure they'd understand."

"*I* don't even understand, why should they?"

"God, you're impossible," Cassie concluded. "I'm hanging up now." And she did.

Jeremy stared at his silent phone. Here was some real breaking news: the beguiling woman he first met that night in front of the old movie house was gone for good.

CHAPTER
17

BY THE TIME Annabelle returned two days later, Jeremy was coasting forward on a new head of steam. A shrink, if Jeremy had one (something he'd been thinking wouldn't be the world's worst idea, and had even made a note to check his health coverage), might say that his last conversation with Cassie was a defining moment in their relationship—or the end thereof.

It's not as if he'd been thinking this might just be a phase she was going through, some kind of middle-age crazy thing in which, instead of buying a sports car, getting lipo, or tattooing a snake on her thigh, she would take a little vacay from her longtime hubby, only to return when she "got over it." No, far from it.

Learning that Cassie was dating again had surely added to the finality of things in Jeremy's mind. But hearing Cassie over the phone with her detached tone and premeditated checklist of divorce chores not only reconfirmed the stark reality of the situation but also made Jeremy realize, maybe for the first time, that he *wanted* her out of his life.

God knows he wasn't the greatest prize, and certainly hadn't been the best partner these last years. But he would have been willing to work on himself, on the relationship, if she had asked, or had given him some kind of rational heads-up. Cassie would later say, If she'd had to tell him, then what was the point? It was like reminding someone to wish you a happy birthday or thank you for a job well done: They either got it or they didn't; you shouldn't have to beg for it.

But Cassie, with her sharp wits and cool self-possession, knew how to walk away and let folks hang themselves with their own rope—rather than be left hanging herself. That may have served her well in legal circles and when bartering a car lease (she was excellent at that; Jeremy would just stand back and let her do her thing), but it wasn't always the most effective way to attack a relationship issue. It was a trait that had slowly made its presence known over their marriage, most acutely, of course, when she cut bait on Jeremy. This time, however, sad as he felt about it all, he would not be the one left hanging.

Although sleep was a nightly crucible (Annabelle suggested he buy a recliner to sleep in; he was stubbornly resisting) and pain was pretty much a constant, Jeremy had started to feel more optimistic and motivated than he had in a long while.

The marathon backyard chat with Annabelle had been invigorating and transporting. It was healing to get an all-new perspective on another person's life and, in turn, his own, from someone as engaging and compassionate as his new therapist. Jeremy could be himself with her. Maybe it was because she'd gotten him at his most defenseless and reflective. Or maybe it was because Annabelle just seemed so genuine that she brought out *his* most authentic side.

It didn't hurt that he was attracted to her. There, he said it. Whew. It felt good to acknowledge it, to embrace it and not be defensive about whatever he was feeling for her (okay, Matty had nailed that; credit where credit was due). And, even though Jeremy told Cassie he didn't need her permission to do whatever he wanted, that she gave it to him in such carte blanche fashion freed him up somehow. Whether she knew it or not, she'd unlocked the door and handed him the key.

Was there something there with Annabelle? Was he actually interested in her that way? Or was he just happy to have another kind and generous person around to help him navigate this strange and difficult time? Who was he kidding? He was way into her, thinking about her more than he was comfortable with, yet comforted by those thoughts just the same.

It might also help if Annabelle was feeling something for him. But Jeremy, pulling his pie out of the sky, wasn't counting on it. For now, anyway.

All that said, he had to figure out how in the world he could stay in the house. That one threw him for a giant loop, one that fell under the heading of: What the fuck had he been thinking? The house was his and Cassie's most valuable asset; she plainly expected them to sell and split the profits. Unless she had another financial plan up her lawyerly sleeve, which was altogether possible. Jeremy could offer to buy her out and stay there, though buy her out with what? *Their* money? It was all in one big pot, so how would that work? Yes, hiring a lawyer seemed inescapable.

Jeremy decided to put it all out of his mind for now and focus on today. This included the grand revival—thanks to a jump start of creative ambition, the urging of others, and the indisputable need to start making bigger money—of his screenwriting non-career.

The night before, unable to sleep, Jeremy had turned on TCM just as one of those famed paranoid conspiracy thrillers from the 1970s, *Three Days of the Condor*, was starting. He'd only seen it in pieces over the years, never in one sitting, and the film, which starred a sturdy Robert Redford in his movie-star prime, sucked Jeremy in from the minute Redford, as a CIA researcher, returned to his Manhattan office from a lunch run only to find all his coworkers mysteriously slaughtered. It was tense and twisty, a little sexy and a little silly, and it reminded Jeremy a bit of his own screenplay thriller—which had been variously titled *Star Witness*, *Human Error*, and *He Acted Alone*—only better. But honestly, not that much better (or maybe time hadn't been kind to the film, which, in retrospect, played fast and loose with much of the plot).

Condor reminded Jeremy of why he started writing his tri-titled movie to begin with, and why he stuck to it for as long as he did—as well as what was wrong with his script that maybe he was finally capable of fixing. He got out his six-years-in-the-making screenplay, read it for the first time in a while and had an epiphany: It was better than he thought. Yeah, it needed work—streamlining of the second act, more vivid supporting characters, a few more ingenious set pieces, sharpened dialogue—but after all this time, he might really have something. Jeremy had let insecurity and ennui get in the way of its success, but not anymore.

He retitled the Final Draft file *Offensive Measures* and got ready to rewrite it for hopefully the last time. He made a vow: on or before the day he removed the mega-sling for good, he would have a polished script ready, willing, and able to show. The thought was so exciting, it gave him a boner. Even his dick agreed he was on the right track.

AS PROMISED, ANNABELLE showed Jeremy how to better navigate kitchen chores in the brace (cooking was doable but had its limits, mostly due to the hurdles of cutting and chopping—and flames), use his left hand to maximum effect and his tethered right to more minimal effect, clean up as needed, and even wrangle the trash, all while protecting his healing arm and shoulder.

"Believe me, the more independent you can be, the better you'll feel," said Annabelle as she surveyed the Luna Pearl (sales speak for speckled gray) granite counters and stainless steel appliances for any danger zones she may have missed.

"I'm actually feeling pretty good, all things considered," Jeremy said, offering a warm smile, which she instantly returned.

They locked eyes for a half second, and then, just as quickly, looked away. Was it Jeremy's imagination or was Annabelle wearing a bit more makeup than usual? And didn't her wavy tresses look more carefully assembled today? And her clothes, though still colorful and eclectic, seemed more measured: witness her snug silk blouse with its perhaps extra-opened button. Whatever was going on, if it even was at all, Jeremy liked it.

Annabelle, maybe picking up on Jeremy's gaze, deflected with her OT rap: "Doing things takes a lot longer now, as I'm sure I don't have to tell you. But, really, what's the big rush, right?"

"Well, I don't have *all* the time in the world," Jeremy said with a sly grin. He went on to tell her about *Three Days of the Condor* and *Offensive Measures* and his newly recharged writing battery, and an approving glint flashed across Annabelle's face.

"Wow, so you're actually doing it! You *must* be feeling 'pretty good.' I'm super happy for you, Jeremy." And with that, she took his free hand and gave it a little squeeze, holding on just long enough for it to be both awkward and stirring. She quietly pulled it away but held onto his eyes. "Sorry, I don't make a habit of grabbing my clients' hands, uh, *non*-therapeutically." But Annabelle didn't look sorry or, for that matter, self-conscious the way she did just minutes before.

Jeremy leaned against the sink and assessed her. He never noticed just how dark her eyes could look, how they could go from brown to near-charcoal with the merest tilt of her head, and then back again without warning. They were deep, inviting pools. He wanted to kiss her.

So he did.

In his mind.

Annabelle moved a step toward Jeremy. Wait, was she going to kiss him? Should he just lean in and—

"I forgot," she said, straightening up, just as Jeremy was about to bravely tilt toward her. What was the kiss equivalent of stopping on a dime? "You wanted me to show you how to adjust that strap around your neck." Annabelle pointed at the bothersome harness. "Hurts, huh?"

Jeremy nodded gingerly. She moved in and, using both hands, swiftly adjusted the strap buckle denting the back of his neck. As they were pretty much nose to nose, Jeremy could smell the faint powdery tang of her perfume: unassuming, yet alluring, like the wearer herself.

She made a few quick tweaks to the wide strap that circled the entire brace at waist level and voilà! Annabelle eyed her handiwork.

"Better?" she asked, still inches from him—or as close as the stupid abduction pillow would allow.

Jeremy nodded yes, praying she couldn't hear his heart pounding, though you'd have to be deaf not to.

"It won't last, the thing moves around so much," Annabelle said, studying his stubbly face. "But at least you'll get some relief."

And, before another word could be spoken, their lips connected in one perfectly synched motion, and they shared a rather terrific kiss. Strangely—or maybe not—Jeremy's heart stopped pounding and started swelling.

They pulled apart and looked at each other with amusement. Jeremy's first thought was to apologize, but Annabelle beat him to it.

"Oh, my God, I am *so* sorry!" she said, leaping back so hard she banged into a dining table chair. "That was so ..."

"Nice?"

"I was going to say ridiculously unprofessional." She scraped the chair back into place.

"Actually, I'd say the way you kiss is quite professional." Jeremy felt like someone else was talking, not him. He smiled at his little joke, but Annabelle didn't.

"You're my client. It's against the law." She started straightening all the chairs at the table.

"What law?"

"*My* law."

"You need a law?"

She stopped, considered that. "I think I do now."

Annabelle straightened the last chair and turned to face him. Her eyes pooled.

"Oh no," Jeremy said. "What's wrong?" Now he'd done it.

She tried to suppress her tears but they wouldn't comply. "I haven't kissed anyone since Gil died," she said. "I mean, *boy-girl kiss*, not, like, my Aunt-Ellen-on-the-cheek kiss."

Boy-girl kiss. Jeremy felt a twinge in his tear ducts. Annabelle started to snuffle.

"Do you need a tissue?" he asked as she sat on one of the chairs she'd just arranged. Jeremy pulled one out of a box perched on the counter. Annabelle took it gratefully, visibly embarrassed by her reaction. She dabbed at her face. Jeremy pulled out a chair and sat next to her, his bulky brace between them.

Annabelle looked up at him with her chocolate eyes. "I think your therapist needs a therapist," she joked through some residual sniffles, eking out a wry smile.

Jeremy took her hand; she didn't pull away. "Just so you know, I'm honored," he said, because he truly was.

"About what?"

"That I was your first real kiss since, well, then." He gently let her hand go. It looked like her tears were about to make an encore, but no. Annabelle folded the tissue in quarters and closed her delicate palm around it.

"I still really miss him," she said quietly. "Still expect to hear him yelling at one of his teams on the TV because they botched a point. Still expect to find his socks and shoes left stranded in the strangest places." She paused and studied the terracotta-red floor. "Still expect his side of the bed to be all rumpled and warm when I wake up. But it's not."

Annabelle looked up at Jeremy who was processing her sorrow, a depth of emotion she'd kept nobly tucked away during their long talk the other day.

"I didn't mean to make you sad," he said.

She rose, her usual poise and pluck slowly returning like a balloon refilled with air. "That's sweet, but you didn't. I don't know what came over me. I usually embarrass myself like that in the privacy of my own kitchen. Just me and a bunch of old photo albums and a box of wine."

Jeremy raised an eyebrow. "*Box* of wine?"

"Okay, a bottle. I was just trying to paint the most pathetic picture I could. How did I do?"

He lumbered up from the chair to face Annabelle and took in that powdery scent, the bottomless depth of her eyes, how her lower lip was fuller than the upper. "I think you have every right to feel however you still feel," Jeremy answered. "I can't imagine what it'd be like to lose someone you loved like that."

"You just lost someone you loved. Didn't you?"

For a moment there, he'd forgotten. What did that mean? It meant that while, at first, Cassie's departure felt like a kind of fatality, she was still very much alive—just not in the way she used to be for Jeremy. Maybe he didn't love his wife the way Annabelle loved Gil; maybe once, but not eternally. And that, he thought in a Frostian moment, has made all the difference.

"I know what you're saying, but I don't think you can compare the two," Jeremy concluded. "Unless you're just trying to be kind." He felt like he was treading tender territory with her, and it was all feeling a bit too much, too soon. Or was it? By what measure?

"Oh, I'd never say something just to be kind," Annabelle joked, though they both knew that was untrue. They stood there a few pensive seconds. "I should go," she said and looked around for her purse. She grabbed it off the counter, avoiding Jeremy's tracking eyes.

"About that kiss," he started. "I just—"

"Jeremy," Annabelle interrupted, "sometimes a kiss is just a kiss." She gave a little eye roll. "Wait, that's from an old movie, isn't it?"

"Not just any old movie: *Casablanca*." He stretched out the iconic title's four syllables in deference. He struck a corny Bogart pose. "Here's looking at you, kid." And Jeremy kept looking at her until they both looked away.

"I have a confession to make," Annabelle said. "I've never actually seen *Casablanca*. I mean, I've seen clips and parts, and I know it's a classic but … for all the movies I have seen, that one escaped me somehow." Before Jeremy could react, she asked, "Do you hate me? Am I persona non grata? Do I belong in movie jail?"

He ticked off the answers: "No. In some circles. I'll see if I can get you a suspended sentence."

"Whew, that's a relief." She smiled, then whistled into her purse for her car key. That second kiss was not in the cards.

Jeremy had a final play tucked up his one normal sleeve: "Anytime you want to watch *Casablanca* let me know. I have it on Blu-Ray. Like any good movie nerd." Once again, Jeremy was trying to attract a woman with the promise of a movie she hadn't seen. He needed a new act.

Annabelle assessed him a moment, started to say something, then reconsidered. She struck a strangely stiff tone: "Is there anything else you need me for, OT-wise? Because personally, I think we've covered the bases—you've been a very good student." She clutched her car key tightly as if protecting a good luck charm—or her only means of escape.

"Thanks. I had a good teacher," Jeremy said. Maybe a kiss *was* just a kiss. "Can I call you if I need help?"

"Maybe it's best to call Dr. Hockstein's office, I'm sure they can refer you to someone. They have a lot of OTs on their list. None with my exact combination of savoir-faire, fashion sense, and mood swings, but you'll be fine. Oh, and you do know you'll have to see a physical therapist once you can send Big Bertha packing, right? And don't blow that off, it's crucial, hear me?"

She was talking so fast Jeremy lost his way … just as he started thinking maybe he'd found it.

"Wait, what?" he asked, catching up. "Another OT? Annabelle, what happened here?" He was pretty sure of the answer, but wanted to hear her say it. From the lost look on her face as she turned around and left, he realized she wasn't going to.

CHAPTER
18

BY THE END of that week, Jeremy had rewritten the first act of *Offensive Measures* and was jazzed about the new pages. Maybe it was because there were any new pages at all. Never mind the fact that he was hacking away with his left hand and a strained assist (as per Annabelle's instructions) from his near-immobile right hand, the painful use of which nearly took his breath away. And if it wasn't exactly taking him twice as long to type and format the script, it sure felt that way. No matter, he was getting it done and, in the scheme of things, that was a big fucking deal.

And no, for those who might have expected or hoped otherwise, Jeremy did not hear from Annabelle after her hasty departure, nor did he reach out to her. Much as he wanted to call or text, he realized he put himself out there with her much farther than he should have—for either of their sakes—and needed to let things breathe for a while or simply die on their own accord. That's not to say he was happy with that "adult decision" or that he didn't think about her much of the time. Okay, all the time. But working on the script was proving a productive distraction, and he was glad for it. (That he changed one of his character's names to Annabelle didn't mean anything, did it?)

One would think that after watching thousands of movies, much less dissecting them in endless reviews and articles, someone—like, say, Jeremy—could easily translate that experience into his or her own screenplay through something akin to creative osmosis. But one would be wrong. It's the difference between riding in a car as a passenger and getting behind the wheel yourself. You'd think you'd know how to do it, until you have to. Then: whole new ballgame.

Jeremy knew a boatload less about, well, everything when he wrote and sold *Parting Gifts*. He banged it out on a wing and a prayer, cribbing from so many other favorite romcoms. It was a genre still in vogue back then for movie stars and studios before these films started migrating to cable TV and streamers, where they reclaimed their popularity.

He also borrowed bits of his relationship with Cassie in creating that screenplay's main characters: a broke, twentyish couple—the guy's an exhausted proofreader, the woman is a beleaguered office assistant—who wins a fortune in the lottery. They quit their jobs, travel the globe, and get sucked into all these crazy adventures that almost end their marriage, only to realize they were happier when all they had was each other. A classic case of "Be careful what you wish for." Everyone loved the screwball script—until they didn't.

By the time Jeremy was done rewriting it (four times, the first two were paid), the story bore little to no resemblance to what the studio originally bought. All that stayed the same were the husband's and wife's names and even those changed when Jeremy was fired and replaced by a high-priced writer who did such a hacky job that the project was immediately shelved.

They say to write what you know, a lesson Jeremy only half took when he wrote *Parting Gifts*. He didn't know a ton about world travel or winning millions of dollars, but he did know what it was like to be young and in love and learning how to adjust to living your best life together. When Cassie read the script she asked, "Is this couple us if we were completely different people?" which may have sounded like a contradiction but pretty much summed up his entire approach.

With the newly christened *Offensive Measures* and its earlier versions, Jeremy knew even less about his subject matter: congressional intrigue, double-dealing scientists, nuclear power. But he took it as a challenge, did lots of homework, and concocted a heady jigsaw puzzle of a story that snowballed into a deadly vortex for an idealistic but obsessive young U.S. senator (paging Jake Gyllenhaal!). If Jeremy could make the rest of the script as good as his just-revised first act, he might actually have something. What he would do with it then was another issue, but first things first: finish the damn thing once and for all.

Plunging back into his old screenplay also gave Jeremy a reason not to think about Cassie or, more specifically, finding a divorce lawyer and figuring out how to keep the house he had no interest in leaving. He was on a writing roll now and didn't want to upset his tenuous creative apple cart, so he figured he could easily put Cassie off another few weeks before being forced to act. Maybe by then he'd have a clearer life plan.

What he couldn't forestall or control was his ex-wife's promised return to Laurel Canyon to gather her things—and presumably some of *theirs*—and erase her footprint from the humble home they once cherished together. So that Saturday, bright and early and— perhaps as a kind of fuck you—unannounced, Cassie let herself in and showed up in the kitchen doorway just as Jeremy was sitting down for breakfast and the *Times*. She scared the hell out of him, appearing like the ghost of weekend mornings past.

For some reason, his first thought upon realizing it was Cassie was how schlumpy he looked, with his bed head of hair, twelve-day growth (he'd given up on his face altogether; electric shaving with one hand doesn't cut it, literally), and whatever baggy old shirt he'd draped over himself and the pillow brace. It's not like Jeremy would have—even could have—spruced himself up in an attempt to make her see what she was "missing," like some abandoned wife might do in the movies. But his self-esteem had taken such a hit these last weeks, and Cassie looked so amazingly pulled together that a more even playing field wouldn't have hurt. Yet why did he even care? Human nature? Competitive spirit? Auld lang syne?

Jeremy immediately went on the defensive. "Thanks for the

heads-up," he snapped, the boxy sling making for a clumsy rise from the table.

Cassie didn't engage, just gazed at her worse-for-the-wear ex-husband. "Wow, I forgot how enormous that brace is. How in the world are you managing with it?"

"I have no choice, that's how I'm managing with it."

"You're acting a little hostile, you know that?" Cassie scanned the tired-looking kitchen, maybe considering what to take with her. Jeremy caught her staring at the coffeemaker.

"I said it before and I'll say it again: You already took one coffee pot, you're not taking another. And if that sounds hostile, it is."

She studied him, took a deep breath, shifted gears. "Look, let's start over, okay? I'm sorry I didn't tell you I was coming this morning, I'm sorry you're stuck in that pillow thing, and I don't need another coffeemaker. Though, I wouldn't mind a cup, if there's extra."

Jeremy was disarmed in the sneaky way only Cassie could disarm him, and he hated himself for it. Still, he decided to try to relax (Can you *try* to relax?) for the short time Cassie would likely be there packing her shit. "Help yourself," he told her with a nod at the half-full coffee carafe.

"Don't mind if I do," chimed in a familiar voice. Matty, carrying a couple of empty cartons, bounded into the kitchen, looking especially fit and tan (beach? bronzer?) in an artfully shrunk Crunch Fitness T-shirt, slim Joe's jeans and red New Balance running shoes. Saturdays were made for this kid. Seeing his father's surprised look, Matty quickly explained, a bit warily: "I'm here to help Mom, hope that's okay." He put the cartons on the counter and watched his dad's expression.

Of course it was okay. Matty was as close to Cassie as he was to Jeremy; they'd always each had their own special relationship with their son, and Jeremy wouldn't want it any other way. Even those times when he and Cassie didn't see eye-to-eye about their marriage or each other, they mostly always agreed about raising Matty: how to guide, support, and love him the best way they could, who they wanted him to be and who they *still* wanted him to be.

With that in mind, Jeremy took the high road. "Why wouldn't it be okay?" he asked Matty. "I always want you to be there for your mother, you know that. This isn't a competition." Jeremy said that last bit for Cassie's sake and even though it didn't seem to outwardly register with her, he knew she heard it loud and clear.

"Okay, cool," Matty answered, on to the next thought as usual. "Mom, want me to pour?" he asked, coffee carafe in hand.

"Sure, sweetheart, thanks. I'll just be in my—*the*—bedroom getting started. Bring it in, would you?" Cassie took the cartons off the counter and made her exit without another word or glance at Jeremy. That wasn't lost on Matty.

"This is weird, huh?" he said to his father as he poured two cups of coffee. "I mean, this must be kind of a mindfuck, y'know, after all this time and all."

Jeremy didn't immediately answer. He didn't want to seem callous or angry, which he was at some level (Jeremy was hardly charming when Cassie appeared just now), but he also knew he had to move on, *was* moving on; his wife of a quarter century certainly had, with little discussion or fanfare. As for right now, he just wanted to finish his breakfast, chat with Matty some more, and get back to his script.

"It's all a little strange, yeah, but I'm muddling through," Jeremy answered as Matty peered into the refrigerator. "If you're looking for almond milk, I still don't have any."

"What? Oh, no, I've started drinking it black. Just getting some 2% for Mom. But I see you only have nonfat."

"You know me: Mr. Healthy," Jeremy kidded as he chewed on a (thankfully presliced) sesame bagel with cream cheese. Joyce had dropped off the skim milk the day before along with some other groceries. Maybe she was trying to tell him something. Somehow Jeremy managed to stay thin without eating particularly well or exercising a lot—make that, at all. Maybe it was genetic (he was built like his dad) or maybe worry kept him lean. Either way, he needed to improve his diet and fitness. Turning fifty was no joke, which he was definitely finding out the hard way.

Matty, still standing at the open fridge, observed his bagel-scarfing father. As if reading his mind, he suggested Jeremy start going for walks.

"Get your heart going," he told him. The phrase made Jeremy think of kissing Annabelle, which made him a little sad.

"With this thing?" Jeremy asked incredulously with a chin nod to his abduction sling. "It's hard enough lugging it around the house much less up and down the hills." Jeremy's street was fairly flat but once you left it, the surrounding blocks, rustic and lovely as they were, were mostly curvy and steep. Or maybe he was just making an excuse. Here was another one: "Besides, I'm not exactly dressed for public consumption—despite my awesome sweatpants." Jeremy hadn't taken off the teal togs since he'd gotten them; it might be time to introduce them to the washing machine.

"Fine," Matty agreed, "then at least do laps out back. It's flat, close, *private*." He gestured out the window at the yard.

It wasn't big, but bigger than the yards of most of the houses on the street, where canyon-view decks were often as "backyard" as it got. Jeremy and Cassie even talked about putting in a swimming pool the first few years they lived there, but the mood—and the money to do so (her law school tuition took over)—passed.

"A half hour a day is all you need," Matty assured his dubious dad, one ready cup of coffee now in each hand.

"I should walk in circles for half an hour? I don't think so." He finished his bagel, guiltily contemplating toasting another half.

"Talk on the phone, listen to music—you have Pandora, don't you? The time will go. And you'll be doing your body a huge favor."

"Frankly, I think my body owes *me* a favor," Jeremy tossed off as Matty was about to exit the room.

He stopped, considered his dad. "Tell you what, let me help Mom pack up, then I'll walk the backyard with you. It'll be fun. We'll bond." Matty flashed a sly grin at Jeremy (he looked so much like Cassie just then it was uncanny) and disappeared down the hallway.

Jeremy called after him: "You drive a hard bargain, pal." He rose to make that second bagel. At least now he had a good excuse: carbo-load for the big walk.

CHAPTER
19

AN HOUR AFTER she so unceremoniously arrived, Cassie left
the house with four packed pieces of their old black Tumi luggage
(which she was doubtlessly not planning to return), a wide kha-
ki-colored duffel bag that Jeremy didn't recognize, three Hefty bags
full of who knows what, and the two cartons Matty came in with,
now filled and sealed. Jeremy would have helped Cassie and Matty
out to the car but, technically, he wasn't allowed to leave the kitchen
(plus he couldn't lift much anyway), so he stayed put and watched
Diners, Drive-Ins and Dives on the Food Network. The show's jokey, tattooed, spiky-haired host was visiting a Vietnamese joint in a
Sacramento strip mall, and he pronounced the food there "pho-no-
menal." The guy could be a little annoying, but he was making a lot
more money than Jeremy.

While Matty was packing up Cassie's car, she returned to the
kitchen to say goodbye. Jeremy had hoped she would just drive
away. No, he didn't. Not really. Much as he didn't want to admit it,
he didn't want to be ignored but also didn't want to ignore her. He
hated this clumsy, unkind standoff. His worry: it was going to get
worse before it got better. That was the nature of divorce, wasn't it?

Jeremy asked, "Get everything?" as he muted the TV.

"For now," Cassie said, placing her and Matty's empty coffee
cups in the sink. Jeremy could only wonder what else she wanted.
He flashed on all those scenes in older movies where divorcing couples split up their books and records, tangling over a dog-eared copy

of *The Grapes of Wrath* or a treasured Billie Holiday album. Technology had rendered a lot of that immaterial (who gets the Kindle?) but who knows what has sentimental value until you have to let it go? How about the marriage itself?

Jeremy offered her a half-assed olive branch: "What's your new apartment like?" Cassie seemed taken aback as if this were privileged information. "What, is it a secret?" he asked, snapping back that olive branch.

"It's nice," she finally answered. "It's just one bedroom, but there's this little sort of den area and a decent-sized balcony so ... yeah."

Jeremy nodded, thinking back on their years together, bits and pieces zipping past like a flicked deck of cards.

He rose from the table to face Cassie. "Hey, can I ask you a question?" he asked, attempting a casual tone. He was a terrible actor.

"Depends on the question," Cassie volleyed with the faintest smile.

"What did you mean that day when you said I failed the test?" And before she could wriggle out of it, added, "C'mon, what did you *really* mean?" It was a question Jeremy hadn't expected to confront today or one that Cassie seemed eager to answer. It hung there like a bat from a rafter.

Cassie studied Jeremy's sallow, expectant face as she composed her thoughts. Her response came in two pointed words: "The party."

"The party? As in my birthday party? *That* was the test?"

"That was the test," Cassie answered with unsettling matter-of-factness. Jeremy, a dull pain coursing through his right arm and shoulder from standing in place, stared at her with such unforgiving puzzlement that Cassie was forced to continue.

"If the party went well, and it made you happy, it would mean that *I* still made you happy. But if you didn't enjoy it, *couldn't* enjoy it and therefore couldn't enjoy—or at least appreciate—what I was trying to do for you, then it would show me that you were not worth fighting for. That *we* were not worth fighting for. Turns out, we weren't."

If it wasn't quite the explanation Jeremy expected, it was yet no great shock that the fucking party was the culprit, a kind of wolf in sheep's clothing that led to such a heedless marital demise. "You set me up," Jeremy realized, part question, part accusation.

"Actually, you set yourself up," Cassie redirected. That law school education sure was paying off.

Jeremy felt a pounding in his chest (forget walking to boost his heart rate, he just needed to fight with his ex-wife) and had to sit down again. It was also a way of restraining himself from lashing out at her, something he knew would open the floodgates of blame, make them both say things they'd regret. To his surprise, Cassie sat across from Jeremy, then took his free hand in hers. It felt soft, warm, familiar. He gently withdrew it.

"I told you I didn't want the party, but you threw me one anyway. What did you expect?" Jeremy said quietly.

"Frankly, exactly what happened."

Her complacent tone was replaced with one of simple resignation. Jeremy wasn't sure which was worse. He also wasn't sure where to go with this. What's done was done.

Fortunately, before anything else needed to be said, Matty bounced in through the back door. "Car's all packed. Amazing how much stuff you can jam into that little—" He stopped short at the sight of his tense, grave-looking parents. "You guys okay?" he asked, knowing the answer but asking nonetheless.

Jeremy, breakfast plate in hand, scrambled up from the table. "Yeah, honey, everything's fine," he said as brightly as he could. "Hey, I meant to ask you, how's that bark mitzvah coming along?"

"Oh, it's a total shitshow," Matty said. "You wouldn't believe it. Couldn't be crazier if it was for an actual person." All in the same breath, he turned to Cassie. "Are you sure you don't want me to follow you to your apartment, help you unload the car?" He swiveled back to Jeremy. "And then I'll come back, and we'll take that walk."

Cassie rose, ready to go. "That's sweet of you, baby, but no need to make two trips. Stay here with your dad," she said. Cassie hugged Matty goodbye and left for the place she would now call home.

JEREMY AND MATTY were on what seemed like their eight hundredth lap around the backyard's imaginary swimming pool, though they'd only been walking about four minutes.

"Having fun yet?" asked Matty, who was in his glory, like a kid who finally got a distracted parent to play LEGOs.

"I feel kind of foolish, especially lugging Big Bertha around," Jeremy said into his abduction pillow. "Think anyone can see us?"

"In Jungleland?" Matty deadpanned as he swept a hand around the overgrown yard with its towering ficus hedges, ivy-shrouded fencing and lofty wall of bamboo. "Maybe someone in a low-flying plane. Or a drone."

"Where did you get your sense of humor, anyway?"

"Not from you," Matty elbowed his dad, "that's for sure."

"I happen to be very funny."

"Your reviews are funny, I'll give you that."

"*Were* funny. And really only the bad ones. Which, I'm not proud to say, were like shooting fish in a barrel."

"I don't know what that means, but if you say so," Matty said, as they entered ridiculous walk, minute five. "Do you miss it?"

"What, reviewing? Like my right arm," Jeremy answered in a timely comparison. It hadn't hit Jeremy quite that bluntly since he was fired (then again, no one had actually asked), but yeah, he did feel pretty wistful about his film critic days—years. Especially when he opened the *Times'* Calendar now and read the work of his fellow reviewers. At least he hadn't been officially replaced yet; that softened the blow.

"And to think *I've* been called a drama queen!"

"You asked, I told you," Jeremy shrugged. "But working on my old screenplay again has helped a lot, so …" He almost walked into the bamboo as he rounded a curve and righted himself. Matty noticed, cocked his head.

"Walk much? Oh, that's right—no!"

"You try getting around in this monster sling, let's see how agile you are," Jeremy retorted, though he knew Matty probably would've used it as some sort of body-strengthening tool.

"All I'm saying is, the more physical you can be, the better you'll be at it," advised Matty with a guru's aplomb.

"Tell you what, let's talk about you," said Jeremy, who, truth be told, was enjoying this cyclic stroll if only to spend thirty uninterrupted minutes alone with his boy who, miraculously, hadn't once checked his phone. "How's Sven?"

"Sven," Matty repeated flatly. "I think Sven is history."

"Oh no!" Jeremy was sorry to hear, though not terribly surprised. He also knew this story would be good for at least fifteen diversionary minutes around the yard. "What happened?"

Here was the deal with Sven: though he was three years older than Matty, he'd had a lot less dating experience and ultimately didn't want to be exclusive the way that Matty wanted to be. Or said he wanted to be, Matty's track record being what it was. Still, as Jeremy had intuited, Matty was pretty hot about this guy and was taking the budding relationship more seriously than usual. "If I meet someone I'm really into, I'd like to keep it going, not fuck it up, know what I mean?" Matty confessed. "I've decided I'm into quality, not quantity."

He may have *just* reached that verdict, but Jeremy would give him the benefit of the doubt.

"Does that mean you deleted your Grindr app?" Jeremy wasn't entirely serious or joking; he wasn't even sure he had the right name. Apparently, he did.

"How do you know I'm on that?" Matty asked, amused, as if his father couldn't possibly know about anything as cool as a gay hookup app much less that his son might use one.

"I think your mother may have mentioned it," Jeremy said casually, remembering that Cassie did recently bring it up. And was it Jeremy's imagination, or were Matty and he walking increasingly faster? "Whatever works, just be careful," Jeremy added. "I'm not judging."

"You shouldn't. A lot of marriages started with a Grindr swipe." Matty pulled ahead of his father. "C'mon, old man, keep up," he said with a smile. They *were* walking faster.

Jeremy quickened his pace. It actually felt good. "Is that what you want now? A marriage?"

"Sure. Eventually. Doesn't everyone?" asked the guy who couldn't commit to how he took his coffee.

Still, what would have once seemed like a perfectly logical question now felt a bit alien to Jeremy. He considered his answer; Matty picked up on the pause. "Maybe not the best topic this very second, huh?"

"No, it's just … well, you're young, you don't need to be thinking about anything as serious as marriage yet."

Matty noted, "You were only, what, two years older than me when you and Mom got married? And you were my age when you met."

"Maybe that was too young, I don't know," wondered Jeremy. "Even if it didn't seem so then." They walked in silence. "Whatever, you fall in love with someone and all bets are off. It's not really something you can predict—or plan."

"Yeah, the last thing I need now is to get married," Matty declared, unraveling the whole thread of the conversation. "But it looks like I *do* need a new boyfriend." He checked the Fitbit on his wrist: "Five more minutes and you're outta jail."

"What if I want to keep walking?" Jeremy challenged.

"You won't," his son rightly predicted with a sideways grin.

Regardless, Jeremy wondered who else he could ask to take these walks with him. Yeah, they were silly, but his workout options were limited right now. He thought of Annabelle. Wouldn't something like this count as part of occupational therapy? How nice it would be to spend this kind of quiet, one-on-one time with her, if under the guise of physical improvement. But did she want to see him or even hear from him? It wasn't looking that way. (Didn't she say as much by suggesting he find a new OT?) But he also knew you didn't often develop feelings for someone who wasn't feeling them back.

"Y'know Annabelle?" Jeremy asked Matty.

"The OT you have a thing for?"

Jeremy paused but didn't dispute that, just kept going.

"She mentioned she had a nephew, Greg or Gavin or something—no, Gabe. Thought you two might hit it off if you were ever looking. So you're looking, right?"

"Did you see a picture?" Matty asked, interest piqued.

"A picture? No, but I could probably get you a phone number if you wanted." Jeremy told himself he was doing this for his son, which he was, but it felt scheming. It didn't stop him.

"Someone's nephew," Matty mulled, as if an aunt or uncle couldn't possibly be a reliably objective matchmaking source (and as if he wasn't someone's nephew himself). "I don't know."

"It was just a thought," Jeremy said, surprised Matty was at all hesitant, maybe underestimating—or overestimating—the selection process of someone who met random strangers on his cell phone. "If you change your mind, let me know."

"Okay, sure, get me his number," said Jeremy's whiplash-inducing son. God bless him.

They finished their walk, and Matty made Jeremy promise he'd do it every day from then on. Jeremy said he would, then they went inside and obliterated the loaf of homemade banana-walnut bread Joyce had brought over the day before. Maybe walking had its perks after all.

JEREMY SAT AT his desk waffling over whether to text or call Annabelle until he finally just dialed her number and hoped for the best. She'd left his house the last time with such vague finality it was like someone writing a long and important letter without signing or sending it. Was her message truly complete or was there a missing P.S. that would have left an opening for Jeremy if he chose to pick up on it? Or was he overthinking the whole thing as usual? He'd find out.

"Jeremy?" Annabelle answered. It was the tone of someone who didn't play games.

"Hi, it's Jeremy," he responded superfluously, a bit too eager and bright. His voice cracked like a twelve-year-old's.

"I know. It says so right here."

Jeremy imagined Annabelle pointing to her phone. He cleared his throat.

"Right," he stalled. "So, how are you?"

"I'm okay. How are *you*?" she asked, with what seemed to Jeremy like concern but could have also just been rote professional courtesy.

"I started walking today. Bertha and I did a half hour around my backyard."

"How did the old girl hold up?" Annabelle bantered. Another good sign?

"Let's just say she behaved herself," Jeremy joked. "I'm putting her on a diet, by the way. I told her, 'If I have to haul you around for another month, you've got to knock off some weight.'" He nervously awaited a chuckle from the other end. There was none.

"So what can I do for you, Jeremy?" asked Annabelle. Jeremy wondered the exact shade of brown her knowing eyes might be at that moment.

He told her about Matty's newly single status and interest in meeting her nephew. Annabelle brightened, and offered to text Jeremy a picture of Gabe and a phone number he could forward to Matty. "I have a good feeling about this," she assured him.

"Great," Jeremy said, "maybe I'll see you at the wedding." He was getting a downhill vibe about the whole conversation. Maybe he *had* developed feelings for someone who wasn't feeling them back.

There was quiet on the line until Annabelle said, "That'd be nice." Jeremy's heart thumped and, what the hell, he dove in.

"I don't want to wait until the wedding, Annabelle. I miss you and want to see you and really think we need to talk. I'd meet you at your place but as you know I can't drive so I'd love for you to come here. Please say yes." Jeremy held his breath. He was tired of not confronting things head on—his last years with Cassie being an obvious lesson.

His words hung in the air like particles in space, swirling around, impossible to grasp, yet even more impossible to avoid. Jeremy shut his eyes tightly as if waiting to be punched. The silence was excruciating, broken only by music blaring from a passing car outside his office window.

Jeremy was about to hang up the phone, avoid the pain and humiliation that was certain to accompany Annabelle's response, when he heard a deep breath on the other end followed by five little words that would change his life: "I'll be there at eight."

SIX WEEKS LATER

CHAPTER
20

FOR THE FIRST time in more than two decades, Jeremy sat across from a film development executive to discuss a screenplay he had written. There were a few key differences, however, not the least of which was that Jeremy was now fifty, and the exec was about the same age—let's say twenty-eight and a half—as the opinionated, self-assured up-and-comers he used to meet with back in the day. How could Jeremy be so much older while the person with the magical and extravagant power to shape his entire professional future could remain so doggedly stuck in time?

It was as if Dorian Gray himself had lived on, graduated from USC's Peter Stark Producing Program and then, in record time, worked his way up to a creative VP for Monolith, which in a few short years had become a major—and majorly deep-pocketed—player in the streaming wars.

There was that too: streamers were not part of the equation back then, not a part of anything yet. It was mainly about selling to the more traditional studios and production companies that were still making films to be seen as God intended: in a movie theatre while scarfing overpriced popcorn and soda with hundreds of other reactive, sometimes deeply annoying, if often equally passionate people.

Suffice to say, at least on the face of it, there were more options now for screenwriters to peddle their wares. "Everyone is desperate for material," was the common refrain in these content-heavy days.

Jeremy would soon find out if that was true, wishful thinking or, like much else in the business of show, complete bullshit.

How Jeremy found himself sunk in a buttery, biscuit-brown leather couch in a bright but indistinct little office overlooking the manicured gardens of Monolith's shiny Santa Monica campus was a long story. But like so much in Jeremy's newish life these days, all roads seemed to lead either to or from Annabelle.

Annabelle.

What a unique, delightful, astonishing, nurturing, beautiful, tender, sexy, and, above all, decent human being she was. But, as Jeremy would discover in their lovely string of days together, she was also haunted and self-protective, watchful and reflective, and not one to plan too far ahead. Which isn't to say that she wasn't unfailingly reliable.

That night six weeks earlier when Annabelle told Jeremy she would be at his house at eight, she was ringing his bell at 7:59 and 59 seconds. She was ridiculously prompt and deceptively organized. She made Jeremy want to be a better man, which, in his and many people's minds (see Helen Hunt's character in *As Good as It Gets*), was one of the best things you could say about someone.

How much "better" Jeremy had become, if at all, he couldn't say. But in ways large and small, thanks to Annabelle; the support of Matty and Joyce; renewed regular contact with old friends Josh, Cliff, Zoë, and his cousin Amie (sadly, and not unexpectedly, Norm was lost to Cassie's side of things); plus his thrilling liberation two weeks earlier from that grotesque abduction pillow, he was feeling lighter, calmer, and far more aspirational.

For as fast as the time sped by, it also felt like much longer than six weeks since Annabelle had accepted Jeremy's hastily delivered invitation. When she did arrive, a bottle of Malbec in hand (a nice and promising touch), the anxiety Jeremy and, he would soon learn, Annabelle, had been feeling since they last spoke melted away, and they spent the next three hours talking incessantly, drinking wine, eating a mishmash of snacks, and falling in love. Or at least allowing their deep like for each other to spring out of its shell and take root in the world around them—which in this case was Jeremy's den, so it felt safe.

Annabelle—loose waves falling around her face, a touch of peachy lipstick, the koala shirt she wore on her first visit, purplish straight-leg yoga pants, and Birkenstock thongs that revealed delicate, aqua-painted toes—got right to the point as soon as they were ensconced on the cushy sectional with their glasses of Malbec.

"I haven't given a thought to another man since Gil died," she started. "No sneaking around Match or JDate, zero interest in being fixed up—and believe me, a few of my friends have been relentless—not even a harmless coffee date. I'd see an attractive guy on the street and I might as well have been looking at a lamppost."

Jeremy was about to say something, but Annabelle raised a hand: "Let me finish." She continued, "But you? You're the first guy I've even given a second look. And, while we're on it, a third and a fourth. And let's not forget that kiss, which was absolutely terrifying."

She gulped some wine and Jeremy stayed silent, no idea where the pendulum was going to swing. "Why terrifying? Because it meant that it might finally be time to stop the pity party, wriggle out of the little cocoon I'd spun for myself, and rejoin the human race."

Annabelle gazed at her glass. Jeremy wondered if it was time for him to jump in. But he waited and a good thing because she was far from done.

"But if that was true, then it also meant that Gil was really and truly gone. That he was never, ever coming back and that nothing I could do was ever going to change that. And that, really, now all I was left with was me. Me without Gil. And that also meant figuring out who I actually *was* without him, who I now wanted to be—or was at least supposed to be." Annabelle leveled her gaze at Jeremy, who still wasn't sure it was his turn. "Is this making any sense?" Annabelle asked, those dark eyes hinting of tears.

"Completely," he said. "And honestly, after everything you went through? I'm not sure how you could've felt any other way." She watched Jeremy shyly, appreciatively. He moved in closer, his fingers grazing hers. "I just hope my ... nonprofessional interest in you wasn't too insensitive. If it was, I totally didn't mean it to be." Annabelle gave a soft smile. Jeremy took her hand. "Not to sound like some compulsive idiot, but I couldn't help myself."

"I guess neither could I," Annabelle said, her smile widening a bit, "which I hope wasn't too insensitive."

"How so?"

"Well, your wife just left you and here I am, swooping in before the body is even cold," she said, placing her near-empty wine glass on the coffee table. "I mean, not that she's dead but you know what I mean."

Jeremy marveled at her empathy. "I do. Nonetheless, she is gone. She's been gone for a lot longer than I've wanted to admit. And so have I. But thank you for saying that." He wanted to fling off that damn abduction brace and hug her tightly, feel her completely in his arms. Of course, he reasoned, if it wasn't for that sling he never would have met Annabelle in the first place. "So are you still terrified?" Jeremy asked.

Annabelle thought about that, longer than Jeremy would have expected. "You're a words guy. What's one step less than terrified?"

He flipped through his mental thesaurus. "Frightened? Anxious? Apprehensive?" He emptied his wine glass as Annabelle mulled adjectives.

"'Frightened' is too timid, 'apprehensive' feels too negative. 'Anxious' sounds too … neurotic," she decided. "What's something that means 'I think I'm into this but just want it to go well because I'm not up to getting my heart broken or feeling weird or stressed and don't want to regret casting off my cocoon for something that may or may not even exist?'"

"Wow, I don't even think Roget himself could answer that one." Annabelle flashed a gentle smile, which inspired Jeremy to say, "How about 'guardedly optimistic?'"

She rolled that around. "I can live with that," she concluded, which gave Jeremy his own flash of guarded optimism. Without another adjective, he took Annabelle's inviting face in his free hand and kissed the living daylights out of her.

JEREMY WASN'T THE only one enjoying newfound partnership. Matty learned that one's aunt could be a perfectly good judge of her nephew's romantic viability, particularly after Matty took one look at Gabe's shirtless photo and deemed him eminently "callable" (though Jeremy suspected that was in place of another more colorful adjective). Matty and Gabe met up the following night—the night after Jeremy and Annabelle's auspicious reunion—and, unlike their respective father and aunt, reportedly got immediately busy, shared ten-grain pancakes and veggie bacon the next morning, and were now shuttling between each other's apartments almost every night.

As far as Matty was concerned, he'd hit the boyfriend jackpot: Gabe was not only charming and funny and looked like Zac Efron but with better abs, he was also a personal trainer who could give Matty a run for his money on the bench press as well as lots of free workout tips. Jeremy had never seen his son so happy and focused; he was positively glowing these days. He even seemed to be enjoying his job more. That bark mitzvah? It went from "shit show" to "event of the month." Matty worked on two more of those dog simchas since, plus a party he invented for the felines called a cat-e-chism. Don't ask.

Jeremy hoped the Matty-Gabe thing would continue: for his son's sake, of course, but also because it might get weird with Annabelle if they broke up. A step ahead of Jeremy's concern, she already told him not to worry, whatever happened was between the boys. And who knows, maybe Gabe was the steadying influence Matty needed. Much as he adored his son, Jeremy needed to start trusting the boy's instincts more, trust that Matty would find his way and better commit to the world around him. And remember that he was still only twenty-three.

So Monolith. One night, about a week into both couples' romantic whirlwinds, they had a double-date dinner at Jeremy's. They all cooked (Annabelle set the menu and picked up the fixings), drank a lot (Jeremy's two-drink ceiling was now a distant memory), laughed their asses off, and traded secret stories in an impromptu truth-or-dare-type round-robin. They learned a lot about each other.

Jeremy could have lived without Matty's teenage story that involved buying flavored condoms at a 7-Eleven, but at least he was being safe, right?

Somewhere between the chicken meatballs with spinach fettuccini and the angel food cake with blueberries and coconut sorbet, Jeremy started talking about *Offensive Measures*, how well the rewrite was going (the second act was taking on an exciting new shape), his plan to finish before the brace was off, and how he just hoped he could figure out what to do with the script once it was ready to show.

"I've been out of the business forever, so the big question is 'show who?'" Jeremy explained, hardly expecting help from anyone at the table.

"Do you know Ian Franco?" Gabe asked, a pensive look on his Efron-like face. Jeremy could easily see what Matty saw in him: Gabe was like supernaturally attractive but in an accessible and disarming way. He and Matty looked good together.

"Is he an actor?" Jeremy wondered. He'd reviewed so many movies with so many performers that everyone sounded like an actor to him.

"I don't know, maybe. But this Ian Franco lives in the apartment next to me. Around my age, decent guy, works for Monolith. I'm not sure doing what exactly, but I know he reads a lot of scripts. Maybe I can ask him to read yours. If you want."

Wow, as if Jeremy didn't already approve of Matty's new boyfriend. "When it's ready, sure! That'd be great, Gabe, thanks so much!"

As soon as those words were out of his mouth Jeremy wondered if he'd spoken too soon. Just hand the script over to some probably lower-level development exec? Chance burning a buyer bridge before Jeremy even found an agent to show it around? Who was he kidding? An agent? Yeah, like they were lining up for him. This was the bird in the hand, take it, you schmuck. It could be a lucky step back into a world he'd left behind.

"Happy to help," smiled Gabe, exposing a fine set of even, white teeth.

"Now, who wants dessert?" Annabelle asked as she rose from the table and winked at Jeremy.

And those were the fateful few degrees of separation that brought resurrected screenwriter Jeremy Lerner to the office of one Ian Franco a few weeks later on an encouragingly sunny Tuesday morning. Though it turned out, Ian had more clout than it first seemed from Gabe's description. When Jeremy checked out the exec online, he learned he was actually Monolith's VP of feature development, which could make him an ideal conduit to move the script forward. That is if Ian even liked *Offensive Measures*. Which, he did—at least enough to schedule a meet and greet with Jeremy. Pretty quickly, in fact, even if Ian did have to reschedule twice. (Jeremy remembered that from years ago: any meeting that didn't change times at least once probably wasn't worth having.)

Back to the age thing: Jeremy was resigned to the fact that he was a generation older than Ian and so many of the studio and network execs he'd meet now in his screenwriting travels. What could he do about that? Not a thing. He was the age he was, they were the age they were.

Still, Jeremy figured he could at least make an effort to not show up looking like Ian's dad but maybe closer to, say, his much—much—older brother. (Notwithstanding, of course, that Gabe surely explained to Ian, by way of introduction, that Jeremy was his boyfriend's *father*.) In any case, Jeremy got his hair smartly cut and, for the first time, colored a passably close shade of dark brown to mask the encroaching gray. He maybe looked a whole two months younger, but he'd take it. Annabelle took one look at the newly shorn and dyed Jeremy, started to fan herself, and dubbed him "His Hotness," so that alone was worth the $140-plus-tip.

Then there was the matter of clothes. What did screenwriters wear to meetings these days? He imagined nothing that different from what they used to wear—what *he* used to wear—which is to say nothing special: jeans, a buttoned-down shirt (in *or* out), up-to-date sneakers (they often provided the personality). Generally, the more casual and unstudied the better; it implied, erroneously, that you spent more time writing than shopping. But Jeremy usually went with whatever he thought he looked best in (he avoided T-shirts, which made him appear kinda bony), while still adhering to the "uniform."

Just to be sure, he called his screenwriter friend, Zoë, who regularly had her share of in-person meetings. She reconfirmed his assumption that, yeah, it was still a come-as-you-are party but cautioned him not to wear anything more than a year old. Jeremy didn't ask why, didn't really want to know (though he had his ageist theory), just dug out a pair of slim-fit Levis and a checkered Bonobos shirt Cassie bought him last Chanukah, and his old black Converse All-Stars that, even he knew, never went out of style. And still, he was dressed better than the compact, baby-faced Ian, who looked like he had just rolled out of bed and into his ergonomic desk chair.

But Ian could have been sitting there stark naked for all Jeremy cared when, after exchanging some pleasantries, which included Ian dubbing Gabe "awesome" and Jeremy praising a new Monolith crime drama he'd squeezed in the night before, Ian leaned back in his chair, took a sip from his Kombucha bottle and said about the last thing Jeremy was prepared to hear: "We love your script and want to make your movie."

"You what?" Jeremy asked, unsure if what he'd heard had even the slightest connection to reality.

Ian grinned. It was one of those rare times someone like him was able to deliver such a totally happy bouquet of news instead of one of those dreaded kiss-offs like "We already have something like it in development" or "I just couldn't get Megan (or Caleb or Aidan or Vanessa) excited."

"We love the world you created, love the whole '70s paranoia throwback thing, think Garfield would be an amazing part for like Adam Driver or Jake Gyllenhaal and want to get it out to directors ASAP. We're thinking Fuqua. Do you like Fuqua?"

"*Antoine* Fuqua?" Jeremy managed to ask. His head was spinning.

He tried to focus on the framed Hockney print of Mulholland Drive hanging behind Ian's desk, but the picture's iconic twists and turns just made him dizzier. Jeremy truly thought this meeting would just be one of those bullshit favors an exec does for his neighbor. He thought that Ian would say nice but noncommittal things about Jeremy's screenplay (if he even read it), ask what else he was working on, offer to keep Jeremy in mind for any open writing assignments ("Though we're all booked out at the moment," was the usual instant backpedal), validate his visitor's parking, and close the door behind him.

But this? This was beyond. *Beyond* beyond! And to think Ian and his bosses had made this momentous decision before any of them even saw Jeremy's clincher haircut. He wanted to call Cassie right then and tell her, and then realized he meant Annabelle and thought he might pass out altogether.

"Who did you say your agent was again?" Ian asked, interrupting Jeremy's reverie.

"Oh. I didn't. I mean, I don't. Have one. An agent." Jeremy sounded like a short-circuiting robot. He'd forgotten how there was so much more to writing movies than writing movies. Reviewing them was a lot less complicated.

Ian stared at Jeremy as if he'd just dropped onto the planet from outer space. "Well, just let us know who business affairs should call to make your deal," Ian finally said with a shrug, taking a last swig of his bottled tea.

"My deal," Jeremy repeated. "Right."

He wasn't even a Writers Guild member anymore, hadn't paid his union dues in a decade. Would he even get the WGA minimum rate? Jeremy didn't have a clue what buyers paid for a screenplay these days that wasn't written by Aaron Sorkin or Diablo Cody or any of the other A-listers making bank out there. And then it hit him like a ton of scripts: if Monolith wanted *Offensive Measures* maybe another company would, too. Someplace like Netflix or Amazon or Hulu or a more traditional studio like Universal, which had bought his first script. If that happened, there'd be competition;

it might drive up the price. A bidding war! Jeremy put the brakes on his ping-ponging thoughts, knew he was getting way too ahead of himself. He should be kneeling at Ian Franco's Vans-covered feet and thanking him for this golden opportunity. Not that that was Jeremy's style, but—Christ, focus, man!

Fortunately, Ian had a crucial reason to break the silence.

"Where do you get your hair cut?" he asked. "I'm looking for a new stylist."

CHAPTER
21

IT WAS ANNABELLE'S idea to gather Jeremy, Matty, Gabe, and Joyce for a celebration dinner at Pace, a quaint and popular Italian spot nestled into a rustic corner of Laurel Canyon just north of Sunset Boulevard. Jeremy, though wary about getting overly excited about his amazing good fortune until the deal closed—Zoë's agent, Juliana, more than happy to jump in to represent Jeremy on the script, had begun negotiating with Monolith and pronounced the streamer's presumptive bid "bearish"—figured he deserved to splurge on the people he cared most about (including Gabe, who, like his aunt, continued to prove a wonderful addition to Jeremy's little circle).

He also considered it a fitting, if belated, way to mark the end of the line for Big Bertha, his freedom to fully use both hands and arms again and to wear and pretty much do whatever he wanted—as long as no heavy lifting was involved. His bad shoulder was still mending, still tender but, like so much else in his life lately, greatly improved. Dr. Hockstein, during a follow-up visit the previous week, said Jeremy was making a "remarkable recovery" and jokingly—or not—took full credit.

When Annabelle suggested Pace (that's *pah*-chay to you: Italian for "peace"), Jeremy went right along with it even though the restaurant struck such a wistful chord in him he had to avoid glancing its way whenever he drove past. And who was the last person

Jeremy would want on his mind while he was feting his script sale over ciabatta-crust pizza and organic beet salad? Cassie, of course, even though he knew that's exactly whose memory would be hovering over the entire evening.

The restaurant had just changed hands—and names—around the time Jeremy and Cassie moved to Laurel Canyon some twenty-plus years ago. They had eaten there a few times before that when it was Caioti, a bohemian hole-in-the-wall famed for serving a salad that, urban legend had it, could kick-start labor in overdue women.

So on the night they closed on their Laurel Canyon house— and with Joyce and Larry babysitting year-old Matty—Jeremy and Cassie thought, where better to honor the occasion but smack dab in their new neighborhood at its one and only official restaurant? While it retained its former woodsy charm, the place now had a bit more elevated menu and the prices to match. But it felt like home to them and, although emotionally zapped from their late afternoon signing spree, they enjoyed a long and languorous meal nestled amid the trattoria's brick-walled warmth.

This is not to say that Jeremy and Cassie, still only in their twenties, weren't more than slightly terrified to be doing something as irrevocably adult as buying a house. And they had no idea that night just how overextended they'd be for the next swath of years or that Jeremy's screenwriting career, which had enabled them, at least on paper, to afford their new homestead, would have the shelf life of sushi. Cassie also hadn't decided to go to law school yet, so those expenses, though they'd prove a wise investment, were also not on their mental tote boards.

As a result, they were free to dream up all kinds of improvements for Chez Lerner: new kitchen cabinets and counters, moving the washer and dryer inside from the garage, relandscaping the front and backyards, retiling the master bathroom, and on and on. They were giddy with creativity, drunk on possibility. They drew sketches on napkins and made lists on their palms. They floated favorite paint colors and wood stains. Money was no object. Need played second fiddle to want.

They were also totally and completely in love—with each other and their wondrous baby son. So much so that after they returned home that night, bid goodbye to Joyce and Larry, gazed in awe at their sleeping child, and then climbed into bed filled with such a heady mix of hope and joy and adventure they could barely stand it, they tried to make a brother or sister for Matty.

Like the indoor laundry room and that new bathroom tile, it would never come to pass.

So as the others gabbed away as they pored over the Pace menu, Jeremy's thoughts sprang back to that night a lifetime ago when he and Cassie sat at a corner booth just two tables down and mapped out the rest of their lives together. It made him terribly sad.

"I just want to give props to my dad," announced Matty, wine glass aloft, "who proves that it's never too late to get your shit together!" They all shared a warm laugh and toasted.

"Oh, I don't know if it's actually 'together,'" said Jeremy as he clinked his glass around the table. "But it's definitely in a much neater pile than it was a few months ago."

"By the way, Mom sends her congratulations," Matty told Jeremy, perhaps a bit too well-timed. It put a slight pall over the table. There was a sudden rearranging of cutlery and interest in the bread-basket. Matty soldiered on: "She's really happy for you, Dad. Knows what a big deal it is."

Jeremy appreciated him trying to normalize things, to keep his family aligned amid its fracture. Annabelle was respectfully silent.

Gabe, quick on the uptake, jumped in to paper over the weird-ness. "Ian told me it's only the second spec screenplay Monolith bought all year. So that's pretty major."

Joyce turned to Jeremy, did her part: "What did you use to say about screenwriting, honey? 'The roulette wheel is always spinning, it's just a matter of whose ball lands in the slot?'"

The exchange escaped Jeremy. He'd been spaced out wondering why Cassie, if she knew about his script sale, hadn't at least shot him a quick text or email. And did she really send her kudos through their son, or did Matty concoct that to make Jeremy feel better?

Then again, Cassie and Jeremy had had next to no communication in weeks. Most notably, not even about their pending divorce, of which Jeremy had still done nothing in terms of hiring an attorney.

This was partly because Cassie, for some unknown reason, had not been pressing him, and partly because Jeremy had been too taken up with the recent whirlwind of his life to deal with it. And though, in theory, he'd come to terms with needing a divorce lawyer, he maybe still naively believed he and Cassie could work things out on their own—even when it came to the house. And maybe, just maybe, he'd begun to think these last few days, the money he'd make from *Offensive Measures* (Juliana said they were circling a healthy six figures, "none of which was a one or a two") could go a ways to making the house his own. And wouldn't there be fitting synchronicity to that, given how he and Cassie were able to afford it in the first place?

Joyce dipped some bread in the pesto-olive oil mix and turned back to Jeremy: "Honey, tell us about physical therapy. How's that coming along?"

As soon as Jeremy's abduction brace was history, he began seeing a physical therapist at a clinic on La Brea covered by his insurance. (That he was still on Cassie's medical plan was a whole other issue.) Dr. Hockstein, Annabelle, the internet, and Jeremy's PT himself, a wispy-whiskered little fellow named Lonnie whose elfin looks belied a powerful pair of hands, all agreed: if Jeremy didn't complete the twelve to eighteen sessions of therapy prescribed to rebuild his strength, it could slow the healing process and leave his rotator cuff susceptible to a retear.

"It's not exactly how I'd like to be spending three hours a week, but I think it helps," Jeremy said, forcing out some halfway upbeat response for Annabelle's benefit. In reality, he despised every painful, tedious minute of PT—those latex resistance bands were torture—and blew off the home exercises Lonnie so diligently diagrammed for him. Jeremy was, however, still doing those thirty-minute walks around his invisible backyard pool, which he found to be great for brainstorming ways to improve *Offensive Measures* and new script ideas altogether. Matty seemed almost more impressed that his father had kept up his daily laps than that he, a relative nobody, had sold a six-year-old screenplay to a billion-dollar streaming platform.

"I've made a decision: the lamb shank," proclaimed Annabelle, closing her menu with such force you'd think she'd just chosen an attack strategy for the Battle of Normandy.

"Caesar salad and the Aphrodite Pie," Jeremy decided. The pizzas were all named for Greek gods, in honor of the adjacent upscale housing development known as Mount Olympus.

"Rigatoni and sausage," declared Matty.

"The snapper," Gabe reported.

"Okay, all present and accounted for," said Joyce, who waved their waitress over from the other side of the room.

Annabelle turned to Jeremy and kissed his cheek, covering his hand with hers. They sat that way, serene and secure, while the others, pretending to ignore the snuggling in their midst, debated the merits of vitamin supplements: Joyce was pro ("They can only help"), Gabe was con ("Eat right, you'll take in all the vitamins you need"), and Matty was on the fence ("Okay, but there's just so much kale one person can eat").

Right as Jeremy was about to change the topic—any other topic, please!—a familiar voice behind him boomed, "Boy, they let anyone into this place, don't they?" Jeremy looked up, startled to see Lucien hovering above him, wife Bonita at his side.

Jeremy disengaged from Annabelle and rose to greet his hapless ex-employer, who'd put on a few pounds and grew an ugly, bushy beard since he'd last seen him at his birthday party. Bonita, with her sleek, super-long dark hair (think Cher in her Sonny days) and turquoise jewelry looked her usual well-heeled earth mother self. Jeremy and Lucien did a half-handshake/half-hug; Bonita tilted her head and smiled, no hug required. Fine by Jeremy. He made quick introductions—or reintroductions—all around, saving Annabelle for last. Without stumbling, he called her his girlfriend, which made Annabelle smile and Lucien study her like a science project. He shouldn't have looked so puzzled: the last time he and Jeremy spoke it was to report that Cassie was spotted on an ice cream date. What did he expect?

"You're doing well, I hope? Recovered from the broken wrist and all?" asked Lucien, one eye on Annabelle.

"Torn rotator cuff," Jeremy corrected him. "And yeah, it's good, thanks." As for the "and all" part of Lucien's question, Jeremy added, because it was too glorious not to, "Actually, this is kind of a celebration dinner."

"Really? Nice. What are you celebrating?" Lucien glanced at Annabelle again.

Joyce, now down to the bottom of her wine glass, brought it on. "My fabulous, brilliant son just sold his screenplay *Offensive Measures* to Monolith, which, I don't mind telling you, only bought two original movie scripts the entire year!"

"Wait," Lucien said, "this isn't the same screenplay you've been working on for ages, is it?"

"One and the same," Jeremy confirmed and, with a sly twist of the knife: "I had some extra time on my hands, as you know, so I pulled out the script again, did a major rewrite, slapped on a new title and, with Gabe's help here"—he swept a hand in Gabe's direction—"got it to an executive at Monolith. And, well, here we are."

Jeremy hoped he wasn't beaming too brightly, but it felt pretty great. Not that Lucien was responsible for his firing per se—Jeremy largely earned that himself—but knowing that the news would likely reach Geneva, whether she gave a shit or not, gave Jeremy a jolt of satisfaction. He wished he could just forgive and forget but sometimes the high road was a lonely, boring place.

Lucien clapped Jeremy on the shoulder (yes, his bad one) and said, with such genuine enthusiasm Jeremy felt like a dope for his preening, "I am so happy for you, man, I really am. You deserve it. Just promise we can interview you first when the movie drops."

"That's a promise," said a humbled Jeremy, remembering now to ask: "How's everything with you?"

"Same shit, different day," he shrugged. "Growing this beard is my big excitement."

"I hate it, he loves it," Bonita told Jeremy with an eye roll. "It's like kissing a sheepdog."

"Hope you got your shots," tossed in Joyce, like she was auditioning for a slot at the Comedy Store.

That bon mot gave everyone, even the impassive Bonita, a laugh.

Lucien offered a final goodbye-and-good-luck to Jeremy and followed his wife to their table.

When they were out of earshot, Annabelle drained her wine glass and said, "Who says success isn't the best revenge?"

CHAPTER
22

"OKAY, THIS IS where we are," Juliana began in an early morning call to Jeremy the next day. "Either they buy you out lock, stock, and screenplay for $275K or you get 150 and the first rewrite at WGA scale, no other guaranteed steps."

Jeremy, pacing the kitchen, wasn't through his second cup of coffee yet so was still a bit fuzzy. Not to be ungrateful, but he had to ask, "What happened to 'six figures, none of which is a one or two?'" He heard keys tapping on the other end.

"I traded $25K upfront for a $75,000 production bonus," she explained. "They don't develop a lot so there's a solid chance they'll shoot it. You'll thank me later." Clack, clack, click.

Annabelle, looking button-cute in Jeremy's oversized old Cannes Film Festival T-shirt (hot tip: you don't have to go there to get one) and lavender cotton panties, her wavy hair twisting into full-on corkscrews, padded in. She'd stayed overnight to continue the celebration—which they did, well into the wee hours. Annabelle, crossing to the coffeepot, wiggled her fingers "hi" to Jeremy, who returned the gesture.

"Okay, that makes sense," he told his agent. "What doesn't make sense is why they'd pay me so much more to do so much less."

Jeremy mouthed "Juliana" to Annabelle. She whispered, "Should I leave?" He waved his hand in a definitive "no."

"They're hoping you'll just take the money and run so they

can bring in another writer immediately, save three, four months. My words, not theirs."

Jeremy noted not an ounce of irony or disdain in Juliana's measured voice. This was her life, and she was more than used to it, each negotiation just a passing car on the freeway.

"Wait, they don't even own the script, and they already want to get rid of me?" Jeremy rolled his eyes at Annabelle, who was getting a crash course in show biz absurdity. For Jeremy, it was an unwelcome refresher course. He spotted some peeling yellow paint on the wall above the stove, wondered if he had a can of touch-up somewhere.

"News flash, Jeremy: Once a director comes on board, they'll want their own writer. Same with a star. It's not about you."

"No, I only wrote the thing," Jeremy said, trying in vain to sound light.

"And you did an awesome job, dude, which is why they're willing to plunk down 300 grand on a script that literally came out of nowhere."

The patrician, pencil-skirted, pushing-fifty Juliana didn't seem like the "dude" type, but Jeremy had to admit it was disarming.

"I thought you said $275?" Jeremy realized.

"You want the buyout, I'll get you 300."

Jeremy swallowed some coffee and processed this. Erstwhile script negotiations crept back into his head, the fight to balance logic and leverage. "What would *you* do?" he asked Juliana. Right now, his agent was Jesus with a headset.

She let loose an uncharacteristic laugh. "C'mon, I'm an agent. I'd grab the money and fuck the rewrite." She turned serious again. "But it's your call."

Gee, thanks. Jeremy sighed and locked eyes with Annabelle, who smiled sweetly over her coffee cup. He had an idea, one he hoped Juliana would talk him out of, but he presented it anyway: "What if there was another buyer?"

"Is there?"

"I'm asking you."

"I didn't know you wanted me to shop it," she answered. "Do you want me to shop it?"

"I don't know, do I?" Jeremy truly wasn't sure he had the stomach for a strategy shift at this point, even if he was the one bringing it up.

"Not if you ever want to work with Monolith again," Juliana told him. Good, he thought, a decision. Or not: "That said," she continued, "I *could* slip it to Sharona at Lionsgate, get a quick read. She's a friend, I trust her. If she likes it, we've got ourselves a ball game."

Jeremy flashed on the tagline from one of his favorite movies: "There's a time for playing it safe and a time for risky business." Okay, but was this really the time to double down, chance blowing the whole thing up? Hadn't he taken enough risks lately, had enough wins? On the other hand, weren't those wins precisely *because* he took those risks? Jeremy glanced at Annabelle, who was answering a text. A client, no doubt. She'd be leaving for her rounds soon.

"The thing is, I've lived with this script for six years," Jeremy told Juliana. "I'd like to be able to do at least the first rewrite."

"Of course you would. The more you write, the better your shot at sole credit and all the goodies that come with. I get it. So does Monolith, hence the deal. But look," Juliana continued after a pensive pause, "let me get creative, see if we can give everyone a tummy rub."

Jeremy wasn't sure exactly what that meant but had had enough agita for one morning. "Okay, well, let me know."

"And Jeremy? Start writing your next script ASAP. This town has a really short memory." Juliana hung up without a goodbye. Jeremy was left staring at his phone.

"That sounded scary," said Annabelle, rising from the table.

"And you only heard my side of the conversation." He met her halfway and kissed her forehead. It was smooth and cool, quite unlike how Jeremy was feeling after that phone call. He wasn't built for negotiating. No wonder he was putting off his divorce.

"I know what'll make you feel better," Annabelle said with a devilish look.

Jeremy narrowed his gaze at his little minx. "Do you have time?"

"To make you French toast? Absolutely."

Okay, not exactly what he had in mind. Still, she looked so excited to get cooking and he was really hungry, so the idea of a great breakfast was nearly as—well, sort of as—enticing. Wow, he was getting older, Jeremy ruefully thought. Right now, anything not to dwell on the *Offensive Measures* wrangling. It would all work out. It had to.

Annabelle went straight to the fridge, pulled out eggs, milk, and a loaf of whole wheat bread, and went to town. "Nutshell me," she said as she heated a frying pan with canola oil.

"What?"

"Oh, that's what Gil used to say to his students before they'd launch into an answer. He was big on bullet points." She shrugged. "It's just a silly expression."

"No, it's funny. And appropriate, since bullet points are about all I have. Basically, Monolith is offering me a lot more to hand over the script and walk away than to stay involved." Just saying those words made Jeremy simmer again, despite not wanting to dwell. "Anyway, Juliana's going to get 'creative,' whatever that means. We'll see."

Annabelle considered this as she cracked a quartet of eggs into a mixing bowl. "Look, I don't know your business, but I know you. And I know you're better than you think you are. You wrote a great script—don't sell yourself short." She started whisking the eggs with remarkable velocity. Her right arm was a blur.

Jeremy was touched and inspired by Annabelle's observation. The truth was, for the most part, he didn't lack confidence in his ability, just people's reactions to it. Though really, wasn't that the same thing? And being thrust back into the screenwriting game only intensified those feelings and reminded him how subjective it all was; how political and yes, superficial it could be. Yet he couldn't deny the thrill of it all—emotionally, creatively, maybe financially—and would do his best to concentrate on that. The universe was sending him a message: "Fucking do this." And you don't want to disappoint the universe.

Jeremy responded assuredly, "I won't sell myself short. I promise." He even persuaded himself.

"That's my guy," she said, dipping bread triangles into the egg mix.

His heart swelled. "Does that make you my gal?"

"Oh, honey, I hate the word 'gal.' Sounds like I should be slinging booze in some old saloon."

Not what Jeremy expected, but okay.

"But yes," she added, "I am otherwise yours. If you'll have me."

Jeremy turned Annabelle from the stove, wrapped both arms around her, and pulled her in close. They kissed as the hot pan hissed behind them.

"Wanna know my secret?" she asked.

"Every one of them," Jeremy replied.

"Don't get too excited," she said, turning back to the frying pan. "I meant my French toast secret."

"The word 'French' is always exciting," he noted with a grin.

"You dip the bread in the egg, stick it in the pan, and then pour what's left of the beaten eggs over it all. Gives it this delicious puffy crust. Then you burn it a little because that's what my mother always did, and she was the world's best cook."

"You haven't had Joyce's roast chicken."

"I'm waiting for an invitation."

"I'll see what I can do. I know people."

This was who they had become. Bantering love bunnies. A mutual admiration society. A guy and his gal—or whatever a better word was. Uncertain start aside, the speed with which they'd bonded, the enchanting familiarity they felt, took them both by surprise.

"Do you think things are moving too fast?" Annabelle asked around week three of their relationship after they'd spent from Friday night (late afternoon, really) through Monday morning camped out at Jeremy's. He was in the waning days of his abduction sling imprisonment, but they worked around it gently and creatively for maximum pleasure on all fronts.

Without discussing it, Jeremy knew they were each experiencing that dizzying rush of new romance in dramatically different ways: Annabelle's reentry into dating was decidedly cathartic, poignant, and cautious; while Jeremy's was exhilarating, empowering, and weirdly vindicating. (*See, Cassie, it wasn't me, it was you,* he thought, somewhat misguidedly.) For both, it was their first time up at bat in ages, yet their physical and emotional muscle memories kicked in like lovers half as young. That each of their previous romantic plunges had led to marriage also went unmentioned but bobbed teasingly beneath the surface.

"I don't know if we're moving too fast," Jeremy answered her. "But I sure don't want to move any slower."

She smiled, relieved. "Okay, I can't argue with that."

Three weeks later, they were eating fabulous French toast and planning their first weekend getaway.

CHAPTER
23

WHEN ANNABELLE FIRST suggested Cambria, a small, tranquil beach town on California's central coast, Jeremy thought it sounded ideal for their little trip. "But I have to warn you," she said, "there's nothing to do there but eat and walk and relax. The beaches are rocky—but the ocean is everywhere. Oh, and if you're lucky there'll be elephant seals. Talk about ugly!"

"Please, you had me at there's nothing to do," said Jeremy. A few days away from the intensity of L.A. would be a well-timed tonic. He also thought mellowing out could help prepare him for the busy weeks that were sure to follow once his script deal closed. (Juliana had texted him halfway through breakfast: "Monolith rethinking $! Stay tuned!"). "Actually," Jeremy realized, "I think I stopped there overnight with Cassie and Matty when we drove Highway 1 to Big Sur one summer. But that's at least a dozen years ago."

"Well, I'm sure it's still exactly the same. Not much changes there," said Annabelle, sprinkling cinnamon on her French toast. "Gil and I must've gone like seven or eight times. We just loved it."

It gave Jeremy pause, so he had to ask: "Are you sure you want to go back? I mean, do you think it'll be hard for you?"

She considered that between eggy bites. "If it is, I should probably get over it, shouldn't I?"

It didn't seem like a question Jeremy should answer, so he didn't.

Annabelle, dark eyes shimmering, announced, "You and I, mister, are going to have the best time."

With a prospect like that, Jeremy couldn't get on the road fast enough. Still, the morning before they were set to take the four-hour drive north, reality came a-calling in a wobbly one-two punch.

First up: as Jeremy was taking his daily backyard constitutional, his phone rang. It was Juliana, who he hadn't heard from in days save a few more "stay tuned" texts, one punctuated with a smiley face presumably so he wouldn't worry. It didn't do the trick. He knew enough to know—and Zoë reconfirmed for him—that when these deals started dragging on it was because the buyers were flexing their muscle, not because the seller was making them sweat. Take the first offer and it's smooth sailing, start tinkering and it's Humpty Dumpty time—it's gonna have to be put back together again and that takes a minute. It's like when you send away your server because you're not ready to order and they don't come back forever. If you'd decided from the start you'd be eating already.

"I have good news and not terrible news," Juliana said. "Which do you want first?"

Guessing games? Really? "Surprise me," Jeremy answered as he walked the yard.

"Lionsgate made us an offer."

"Wait, what? Lionsgate? You showed it to Lionsgate? Why didn't you tell me?" Jeremy stopped dead in his tracks near the withering grapefruit tree.

"We talked about submitting it. We never talked about *not* submitting it," said Juliana in her best agent-ese. "Anyway, it's irrelevant because, as I predicted, Sharona went crazy for the script. Wants to get it to Jake Gyllenhaal."

"So does Monolith," Jeremy reminded her.

"Monolith doesn't have a deal yet."

"Does Lionsgate?"

"No, because they're offering less than Monolith," Juliana told him. Jeremy was baffled. There went the keyboard clacking again. "But it doesn't matter," she asserted.

"It doesn't?" Why did Jeremy feel like he lost IQ points whenever he talked to his agent?

"No, the whole point is I can use it to drive up Monolith. They don't know what Lionsgate offered." Juliana then said "Two minutes" to someone who wasn't Jeremy, so that was apparently how much time was left to sort this out.

"In that case, can't you also use Monolith to drive up Lionsgate?"

"Gee, why didn't I think of that?" she answered, dry as a bone.

Jeremy could practically hear her rolling her eyes; he could certainly picture it.

"Tried it, didn't work. They're not stockpiling like Monolith. Anyway, you just have to know there's a limit to what anyone will spend on you, Jeremy."

"Okay, I'm confused. Have we gotten to the good news yet?"

Juliana snorted. "You're funny. You don't look funny, but you are." Which was funny, because he wasn't trying to be funny, so where exactly did that leave him?

"Honey, Lionsgate *was* the good news." Clack, clack. "The not terrible news is that even though Monolith won't move on any of the points yet, they haven't taken the deal off the table."

Jeremy stopped again. "Wait, was that even *on* the table? To take it *off* the table?" Jeremy had to drop into a patio chair. He was getting lightheaded.

"Of course. It always is! But I talked them out of it. Your friend Ian also put in a good word with business affairs. He wants to make your script. He likes you."

"He's not exactly my friend."

"Not with that attitude. And by the way, it wouldn't hurt to have a few younger friends in the business, know what I mean?"

He knew what she meant, and it made him rub his temples. "I still don't get it. Your last text said Monolith was rethinking the money."

"They were. They did. They decided they weren't going to budge. They probably never were. It's a war out there, Jeremy."

He imagined Juliana sitting at her desk in an Armani camisole and an army helmet. "So where does this leave us?"

"I go back to Monolith one last time about Lionsgate, and you go back to thinking up your next great script idea. Gotta jump, dude." And she did.

Dude. Again.

Jeremy finished his backyard laps, contemplated the fate of his resuscitated screenwriting career, then went inside and fixed himself a Bloody Mary. It was 10:30 a.m. He pretended it was a Sunday.

But his convo with Juliana was a party compared with what came later as he was driving to a physical therapy session. Cassie's name came up on the phone display, and he was about to send her to voicemail. But his parental reflex kicked in—What if Matty had been bitten by a rabid bark mitzvah boy?—and Jeremy answered.

As always, he should have trusted his first instinct.

To nutshell it, as Annabelle—or her Gil—might have put it, Cassie decided to go with a different divorce lawyer than she'd first planned, and it had taken awhile for her to get the new one. Jeremy had not even begun to look into attorneys, but his feet-dragging days were clearly kaput. And Cassie again squelched the mediator option, which made Jeremy wonder if he shouldn't hire one to mediate the whole mediator concept. When Jeremy brought up the potentially huge cost of legal fees, Cassie said that was why it was incumbent upon them to be smart, fair, and decisive and not drag out the proceedings any more than necessary. Which was to say *he* should be and do all those things.

"We don't have to worry about custody so that's a giant savings right there," Cassie said, as if they were shopping for a new bedroom set. "But, look," she added, "we have assets. We have history. We have the house. So."

"What if I said I'd buy you out of the house?" Jeremy asked out of his ass.

"I'd say 'with what?'"

Yes, that *was* the question. Jeremy stopped at a light in front of Pink's, a legendary hot dog stand that was never without a line of customers snaking out onto La Brea. He hadn't been there in eons; last time was, natch, with Cassie who, in their early days together, made it her monthly guilty pleasure. For Jeremy, it was all pleasure, no guilt, but he always kept that illusion of "forbidden indulgence" going for the sake of his more health-conscious wife. He used to love watching the sexy, fit Cassie eat those messy, delectable, nitrate-loaded treats like it was the ultimate sin. They'd go early on a Saturday, almost beat the opening crowd, and chow down on chili cheese dogs or some other obscenely wonderful concoction, onion rings on the side. They continued the tradition for a while after Matty was born, but it eventually petered out as many things did.

"I think you know I sold my screenplay," Jeremy finally said to Cassie as the light turned green, and he continued south across Melrose Avenue.

"I do. Congratulations," she replied, with guarded enthusiasm. "Was it for $1.8 million? Because that's what the house is apparently worth, which, let's face it, is un-fucking-believable given what we paid for it."

Jeremy thought she was sounding awfully cavalier, and it hit him that he totally hadn't been thinking clearly—if at all—about how he would work out staying in the house.

"I'll ask again: Did the script sell for $1.8 million?"

Jeremy clenched his jaw so tightly he thought it would lock. "I think you know the answer to that," he said, matching her patronizing tone. "And you also know that's twice what I'd have to pay you." Like that was even remotely doable either. But still.

"Just get a lawyer, Jeremy, okay? And we'll go from there. It's enough already."

"It was apparently enough a long time ago," he sniped back. But she had already hung up.

As soon as Jeremy got home, Juliana called, sounding like she'd just been made queen of England. "I have splendid news, Jeremy! Our friends at Monolith gave way, offered up a guaranteed polish! Isn't that smashing?"

He didn't really know: was it great, or was he being placated? He knew he should be thanking his lucky stars—his and everyone else's. And he believed Juliana was doing her best, even if he couldn't let her know that just yet. So he had to ask: "And what would that bring the total to?"

"About 210. Minus commission, of course," his agent happily reported.

That was certainly a bundle, definitely way (way) more than he'd made any year since, well, he'd sold his last screenplay. Except there was still the matter of that extra hundred thou if he would simply bid farewell to his script as it was. And also as it was, he needed the dough for the divorce.

Just when he was about to bring that up, Juliana jumped back in more bluntly: "It's take-it-or-leave-it time, Jeremy. Final offer, no returns, exchanges or refunds."

Don't be an asshole, he thought, just say thank you and get to work.

"And the $300,000?" Jeremy asked like an asshole because he couldn't help himself.

"You're kidding, right?" There went those clacking keys again. She was checking out.

"Yeah, I'm kidding," Jeremy lied. "But, for the record, let's say I wasn't."

"Oh, honey. That ship has sailed so far away you couldn't get it back with all the radar in the Pacific." She agent-spoke again: "Shall I tell Monolith to paper you up?"

A moment, a swallow, and then, from Jeremy: "Yes, with a nice red bow."

CHAPTER
24

IT WAS SUCH a beautiful summer morning—warmish, breezy, unusually clear—when they packed up Jeremy's Prius and began the drive up to Cambria that his festering worry about all things Cassie quickly took a back seat.

Annabelle had planned out the trip with such endearing precision and care that all Jeremy had to do was breathe. Annabelle said it felt like she was introducing a wonderful new friend to a favorite old friend. And she couldn't wait for them to meet.

Nope, negativity didn't stand a chance this weekend, not with Ms. Annabelle Eve Duran in the house. Jeremy had just recently learned her middle name and was determined to use it as often as possible. That's because his, believe it or not, was Adam. Really, what were the odds? They joked that if they had a daughter they'd name her Eden, even though in *this* life a cocker spaniel was far more likely.

They were out of L.A. County within an hour, Friday morning freeway traffic proving thankfully lighter than normal. They continued up the 101, past coastal Oxnard and later, affluent Santa Barbara where Annabelle planned for their first selfie stop: the town's vast esplanade overlooking a gorgeous beachfront on one side and the luxurious Biltmore Hotel across the way. It was all set beneath a cloudless, azure sky that lit Jeremy and Annabelle like movie stars. They sat on a low wall, the Pacific behind them, and took photos: sunglasses both on and off, taking turns in Annabelle's floppy flowered sun hat, and doing their fair share of mugging.

"See that patio restaurant," said Annabelle, pointing beyond the adjacent road toward the Biltmore's plush, open-air dining area. "Gil and I celebrated our fifth anniversary there with the most fabulous Sunday brunch, preceded by a ridiculously pricey overnight in one of the hotel's amazing cottages. I was like, 'Honey, no, we *cannot* afford it,' and he was all 'I know, Anna B.'—he called me Anna B.—'but you only live once.'"

"Unless you're James Bond, then you only live twice," Jeremy joked, realizing as the words were exiting his mouth that he was stepping on a tender recollection with some silly movie trivia.

But Annabelle, undeterred, pivoted back to the land of the living with the admission that she'd never seen a James Bond movie. "Wait, how does that compare to never seeing *Casablanca*?" she asked. "And how come we haven't watched that together yet? You promised!"

"Tell you what, next weekend, a double feature: *Casablanca* and either *Dr. No*, which was the first Bond film ever or maybe *Goldfinger*. The early ones are the best because, y'know, Sean Connery. And the '60s, of course."

Annabelle: "The '60s? We weren't even born then."

"Yeah, but they were cool and crazy and crammed with conflict," said Jeremy as an attractive young family of five breezily bicycled past.

"That's a lotta c's, cowboy," Annabelle noted, adjusting her sun hat. "Wait, that's another one!"

Jeremy grinned back. "So—Bogey and Bond? Next Friday night?"

"It's a date," she promised, as her eyes drifted back to the site of her fifth-anniversary retreat. A faint shadow crossed her face as, Jeremy could tell, Gil's ghost was threatening to invade her newfound island of bliss. Would he get through this time?

Annabelle sprung up from the wall, slapped on a happy face, and announced: "We're not gonna get there by lunchtime if we sit here all day!"

JEREMY HADN'T TALKED to anyone, particularly Annabelle, about his fractious chat with Cassie the day before, not wanting to give it any more air than it needed. Even so, he knew he'd have to deal with finding a lawyer when he returned to L.A. Cassie was right about one thing: it was enough already.

Annabelle was circumspect about Jeremy's dealings with Cassie, never prying and mostly just listening with concern the rare times he brought her up. But with her finely tuned emotional radar, Annabelle seemed able to tell when the divorce—or anything troubling—was on his mind and would gingerly ask what was up. Loath to draw her into his mess, especially at this early stage of their relationship, Jeremy usually sloughed off a pensive mood on his scriptwriting ("Just thinking about this scene I'm trying to fix"), which Annabelle, whether she believed him or not, would at least outwardly accept.

The irony was that he had begun to trust her judgment—and objectivity—so implicitly that her input might have been an enormous help as he floundered through the dissolution of his marriage. But there were a few other factors at work. If Jeremy were to be completely truthful with Annabelle about what went down with Cassie, it might mean revealing more of his faults than he cared to; he was still reconciling them himself. If they stayed together, Annabelle would spot them on her own soon enough, if she hadn't already. Did that make Jeremy selfish or controlling or insecure? All of those things? Or was he just being considerate of Annabelle's feelings, her own sense of well-being? Still, he wondered, of the two of them, who really needed protecting?

Jeremy also didn't think complaining about the last woman in his life to the new woman in his life was exactly the coolest thing to do, especially when that new woman had lost the love of her life to an untimely death just the year before.

All this by way of explaining how, as they made their way north to the next photo opportunity—the notoriously gaudy Madonna Inn in San Luis Obispo—it didn't surprise Jeremy when, after a patch of silence, the astute Annabelle turned down the Pandora

Broadway Showtunes station (he was a fan, but she was a full-on theater geek) and said, "Okay, a penny for your thoughts."

"Five bucks and you're on," Jeremy quipped, a part of him secretly hoping she'd pull out a fiver and call his bluff.

"Look, let's get this on and off the table, alright? Our previous spouses are traveling with us this weekend whether we like it or not, so we have two choices: say what's on our mind or let it all pile up inside of us and sit there like a brick."

That was way better than five bucks, thought Jeremy: Honesty. Maybe they had been acting a bit too nobly for their own good. Really, who comes into a relationship, especially at their ages, without some kind of baggage? And what if, to paraphrase a lyric from the musical *Rent* (the rowdy "La Vie Boheme" had coincidentally—or maybe not—just streamed on Pandora), their baggage went together, was actually a strangely matched set?

"Does this mean we're entering a new phase of our new relationship?" asked Jeremy. "The no-bricks phase?"

Before Annabelle could answer, she was diverted by something out the window. "Jeremy, look! The Pea Soup Andersen's sign!"

"The what?" He followed her gaze, but all he saw was a billboard slipping out of sight.

She turned back to Jeremy, dark eyes sparkling. "It's this sweet old restaurant that's known for its pea soup. Has kind of a Danish thing going on. We ate there once, food was okay, but you don't really go for the food."

"What do you go for?" wondered Jeremy, whose least favorite soup was split pea. *The Exorcist* ruined it for him as a kid; there was no turning back.

"It's famous!" she answered as if that was enough.

"Not that famous." The place was news to Jeremy, though he was enthused by her enthusiasm, as always.

Annabelle poked him playfully in the side. "To answer your question: yes, we're definitely entering our 'no-bricks' phase." She studied Jeremy a moment; he was quiet. "Is that okay?"

He waited a dramatic beat and said, "Yes, on one condition."

"What's that?"

"We don't have to stop at Pea Soup Corrigan's or whatever the hell it's called." He broke into a smile. She returned it.

"Andersen's! And no—you are officially spared." She added dryly, "Even if it is a vital piece of California history."

Jeremy leaned over, kissed her cheek and then, as they sped along the sunny, sparsely trafficked freeway toward San Luis Obispo, proceeded to unload about his last talk with Cassie. He began cautiously, in a kind of self-editing mode. But that soon gave way to a far more unvarnished take than he'd ever given Annabelle about the divorce: how he and Cassie got there, who they once were and who they'd become, and what he now faced both legally and financially. It was a mouthful, but Jeremy was grateful to be expunging this particular brick.

Annabelle listened quietly, occasionally glancing out her window at a passing vineyard or field. Her serene face betrayed little by way of surprise or appraisal, which encouraged Jeremy to expound. He finished up just as the last jaunty bars of "You Could Drive a Person Crazy" from Sondheim's *Company* played over the Bluetooth.

"There, now, was that so difficult?" Annabelle asked with a smile, knowing just how difficult it was.

"Actually, yes," he answered. "But you made it easier, so thank you." He gave her a long, appreciative look, awaiting a further response. "So what's your verdict, counselor?"

She spun back, pointing: "This is it—the exit!"

Jeremy, startled, swerved across several lanes and almost crash-landed onto the Madonna Road exit.

"Gee, thanks for the notice," he said, straightening out the car and catching his breath.

"Sorry, sorry, it just came up so soon! But, hey—good reflexes!"

He shot her a wry look; Annabelle shrugged.

"Anyway, my verdict," she considered. "Honestly? Same thing I thought after you gave me the abridged version when we first met."

"Which was … what?" he asked, turning left off the exit ramp and following a sign to the Madonna Inn.

"Don't take this the wrong way," Annabelle began, "but I thought, 'Wow, Gil and I were so lucky.'" She offered a cockeyed half grin and added: "Except for the he-got-sick-and-died part."

Jeremy didn't know how to react, she could tell. "Laugh, sweetie, it's a joke."

He relaxed, flashed a wistful smile.

She continued: "I also thought: 'Why is he procrastinating on finding a lawyer? Is he not really sure he wants a divorce? Does he still ...?'" Annabelle let her eyes complete that sentence.

The question unnerved Jeremy. A part of him would always love Cassie, but not in the way Annabelle seemed concerned about.

"I definitely want the divorce," he answered. "At first, I didn't. I mean, look, I was caught totally off guard. Cassie was like ten giant steps ahead of me. But I feel like I've caught up." He added, from a recess in his mind that surprised even him, "I'm not going to beg anyone to love me." Jeremy stopped, realized: "I didn't mean—that sounded harsh, I'm sorry."

"Not at all. You can't force anyone to love you any more than you can force yourself to love someone back. You either do or you don't. I get it." She indicated out the windshield, as the garish hotel loomed ahead: "Take a left and then a right into the driveway."

Annabelle went on to tell Jeremy about an ex-client who was a divorce lawyer with an excellent reputation.

"Just tell me," asked Jeremy, "is he anything like Laura Dern in *Marriage Story*?"

"You mean a shark in stilettos? I can't vouch for his footwear, but I could see him being plenty tough. I mean, he's from the Bronx."

"So is Jennifer Lopez, but I'm not sure I'd want her defending me in a divorce," Jeremy joked.

They took a few selfies outside the benign, almost stately looking inn and a bunch inside where the real ugly happened. Jeremy dubbed the hotel's eye-popping, pink-and-orange-splattered décor "turn-of-the-century whorehouse." Though his artistic side appreciated the site's eccentric, super-kitschy appeal, he was secretly glad Annabelle's itinerary didn't include an overnight stay. His dreams lately were weird enough.

CHAPTER
25

JEREMY AND HIS parents didn't travel much when he was a kid. No summering in Europe, Christmases in Hawaii, or winter breaks in Aspen like so many of his better-off classmates and neighbors. He never thought much of it, knew that his parents' firmly middle-class status and salary limitations—Larry worked for several chain accounting firms, Joyce comanaged a Tarzana podiatrist's office—didn't leave much leeway for excess luxury or financial frivolity. Jeremy once overheard Larry tell Joyce that if they didn't have to spend so much "goddamn dough" on their son's private school maybe they'd be able to indulge a bit more.

Once Jeremy married Cassie he realized, at least compared with his wife, how little of the world he'd seen. They began to rectify that once they had the money to do so—that being before and well after Cassie's time-, savings-, and freedom-draining law school years. (For the record, despite the initial sacrifices, Jeremy was always on Team Cassie when it came to her decision to make the leap from paralegal to attorney. He found her drive to do so inspiring and sexy.)

But vacationing with Cassie was a far more seat-of-your-pants affair than he'd ever experienced with his parents, trekking on his own across western Canada after college, or even in the few hours he'd spent that morning on the road with Annabelle.

"I'll take care of everything," Cassie would announce and then

176

proceed to do little beyond arranging their plane tickets. She took the word "vacationing" seriously. That meant no set schedule, no laundry list of must-see attractions or eateries, no maps or *Fodor's Guide* tumbling around her backpack, and, perhaps most loosey-goosey of all, no hotel reservations. The latter always struck fear in Jeremy's chicken heart, especially once Matty began to travel with them. (Would they end up sleeping with their child in some strange park?)

But Cassie, excited by the unknown, would pick a desired neighborhood (that much she'd research), tell the cab driver to take them there, yell "Stop!" when she liked the looks of a passing inn, and off they'd go. It almost always worked out and, Jeremy had to admit, they ended up in some pretty cool lodgings over the years. When Matty got older Cassie would sometimes let him shout "Stop!" and only once did she have to overrule his selection: a narrow and darkish red-brick building in the heart of Amsterdam that, if it wasn't a drug den or a brothel, it might as well have been. Matty was drawn to its peaked roof, colorful leaded glass windows and neon sign that winked *Gasthuis* (guest house), but Cassie smelled a rat.

Walking past it a few days later they learned it was once a tony bed and breakfast but now served as a private assisted living facility; they'd never replaced the signage. It had been all part of the fun of traveling with Cassie who, in real life, was far more organized than the carefree explorer she became once she left L.A.

Except for a sporadic weekend away—Palm Springs, Scottsdale, Seattle to see her dying great-aunt June—Jeremy and Cassie hadn't taken a meaningful vacation together in four or five years. They stopped even talking about going anywhere, just immersed themselves in work, Matty, and life's day-to-day. Their relationship became like a tire with a slow leak: it gradually, imperceptibly ran out of air.

THOUGH IT WAS just before one when they rolled into Cambria, a fine layer of fog still hung over the coastline and a mild but persistent breeze blew in from the ocean. They made their way up

Moonstone Beach Drive, a scenic stretch of tidy, low-slung hotels and motor inns on one side and a mile-long wooden boardwalk traversing scrubby, herb-scented fields on the other. It was all perched above a rugged beach that gave way to a lightly choppy swath of the Pacific. It was nothing fancy or overly dramatic, more like a mellow little slice of paradise.

Not only did Annabelle make hotel reservations—there would be no madcap shouts of "Stop here!" on her watch—but she preselected the exact room she wanted for them, no substitutes accepted. It seemed that at her favorite Cambria lodge, the snug and welcoming Hearthside Inn, the primo spots to stay were in the row of oceanfront, ground-floor rooms with, as she put it, "must-have" attached patios. Experience taught Annabelle that room 108, at the westernmost edge of the hotel, was angled in such a way that it offered the most privacy plus the best view of the Pacific, free and clear of the twisty old Monterey cypress trees that dotted the landscape. Lo and behold, 108 was available—and it was theirs.

After settling into the room, which was clean, charming, and casual with a cushy, queen-sized mattress and gas fireplace that Annabelle promised would get a workout that weekend (the fireplace, not the bed, because that went without saying), Jeremy and Annabelle strolled up to the Moonstone Bar and Grill for a late, ocean-view lunch of chicken taco salads washed down with a couple of Modelos. They lingered on the patio deck, nursing their second beers, and gazing out at visitors ambling along the boardwalk as the Pacific shimmered beyond them, the gray-blue sky finally fog-free.

"Do you remember any of this from when you were here with Cassie and Matty?" asked Annabelle, hidden behind a kicky pair of vintage cat-eyed sunglasses she'd found recently on eBay.

"Little to nothing," Jeremy admitted. "I think by the time we got here it was dark, and we left first thing in the morning."

It occurred to Jeremy that, as usual, Cassie hadn't planned where they would sleep that night. They could have stayed in room 108 at the Hearthside Inn for all Jeremy recalled. He texted Matty from lunch: "Do you remember where we stayed in Cambria that time we all drove up Highway 1?" Matty's response: "Couldn't tell you with a gun to my head." That made two of them.

Jeremy watched Annabelle staring out at the ocean from their plum spot on the veranda as she downed the last of her beer. She looked lovely, peaceful, distant.

"Did you and Gil come here a lot?" Jeremy asked. He wouldn't have intruded on her reverie if she hadn't already given him permission, if not downright encouragement, to do so. And yet, it still gave him pause.

"Oh, sure, all the time. I mean, everyone does. You stay on Moonstone Beach, you end up here." She gave him a tender smile, dark eyes aglow. "Just like us." Then, as if she could read his mind, added, "I'm fine, Cookie. I promise I'll tell you if I'm not. That's the deal, right?"

He nodded yes. How could you disagree with someone who called you Cookie?

They held hands as they wandered along the narrow and curvy Moonstone Beach boardwalk, making way when joggers and dog walkers passed in the other direction, and amused by the intrepid rabbits and ground squirrels that darted over and under the wooden planks. The late afternoon sun was lush and bracing; Jeremy felt more relaxed and hopeful than he had in ages. He stopped, leaned in, and gave Annabelle a long, award-winning kiss right there in the middle of the boardwalk. People had to step around them. One whistled, another grumbled.

When it was over, Annabelle, looking as smitten as a schoolgirl, gazed at Jeremy. "Wow, Rhett Butler was right."

"Yeah?" Jeremy asked, still a bit breathless. "About what?"

"When he told Scarlett, 'You should be kissed, and often, and by someone who knows how.'"

Jeremy could feel his face flush, his heart flip. You'd think he and Annabelle hadn't already kissed like that a hundred times. Just never in one of her favorite places. He regained his cool and gave her a sly look. "Full disclosure: I plan on taking the 'and often' part of that quote very seriously."

Striking her best Scarlett O'Hara pose, Annabelle exclaimed,

"Why, Mr. Butler, as God as my witness, I should certainly hope so!"

WILDLIFE WAS KIND of a big thing around Cambria. Or at least for a city girl like Annabelle. She had already slotted in a visit to see those legendary elephant seals, which would hopefully be beached up the coast a bit in San Simeon, a town perhaps better known as the home of Hearst Castle. Surprisingly, Annabelle had not scheduled them for a stop at the famed publishing magnate's onetime estate. ("165 rooms! 123 acres of gardens!" barked the landmark's website.) Jeremy was sure it would be at the top of her list, but she declared the place "wildly overrated."

Jeremy reminded her that the great movie *Citizen Kane* was based on Hearst, as if that alone was reason enough to see the tycoon's grand digs, but Annabelle wasn't sold.

"Still," she said, "I'll go if you want to. Wouldn't want you to feel like you missed out or anything."

"Gee, why would I want to see one of the most famous homes of all time when a few minutes away are these grotesque sea creatures flopping around the beach?" In truth, Jeremy didn't care if he saw either attraction, but couldn't resist teasing.

"Did you know they're the largest seals in the entire Northern Hemisphere?" asked Annabelle with delightful earnestness.

"Now how would I know that?" Jeremy answered.

"You're a writer. Writers know things. And now you know something else!" She smiled that smile and he was putty. He'd happily visit the elephant seals.

It was twilight, and they were driving to Annabelle's favorite restaurant in town for dinner, an Asian fusion place called the Wild Ginger Café located on the eastern half of quaint, laid-back Main Street. But first, back to the local wildlife: one of Annabelle's (and presumably Gil's) rituals was to search for the deer that would emerge around early evening to forage for food in a nice residential neighborhood near a grassy tract called the Fiscalini Ranch.

With Jeremy at the wheel, Annabelle directed him through the dimming grid of sidewalk-less streets. She was on the lookout for the mini herds of deer that, she promised, would near-magically appear in driveways and yards chomping away on fragrant grasses, weeds, and wildflowers.

Oh, and there was a kind of game attached to these sightings. "You pick a number," Annabelle explained, "say, twenty. Then you pick something good that will happen if you see twenty deer."

"Is that twenty total or twenty all at once?" Jeremy asked in full sincerity. He wasn't one to look a gift deer in the mouth.

"Well, either, I guess," she considered. "As long as you hit twenty. Of course, the higher the number, the bigger the wish. You can't say, like, 'If I see one deer I'll win a million dollars.' That'd be ridiculous."

Jeremy was tickled. There were actual rules. "What *would* one deer buy you? Just for argument's sake."

"Oh, you'll never see just one deer."

"Okay, two then."

"Not much: a good song will come on the radio next. It won't rain tomorrow." She pointed out the passenger window at a thatch of willowy pink flowers. "Jeremy, stop, look!" And there, like they just stepped out of a storybook, stood a trio of leggy deer, busily chewing grass and gazing back glassy-eyed. She snapped photos of the lithe animals just before they vanished.

Annabelle turned to Jeremy with a wide-eyed grin. "Huh? Did I tell you?"

Jeremy had to admit he was a bit gobsmacked by the sight of the deer. There was something otherworldly about them. Had he ever even seen one up close like that? For real?

"Wow," he told Annabelle, "that was cool."

"Right?" She grinned. "Okay, we saw three. So what's the total number we're shooting for tonight? And what's our wish?"

"I don't know, you decide. Or is it like a birthday wish? You have to keep it to yourself or it won't come true?"

Before she could answer, Jeremy noticed a cluster of neighbors hanging out in a shared driveway, drinking wine and eyeballing a passing deer as if it were the mailman. "Look, number four!" called

Jeremy with glee. He was into it now.

"So cute!" Annabelle turned to him, excited. "Let's go for twenty-five deer in ..." she checked her watch, "the next fifteen minutes. If we get there, *Offensive Measures* is going to get made and be a big hit!"

Okay, now Jeremy was really into it. "You're on!" he declared. "But does that include the four deer we already spotted?"

Annabelle thought for a second and brightened. "Why the hell not?"

Thirty-six deer later and a guaranteed movie smash under his belt, Jeremy followed Annabelle's directions out of the darkening neighborhood and across Highway 1 to Cambria's East Village for some delectable Vietnamese BBQ pork, prawn curry, and banana-mango sorbet.

CHAPTER
26

WHEN THEY RETURNED to the hotel, Jeremy and Annabelle parked and went for a late stroll on the boardwalk, which they had all to themselves except for a pair of hearty joggers and a teenage boy walking a rowdy springer spaniel. It was chilly and pitch-dark save the dim light emanating from the row of hotels across the way and the occasional pair of headlights sweeping down Moonstone Beach Drive. The ocean, with its steady melody of crashing waves, was inky and only vaguely moonlit. Annabelle brightened their path with one of those boxy floating lanterns, which she wielded with authority.

They replayed the past few hours: the deer hunting; the tasty, strikingly plated food at the Wild Ginger Café; its charming outdoor patio where they sat under twinkle lights and a welcoming heat lamp; Jade, the eatery's chatty if self-effacing Singaporean owner and chef who admittedly lived for her business; and the cheery lesbian couple from Bakersfield at the next table who told Jeremy and Annabelle their life stories between courses.

The evening had been free of any particularly deep discussion; Jeremy just assumed Annabelle and Gil feasted at the Wild Ginger many times and that Jade was circumspect enough not to mention the late professor in front of his widow and her new guy. Annabelle, for her part, never brought up Gil throughout dinner when she certainly could have. In return, Jeremy kept Cassie tucked away in his mental vault, and just enjoyed Annabelle.

But wasn't that counter to what they'd agreed upon just that morning in the car? Cards on the table? Hearts on their sleeves? Jeremy had questions; shouldn't he be asking them? Certainly the thoughtful and observant Annabelle had more memories to share, reveries to reveal. Yet she promised she'd let Jeremy know if she wasn't "fine," so wasn't that enough? Did he want her to bring up Gil right there on the shadowy boardwalk so he could talk about Cassie, who he was feeling a bit sentimental about and had no idea why?

Until it hit him.

His hand laced in Annabelle's, Jeremy stared up at the black-ish sky with its sprawl of winking stars and recalled one of his and Cassie's dating rituals. Now and again, on a particularly clear night, they'd drive up Laurel Canyon to Mulholland Drive, park in one of the famed road's many scenic turnouts set above the twinkling San Fernando Valley, sit on the roof of Jeremy's old Volkswagen Jetta, and make out like they had the last tongues on earth. Sated, they'd then try to identify as many of the sky's most visible constellations as they could, and even made up a few goofy ones of their own ("Look, it's Rectumulus!" "There's Sergeant Major Minor!"). He hadn't thought about their stargazing ritual in ages.

So he told Annabelle about it.

She listened intently, even laughed at his and Cassie's fake constellation names. From the boardwalk, they gazed into the heavens and successfully located the dippers, Orion, and Cassiopeia (which, of course, further evoked Jeremy's ex-wife, but what could you do, that's what the thing was called).

It turned out Annabelle was an astronomy buff as a teenager, though all that remained was a passing interest in astrology. She'd been promising to read Jeremy's natal chart and made a mental note to do so when they were back in L.A. "I have to see if we are 'official-ly' compatible," she joked. But Jeremy, who was both intrigued by and skeptical of the pseudoscience, hoped she'd pass on the reading and had already hinted as much. Which only made her want to do it more.

Here was the difference: Jeremy worried an astrological reading might reveal too many incompatibilities (okay, maybe he believed a tad more in astrology than he let on), while Annabelle was sure it would show just how suited they were for each other and was excited to be proven correct. It made Jeremy realize that, once again, he feared being exposed as an imposter: not the husband, boyfriend, dad, son, film critic, screenwriter, provider, or overall man (pick one or more) that he imagined himself to be. But just because he disappointed Cassie didn't mean he'd ultimately disappoint Annabelle. Did it?

Jeremy pondered all this as they walked back to the Hearthside Inn, Annabelle's bobbing lantern bisecting the murk. She was quiet as well, either respecting Jeremy's reflective silence or lost in her own tangle of late evening thoughts. Even so, she winked promisingly at Jeremy as he slid the key card into their door lock. Annabelle lit the gas fireplace as soon as they got inside; the faux hearth threw off more atmosphere than heat but that was okay—it was chillier outside than in.

Annabelle turned from the fireplace and looked at Jeremy, who was sitting on the bed, taking off his shoes. "I'm going to ask you something, and you need to tell me the God's honest truth, okay?"

Jeremy didn't love the sound of the question. "Is this another no-bricks thing?" he asked, truly not sure if he was up to utter candor right now.

"I know we talked about this earlier, and it may not be fair of me to ask again, and I totally don't want to ruin the vibe now—but is there any part of you that thinks he may still have feelings, real feelings, for Cassie? Because I'm getting invested here, and if you think there's even the slightest chance you'll wake up one day and wonder, despite what you said earlier, if you should have talked Cassie into loving you and that's what she's been waiting for all along and this has all just been more of a trial separation than a parting of ways, then you really have to let me know so I can, well … recalibrate my investment." Annabelle plopped onto the bed in emotional exhaustion and stared into her hands.

That was hardly how Jeremy expected the lovely night to end, and he wouldn't allow it to. He sat down next to Annabelle, took her delicate hand in his, and verbalized the words he had thought to himself earlier.

"There's a part of me that will always have special feelings for Cassie. She was my first love, the mother of my child; we became full-fledged adults together, went through so much: twenty-seven years start to finish. That's a lifetime, Annabelle."

Her eyes were welling up with either uncertainty or hope. Jeremy knew he needed to wrap up before the floodgates opened.

"But no, I don't love Cassie anymore—and I don't want to. I want to love you." He wrapped his arms around her and kissed her gently, his lips grazing the salty tears rolling down her cheek.

"Good answer," Annabelle said, smiling through her misty eyes.

"Feel better?" Jeremy asked, stroking the waves of her hair.

She gave an appreciative nod and dabbed at her eyes. "Okay," she said as she slithered out of her jeans. "Now let's get busy, shall we?"

THE REST OF the weekend mirrored that first day in Cambria, a mix of long walks along camera-ready locales, shared stories about their pasts, discussion of the present, good eats, a bracing swim in the ocean, a trip to see the elephant seals (homely, prehistoric looking, oddly fascinating), moonstone collecting on a San Simeon beach, a visit to a picturesque winery, random chats with fellow tourists, and a second round of twilight deer spotting (they topped out at a mere twenty-two). They proved well-matched traveling companions, though Jeremy had to admit he said yes to a few more activities than he truly wanted to (he would've loved a post-lunch nap) just to make Annabelle happy, which also made him happy. She was an energizing force and that was a good thing for a guy with a history of momentum issues.

They did, however, hit a speed bump late Saturday afternoon. As they lounged on their private patio and sipped winery-bought Syrah from borrowed Hearthside Inn wine glasses (which they would eventually purloin—*shh*!), the topic of Matty arose.

"You did a wonderful job with your son. He's a terrific man."

"Thank you, but I can only take half the credit. Cassie was—*is*—a really good mom. I can't fault her there."

Annabelle was about to pour herself more wine, and then passed. "It's admirable, you know."

"What is?"

"How you give credit where it's due. Not every jilted husband would do that." She reconsidered, poured them each another half glass.

"Yeah, I'm a frickin' saint," Jeremy said, his mood darkening.

Annabelle hesitated. "Did I say something wrong?"

"No. Though, frankly, the word 'jilted' sounds a little weird. It's not like I was left at the altar or something."

"Of course not but, well, I think you know what I mean."

"I know what you think you mean but it makes me sound like kind of a ... what's the word? A cuckold." Jeremy drained his wine glass in one gulp and set it back down on the little glass table that sat between their mesh-back chairs.

Annabelle studied him a moment over her wine glass. She watched him eyeing a pair of joggers sprinting along the boardwalk. A flock of gulls—or were they sandpipers?—soared overhead.

"I was giving you a compliment," she finally said. "Sorry if it didn't come out that way. And not to debate someone who uses words for a living, but I don't think cuckold is the right one. Unless she was cheating on you behind your back. Was she?"

Jeremy sighed. "I don't think so, no. And, look, I didn't mean to snap. At you of all people. *You* are the saint." He leaned over and kissed her forehead. "But this divorce ... I have a lot of work ahead of me, a lot of stress and, if I'm being completely candid—"

"That is the weekend theme."

"So, talking about it like we did—and don't get me wrong, I'm glad we did—but it only reconfirmed for me what I've known all along and what I've been trying to avoid: that it's going to be a shit show and I'm kind of freaking out about it." He looked back out at the churning Pacific over the patio's waist-high banister, a brooding look on his face.

Annabelle rose and curled an arm around his waist. They took in the splendid view that added a hundred bucks to their room rate. "Who wouldn't freak out about what you're going to have to go through?" she said. "You think Cassie's not freaking out?"

Jeremy looked at her inquisitively.

"Did you really buy what she told you about changing lawyers delaying her from getting started? As my grandma Iris used to say, usually accompanied by the world's biggest eye roll, 'Please, Eloise.'"

"Actually, yeah, I did buy it. Why not? She's a lawyer herself, I'd say she knows what she's doing. A lot more than me, anyway."

"Maybe she does, maybe she doesn't. But trust me, she doesn't want to be facing this any more than you do. And if you were in touch with her more, you'd probably see that." Annabelle grabbed the wine bottle and their glasses and took them back inside. Jeremy followed her.

"You think I should be in touch with her more? I mean, it seems like she wants as little to do with me as humanly possible."

Annabelle corked the wine bottle. "I think you're going to have to grab yourself by those lovely balls of yours, straighten your spine, and prepare to do battle. It'll hurt, it'll piss you the fuck off, it'll make you say and do some things you won't be proud of, and it'll be over."

She moved off to the bathroom, rinsing out their wine glasses in the sink. Jeremy appeared in the doorway. "Are you talking from personal experience or just your general wellspring of common sense?"

"You mean from when I divorced Andy? Not really. We were kids, we had virtually nothing. We just said 'I'll take this, you take that,' and he was off to Canada." She dried the glasses with a wash-cloth. "I'm actually talking from getting to know the kind, sweet, brainy, sexy, slightly neurotic, and strangely under-confident man I see before me."

Jeremy raised an eyebrow and leaned against the counter.

"You think I'm sexy?" he asked, fishing for a punch line, not a compliment.

"What do you think I'm hanging around you for—a part in your movie?" Annabelle put her arms around his waist and gave him an informative kiss.

"See, even you know no one ever sleeps with the writer to get ahead," he joked, and kissed her again.

"Well, they don't know what they're missing."

CHAPTER
27

A FEW DAYS after he returned from Cambria, Jeremy found himself hiring his first and—please, God—last divorce lawyer, the unfortunately named but otherwise agreeable Arvin Box.

The attorney's neat, understated office was in a high-rise building in Encino, unlike Cassie's lawyer who worked in the swankier Century City, in one of the Westside area's many elite mega-towers. It meant nothing to Jeremy, who was simply happy that if he had to drive over the hill and into the San Fernando Valley he could pay a visit to his mother, who lived near Box's building, following his appointment.

After a few minutes of chitchat about Annabelle—Arvin already knew that she and Jeremy were an item ("Please take good care of my boyfriend," she no doubt told her former client)—and show business (his daughter-in-law's sister wrote sitcoms, did Jeremy know her?), the natty, sixtyish Arvin got down to brass tacks. His genial manner turned appropriately steely as he asked Jeremy a fusillade of personal questions, laid out the pros and cons of Jeremy's legal prospects against Cassie, explained his fee structure and promised a swift and mutually satisfying conclusion to the proceedings—as long as Jeremy and his ex-wife stayed as practical, realistic, and unemotional as possible. (Shades of Cassie's warning to Jeremy; must be a lawyer thing.)

"Just know, knock wood, that I have more work than I need, so it's also in my best interest to wrap this up as quickly and amicably as possible. If that sounds like bullshit, I assure you it's not. That being said, I'll fight like a motherfucker to make sure you don't get taken to the cleaners and can walk away with the most intact and dignified life you possibly can."

As if in punctuation, Arvin popped a few gummy bears from a jar on his desk. He offered the candy to Jeremy, who declined, too queasy to ingest more than the overwhelming reality of his case.

That, unfortunately, included the confirmation that yes, given California's community property laws, Jeremy would have to buy out Cassie's share in their Laurel Canyon home—at current market value—if he wanted to stay in it. It wasn't impossible, but it also wasn't recommended.

"You can put yourself in total hock if you want," said Arvin. "But unless you've got unlimited funds, it's cleaner and frankly smarter to just sell and start the hell over on your own."

Jeremy's shoulders sagged.

There was a ray of sunlight for Jeremy: the fact that, at least until just recently, Cassie made significantly more money than he did, even with her modest lawyerly earnings from the nonprofit sector. So she may be legally obligated to pay temporary alimony until the divorce was finalized. On the downside, because, of course, there had to be one, Cassie would get to share in any and all profits from *Offensive Measures*, even if Jeremy didn't receive any actual money from the sale until after the split.

"You wrote it while you were together, so Cassie can claim she was your motivator, cheerleader, muse, dick stroker, whatever, and deserves to share in its success. Tale as old as time," explained the attorney, dipping into the jar for a gummy bear refill. He seemed to favor the green ones.

"Technically," Jeremy thought out loud, "I rewrote the script after she left, and sold it based on that draft, not the early ones."

Arvin scribbled a few notes, then looked back up. "Irrelevant, counselor!" he shot back like a bad actor in a courtroom scene.

"Wish it wasn't, but the law's the law. And some things you can't argue."

"Don't you just hate it when that happens?" Jeremy joked, but his heart wasn't in it. Still, his general terror aside, Jeremy got a good feeling about Arvin. He found him supportive, direct, and helpfully unequivocal. In truth, Jeremy needed as few choices to make as possible; things would go faster that way and it would keep his head clear for all the major non-divorce items he'd be dealing with over the next few months.

Arvin rotely outlined next steps—serving and responding to divorce papers was up top—and tossed out a string of terms like "petitioner," "temporary orders," "disclosure," "discovery," "settlement," "hearing," and "trial," all of which landed for Jeremy in a big, blurry mental heap.

"Oh, and the second you get home," Arvin added, "you must change the passwords to all your personal accounts—and don't forget everything on the goddamn cloud."

"Okay, but Cassie would never go in and steal anything. She's not that type of person. I mean, she's a lawyer herself, so." Jeremy could see Arvin's gaze withering in real time. Jeremy, sufficiently cowed, said, "Okay, got it," then handed over his Visa card to pay his new lawyer's ample retainer.

"GUESS WHO CALLED me today?" asked Joyce with nothing short of self-satisfied glee.

"Barack Obama. He heard he was the one person in the world you'd most like to have lunch with, and he's ready to take you up on your offer. What are you going to wear?" Jeremy was fixing Joyce's oven door; the screws on each side had simultaneously popped out, and she was left with a lethal accordion of metal and glass.

"That's still one of my fantasies, but no, guess again," she answered as she watched Jeremy try to align the door's trio of weighty slats. "And for God's sake be careful with that thing. I really should have called a repairman."

Jeremy gritted his teeth as he squeezed the panels together and, one at a time, carefully reinserted the Phillips-head screws that held them in place. What a piece of shit, he thought, but kept that to himself. He didn't want to offend Joyce. She was so proud of every major purchase she'd made on her own since Larry died. "I don't know, Ma, who called you today?"

"Your soon-to-be ex-mother-in-law, that's who!"

"Rhea called you? Really? She and Henry haven't even called me all this time." Jeremy gave the oven door screws one final tighten and declared victory. "Gotcha, you bastard!"

Joyce eyeballed the mended door. "I take it back, I didn't need a repairman. You're my hero."

"Just call me Superson," her hero quipped, relieved he had actually fixed the damn thing. "So what did she say?"

"Who, Rhea? Oh, just that she and Henry felt terrible about you and Cassie and hoped we could still be friends." Joyce opened and shut the oven door a few times with a wondrous look.

"That's it? After twenty-seven years?"

"Sounds like it was more than *you* got."

Jeremy glared at his mom's unlikely flippancy.

She squeezed his arm. "Sorry, sweetie, I'm just saying."

"Okay, but you were never exactly friends, so why now?"

"Well, we were friend-*ly*. And God knows we've spent enough time around each other. But, y'know, your father never got past them backing out of paying for the wedding, so he mostly just put up with them for appearance's sake." She grabbed the kettle off the stovetop. "I'm making some tea. Want some?"

Jeremy checked his watch. "I'll take a beer if you have one."

"Ooh, good idea. It's too hot out for tea, anyway." Joyce flung open the fridge, dug out a couple of bottles of Corona, and handed one to Jeremy.

They sat across from each other on stools at the squat granite peninsula that stuck out like a thumb from the kitchen wall. Joyce had lived in the two-bedroom-with-a-den condo since she'd sold their longtime Sherman Oaks ranch house the year after Larry passed. Her unit, on the top floor of the two-story, courtyard-style complex, was a bit sterile and boxy, if unusually roomy for its relatively new age. But Joyce snugged the place up with lots of warm colors, cushy furnishings, wood-framed artwork, and several walls of packed pine bookshelves. Some of the décor was from the Sherman Oaks house while much was bought new when she moved into the condo. "I don't want too many old memories hanging around me," Joyce had explained at the time. Plus her shopping jaunts helped keep her mind off her loss and focused on the future. "Forward march!" she called it.

Jeremy felt a belated wave of defensiveness toward his parents. "Cassie was mortified, you know, the way Henry shot his mouth off about footing the whole wedding bill—when no one even asked him to—and then, in the light of day, deciding the families should split it. I don't blame Dad for being pissed off."

"Oh, we all had too much to drink that night celebrating your engagement, who knows what we said," Joyce recalled between ironic sips of beer. "I couldn't hold it against Henry, even if your father did. Besides, Dad and I were happy to pay our share. Your wedding was … well, it was a glorious night, wasn't it?"

The question sat there like an ill-timed stink bomb until Joyce, realizing the faux pas, waved a hand and said, "Anyway, I thought you liked Cassie's parents. At least more than Cassie did."

"I did. I do," answered Jeremy. "I always thought Cassie was overly hard on them, especially given how devoted they tried to be to her and Matty. Even if, when it's all said and done, he is closer to you."

"Well, I am just so much damn fun," Joyce said, only half-kiddingly, then raised her bottle to Jeremy and took another swig.

"It's just weird to be so involved in people's lives for so long and then poof—it's like you never were."

For a guy who had an awesome new girlfriend and had just sold a screenplay to a major buyer (Juliana left a message today: he'd have the contract by week's end), Jeremy was looking awfully glum.

Joyce stood. "You're depressing me, you know that?"

"Sorry, Ma. Where are you going?"

She gestured with her half-full Corona. "Let's finish these out on the lanai, okay?"

That's what Joyce miscalled, as if she were the fifth member of the *Golden Girls*, the compact balcony off the living room that had just enough space for two deck chairs, a little table, and a potted plant or two. Jeremy followed her out. They sat and looked out at the symmetrically planted, overly pruned courtyard beneath them. It was so precise it almost didn't look real.

"So tell me about Cambria," said Joyce, nestling into the soft canvas of her chair.

"It couldn't have been more relaxing. I've never spent so much time communing with the ocean. The place was lovely." He finished his beer and wouldn't have minded another, but knew Joyce would tell him he shouldn't drive home tipsy, and she'd be right.

"I meant something interesting," she said with a cagey grin.

Jeremy had no idea what she had in mind.

"Like where's this going? With Annabelle. You go away with someone new, you learn a lot about them. What did you learn?"

Joyce waved down at a woman around her age crossing the courtyard beneath. The neighbor waved back and kept going. "That's Helene Darvell, she's one of your fans. She's Australian, you know."

"No, I didn't know, and one of my fans of what?"

"Your movie reviews, of course!"

Oh. "Did you tell her I was fired?"

"I didn't have the heart. She'll figure it out herself, I'm sure." Joyce sat upright. "So we were talking about the darling Annabelle."

"Were we?" Jeremy asked dubiously. Joyce had that look on her face he knew all too well: she wanted answers and she wanted them now. It's not like he had anything to hide. "She's fantastic. I'm crazy about her."

A tear bubbled up in Joyce's eye. "Honey, I'm so thrilled for you. She feels the same, I hope? I mean, how could she not?"

"Cassie didn't, so clearly I am resistible in some circles," he offered dryly. "But, yeah, I think—I hope—we're on the same wavelength, romantically speaking."

Joyce's expression turned somber. "Promise me you won't hurt her. That's all."

He looked astonished. "Why in the world would I hurt her?"

"Oh, darling, you're taking this the wrong way, I can tell."

"What way should I take it?" Now he really wanted that second beer.

Joyce chose her words carefully. "I know you wouldn't do it on purpose. Of course you wouldn't. You're a good person, too good sometimes." She took Jeremy's hand. "It's just that no matter how sweet and kind and considerate Annabelle may seem, when you lose a spouse it leaves you far more vulnerable—let's call it what it is: crazy—than even you yourself could ever imagine. It's unpredictable and raw and bone deep. It's been six years, and I'm still astonished at how your father's death can hit me sometimes. Do you see what I'm saying?"

Jeremy did—and he didn't. He and Annabelle had discussed Gil's absence, so Jeremy felt the issue had been sufficiently road tested (maybe literally). He completely grasped the loss and trauma involved, but also believed Annabelle wouldn't be in a new relationship if she was that emotionally or romantically incapacitated.

"I do, Mom, I know what you're saying," Jeremy semi-truthed, "but I think Annabelle and I are good on that front."

Joyce gazed at Jeremy in that grave, fixed way that reminded him of when he was small, and she'd impart some key life lesson ("Never let anyone tell you what you're thinking!" sprang to mind). Watching his mother now, Jeremy noticed that she looked tired, slightly distracted; her gray-green eyes were a bit rheumy, her normal joie de vivre low on the *joie*.

"Good, I hope so," Joyce finally said in response. "You both deserve to be happy. And, guess what? Cassie does, too. I'm just sorry it couldn't have been with you."

"We had a good run, Mom. Just wasn't meant to be, I guess."

"That's awfully equitable of you, sweetheart. Still, there's something special about living out your life with one person, someone who knew you when you were young and knows you when you're old and rickety."

"You're hardly rickety, Ma."

"I wasn't talking about me, sweetheart." She smiled wistfully.

CHAPTER
28

JEREMY'S DEAL CLOSED that Friday as Juliana promised. He happily signed his contract electronically and emailed copies to his agent and the business affairs department at Monolith. The last time he'd signed a screenwriting deal it was in person, in pen, on paper, and in triplicate (oh, and notarized).

Twenty minutes later, Ian's assistant, Xani (somehow short for Alexandra), called Jeremy to set a notes meeting with her boss for Monday morning at eleven. "You'll be working through lunch so we'll order in. Anything you don't eat?"

"Crow," Jeremy answered to a forest full of crickets. He guaranteed Xani was straining to figure out if that was in the poultry family without having to ask. He saved her any further brain power and quickly added, "Anything is fine, thanks." He was more concerned about the fact that Ian had so many notes they'd have to eat their way through them.

"Look, the notes are just a way for execs to justify their existence—and, to be fair, sometimes they do have good ideas—while *you* work off the rewrite and polish fees you fought so hard to get," said Zoë that afternoon, as she accompanied Jeremy on his daily backyard walk. He'd increased them from thirty to forty-five minutes a whack, and had even convinced several friends to join him on his quirky routine when they'd stop by to visit.

"Juliana did the fighting, I did the nail biting," joked Jeremy.

"As it should be," said Zoë, who had just been hired to adapt a best-selling novel for a Showtime miniseries. Her career had had its share of ups and downs but was on a major upswing. She credited Juliana, thought she was a whiz; Jeremy would find out.

"That thing looks like it's seen better days," she noted as they passed the old grapefruit tree.

Jeremy stopped to pay the tree homage. "Yeah, it's been in bad shape lately," he said, taking in its crumbly leaves and sad-looking fruit. "I keep thinking it'll get better all by itself, but I clearly have no predictive skills."

"You're just being an optimist, nothing wrong with that." Zoë studied the blighted tree. "Tell you one thing, you can't be a writer without it—hope, that is. Especially when you get to our age and the deck's increasingly stacked against you."

"'Our age?' Wow," said Jeremy with mock indignance. "I'd like to think my best work is ahead of me. I mean, it better be, or I'm barking up the wrong tree, all puns intended."

He started walking again and Zoë followed. "Just keep your eyes on the prize," she advised. "You'll be fine."

"You mean, get my movie made?"

"Well, sure. But it's all about parlaying this sale into bigger, better-paid work. The window's open, pal, but it shuts crazy fast. Today you're on the hot-shit list, tomorrow you're answering ads on Ink-Tip," she said, referring to a popular website where lesser-known producers search for unsold scripts.

"Juliana wants me to start writing a new screenplay," said Jeremy, with a glance back at the grapefruit tree. He wondered if he should finally bring in a tree doctor, or whatever they were called. Maybe it could still be saved.

"Oh, fuck that. Sure, go spend six months writing another script with no guarantee of a sale. No skin off her back, right? She just says that to cover her ass if she doesn't get you another job, which is her job this very second. She knows that, and now you know that. Besides, it's not like you don't have plenty of work ahead of you on *Offensive Measures*. So while you're sweating that, she can be lining up your next gig. Capeesh?"

"I thought you liked Juliana."

"I fucking love Juliana. But sometimes she's a heinous cross-breed of Teflon and bullshit. So, sure, come up with some new script ideas to pitch in case you need them, but never let Juliana forget that she works for you. Right now, you've got the boat and the oars." She stepped off her proverbial soapbox and shrugged. "That's my take, anyway."

As Jeremy absorbed all that, Zoë scanned the yard. "So you definitely have to sell, huh?"

"Looks like it. Financially, it's just too complicated. It'll be cleaner this way. Or so I'm told."

Cassie had presented him with two realtors to choose from this week. Jeremy flipped a coin and picked Marjan Khan, whose face he recognized from countless bus bench ads and neighborhood lawn signs, one of which now swung from its perch in Jeremy's front garden. (Katie and Crash were "super sad" when they saw the for-sale placard, even though Jeremy had warned them it was coming. It hit Jeremy hard as well.)

Zoë gave him an empathetic look as they passed the grapefruit tree again. "Maybe you could move in with Annabelle," she half joked. "Or get a new place together. Wouldn't that be fun?"

That took Jeremy by surprise. He'd just assumed he'd rent something small and affordable until he figured out a longer-term plan. Live with Annabelle? That seemed premature and presumptuous. Didn't it?

INSTEAD OF MEETING in Ian's office, the executive led Jeremy down the hall to a corner conference room with a multi-window view of the city and the mountains beyond. An immense, rectangular wooden table for twenty, around which sat ergonomic swivel chairs, filled most of the echoey room. At one end of the table was a stack of blank notepads, ballpoint pens, Sharpies, and good old-fashioned pencils that, to Jeremy, looked more for show—"See, the great ideas just flow around here!"—than actual use.

"Sit anywhere you'd like," said Ian, who plopped himself down in a chair at the center of the table and took all the guesswork out for Jeremy, who settled in across from Ian. The ever dutiful Xani, who Jeremy decided might actually be older than her young boss (those were not the worry lines of a twenty-something), followed them in carrying a MacBook Air, more pads and pens, two phones (hers and Ian's?), a sheaf of Xeroxed notes pages and a printed copy of *Offensive Measures*. She handed a set of the notes pages and the script to Ian, who, Jeremy would later realize, didn't look at them once during the meeting. Like the pads and pens, they were props.

"There he is!" announced Ian, sounding eerily like Dr. Hockstein greeting Jeremy post-surgery. Jeremy watched as the exec sprang out of his chair and opened his arms to the skinny, thirtyish guy in a white T-shirt, holey jeans, and tattoo sleeves who had just entered. "Jeremy, do you know Laz Huddlestone?"

The name sounded familiar. Too familiar. Jeremy realized who he was: a director whose first film, a convoluted action-thriller called *Time Bomb*, he'd reviewed last year for the *Times*. Jeremy recalled the closing line of his critique: "Save your time, avoid this bomb." What was this hack doing here? Unless ...

"Laz loves your script and wants to direct it," explained Ian. "Which is awesome because we love Laz and want him to direct it." He shot the filmmaker an unctuous grin that seemed a bit much, even for a glad-handing film exec.

"Oh, okay, that's great," said a startled Jeremy. He stood to shake Laz's non-extended hand and added, "Thanks, man, really glad you liked the script." Couldn't Ian have warned Jeremy they'd picked a director and that he'd be in the meeting?

Laz eyeballed the writer as he returned the handshake. "Are you the same Jeremy Lerner who writes for the *L.A. Times*?" he asked, his accent somewhere between English and South African. Or was it Australian?

Okay, this was a case of good news/awful news. The good news was that Monolith was already attaching a director to his script, so it was likely on the fast track to getting made. Booyah! The awful news: Laz Huddlestone knew who he was and, if the vague snarl in his voice was any indication, was aware that Jeremy hated his debut feature—a movie that presumably (if inexplicably) gave him the cred to direct this one. Meantime, what the hell happened to Antoine Fuqua?

"Yep, that's me," Jeremy answered as breezily as he could, steeling himself for the blowback.

"Wait, you write for the *Times*?" asked Ian. "Wow, that's amazing. How come I didn't know that?"

Because you've probably never read a newspaper in your life, thought Jeremy, maybe unfairly given how few people read newspapers anymore (except apparently Laz Huddlestone). He glanced at Xani, who was earnestly documenting all this on her laptop.

"I did, until recently," Jeremy admitted, frozen in place.

"Yeah, gave *Time Bomb* a bloody shite review this one," said Laz, his accent shifting into full-on Brit. His eyes were boring holes in Jeremy.

Ian looked like a deer caught in headlights. "Wait, what? Seriously?" This was a diplomatic snafu that, frankly, only Laz could dig them out of by simply taking the high road and blowing it off. Turn it into something they could all laugh about during awards season.

"Serious as a fookin' heart attack," Laz answered. So much for the high road.

Ian, struggling to read the room, forced out a careful chuckle. "Really, what are the chances?" he asked. He looked at Jeremy for a lifeline.

In the end, Jeremy refused to get sucked into this silliness. He wasn't the only critic who roasted *Time Bomb*; he'd just been doing his job. And had Laz done his better, maybe reviewers would have liked the film more. Who's to say? Regardless, the guy was being asked to direct a big movie for Monolith—and it was because of Jeremy's script—so what's the complaint? Still, Jeremy needed to say something to ease the tangible tension.

"Sorry about that, Laz," Jeremy offered with an innocent shrug. "It was just an opinion, that's all. Nothing personal." Which, of course, was bullshit, because how could someone not take a slam like that personally? It was your work being judged. But what else could Jeremy say?

The men stood there a few painful seconds (Xani stayed seated, her pen still) until Laz broke into a dark grin. "Ah, what the fook. Bygones be bygones, and all that shite. We have a sodding movie to make, right? And it's going to be fookin' brilliant!" He gave Jeremy a devilish wink that said: "I may be cool now, but I'm watching you."

Jeremy relaxed and took his seat again, as did an enormously relieved Ian. Laz came around and dropped into the chair next to Jeremy. "Gonna sit next to my new best mate if that's okay," the director said. He stopped short of throwing his arm around Jeremy, who rolled his chair back to make room for Laz while trying to decide whether "détente" or "truce" was where he and the scraggly-hip director had landed. Whatever. As Laz said, they had a "sodding" movie to make, the idea of which made Jeremy want to pinch himself awake.

"Alright," said Ian brightly, "let's dive into this baby!"

CHAPTER
29

FIVE HOURS, FOUR phone breaks (Ian: 3, Laz: 1), numerous bathroom duck-outs, and an assortment of grilled panini sandwiches later, Jeremy had his marching orders on the script rewrite. Ian and Laz went page by page, tossing out a dizzying—and only occasionally infuriating—combination of suggestions and directives, though Jeremy knew even the suggestions were directives. He took a load of notes, pushed back on a few requested changes (though carefully picked his battles), and stayed as calm and open-minded as any outnumbered screenwriter could under the circumstances.

Laz, despite his brash observations and sporadic torrent of curse words (he said fuck—or in his case, fook or some variation—seemingly more times than in all of *Goodfellas*), was strangely deferential to Ian and Jeremy. It made Jeremy question if Laz really had the gig or if this meeting wasn't some kind of audition. (Turned out it wasn't. His deal closed the day before Jeremy's; Ian was quite the little secret keeper.)

Jeremy relaxed more as the meeting progressed, largely because Ian, at least for now, treated him as indisposably as he did Laz. By the end, Laz was even joking around with Jeremy, quizzing him on which movies he reviewed worse than *Time Bomb*. Fortunately, there were many. No matter, Jeremy knew that in features, it was the writer, not the director, who was the disposable one—unless the writer *was* the director then: checkmate.

There was only one truly giant curveball thrown at Jeremy and it was from Ian. "I'm just spitballing here," he began, "but *what if ...* what if ... we made Senator Garfield a woman instead of a man?" Jeremy hated the idea but said nothing at first. That's because Laz beat him to it.

"That is fookin' brilliant. I bloody love that. A fookin' ton!" enthused Laz so quickly that Jeremy wondered if it wasn't the director's idea all along. "I know Emily Blunt," said Laz. "I can text her right now!"

"Love Emily Blunt!" agreed Ian. "Jeremy, what do you think?"

"Who doesn't love Emily Blunt?" he answered. But he loved Jake Gyllenhaal or Ryan Gosling more for the part of a pipe-smoking, male senator suddenly stricken by paranoia and erectile dysfunction.

"Why the hell would they want to do that?" asked Annabelle with layman's outrage—and logic—when Jeremy got her up to speed over dinner that night on the marathon Monolith meeting. "I mean, doesn't that change everything?"

"Well, yes and no. Lots of parts written for men have been switched to women. It can bring a twist to things we've already seen a million times," Jeremy said, further reconciling the concept in his head.

They were sitting in Annabelle's dining room over a delicious home-cooked meal of grilled mahi-mahi, rice pilaf, and sautéed Brussels sprouts, accompanied by, as Hannibal Lecter would have called it in his inimitable way, "a nice chianti" (hold the fava beans). Jeremy found himself studying Annabelle's cottage more closely that night than he had during his previous visits. It was a small, Craftsman-style place on a cramped side street on the border of Hollywood and Los Feliz, a town or so over from Jeremy and Cassie's first apartment.

Annabelle and Gil bought the two-bedroom house just before they got married. According to Annabelle, it was a steal because it was "a total dump" that she, Gil, and his contractor brother, Ramón, ended up restoring to its earlier glory—or to at least a far more livable condition. The result was a charming, eclectic little spot that was worth more now than Jeremy's larger cottage given its hip and desirable (if congested) location.

Jeremy had been thinking a lot about what Zoë had said about living with Annabelle and, while it appealed to him on so many levels, it felt like too big a leap—and commitment—to even consider floating at this point. And yet, over that fish dinner, he couldn't help but imagine what it would be like to put his shoes under Annabelle's bed, so to speak. She had apparently lived in the compact house quite comfortably with Gil, so why not Jeremy? They could split expenses and duties and otherwise join forces. Make a life together. The downside was there was no immediate place for Jeremy's office or, as far as he could see, even a quiet corner to set up shop. There was the second bedroom, but that was spoken for as an exercise/craft room combo with a sofa bed for visitors.

Besides, what made Jeremy think Annabelle would jump at the chance to live with him? She seemed to want their relationship to move forward, but was this what she had in mind? And would Jeremy even be thinking about it if he didn't have to move this fall? It made him feel like some kind of opportunist. Still, how would he react if the roles were reversed, and Annabelle asked to move in with him?

He decided to table it all for the time being and focus on the amazing hot apple crumble Annabelle had whipped up for dessert.

"What if you said you didn't want to make your main character a woman? What would happen?" asked Annabelle.

"I could fight it," he answered, swallowing a spoonful of the apple-cinnamon treat, "but I'd lose and have to make the change anyway. And then I'd be branded 'difficult' or 'uncooperative,' which would give them ammunition to fire or replace me—which they'll probably do anyway at some point. This crumble is fantastic, by the way."

"Thanks, it's really easy to make." She smiled, enjoying a big bite of the dessert. "Your business is a little crazy, isn't it? Mine is so simple: someone has a problem, you help them fix it. They feel better, and you go on your way."

"Unless you start dating them." Jeremy flashed a grin.

"Oh, that would never happen." She returned the smile.

"Anyway, as Zoë told me, once these people get something in their heads, they rarely shake it loose. You're just better off riding the horse in the direction it's going."

"Off a cliff?"

"Honestly? I'm thinking that changing Garfield to a woman isn't a bad idea. I'm kind of sorry I didn't write it that way from the start."

"Then they'd want to make her a man."

Jeremy laughed. "You're catching on." He scraped the remains of his crumble out of the dish and savored it. "I'm surprised you don't think a female lead would be a good thing. You being a woman and all."

"I'm *your* woman first. I want what's best for you. But if you're good, I'm good. I mean, I'm not the one who has to go in and tear the whole thing apart." She began to collect the dinner plates.

Jeremy rose to help. "Bottom line, I'm lucky to have this job. Almost as lucky as I am to have you."

Annabelle couldn't help but smile. "Listen to you."

Jeremy leaned in to kiss her. Annabelle set the plates she held in each hand back on the table, put her arms around her guy, and returned his kiss. "You taste like cinnamon."

JEREMY AND CASSIE'S realtor, Marjan, had already traipsed several prospective buyers through the house, each time requiring Jeremy to disappear for the hour-long intrusion. He promised to silently hole up in his office and not get in anyone's way, but Marjan put the kibosh on that tout de suite: "Trust me," she told him in a practiced tone, "you'll hate being here, and my clients will hate having you here. Any questions?" Sure, but did it matter?

Jeremy either went for a long walk up and down the neighborhood hills (way better aerobic exercise than his backyard jaunts; Matty heartily approved, even joined him a few times) or ducked in next door to hang with Katie and/or Crash. It was proving a good way to spend quality time with his favorite neighbors; they all knew, without verbalizing it, that they'd likely lose touch once they were no longer living next door to each other. It was just how these things went.

He would always return to his house feeling a bit violated (Did a stranger use my toilet? Rifle through my nightstand?) and wondering what kind of cruel comments his anonymous visitors made about his home of twenty-two years ("Ugh, that wall color is awful!" "Who would ever choose such ugly tile?"). Jeremy soon understood why Marjan discouraged his presence during those tours. Mostly, though, he hoped a buyer would surface sooner than later and not drag out the pain of the process. Until then, Jeremy found himself taking stock of his abode and trying not to get too overwhelmed by the raft of memories that lived within its walls.

And suddenly, there was an offer, one just shy of the asking price. A couple in their forties—he was in finance, she was in insurance— who recently relocated to L.A. from Denver with their six-year-old daughter and hypo-allergenic Wheaton-doodle, were looking for something comfy and bucolic with a good public school nearby and Chez Lerner handily fit the bill, quirks and all. Cassie wanted to accept the offer and Marjan, of course, agreed ("Hold out for full price and you could be waiting forever!"), so Jeremy ultimately made three. It was a dark day for him but, fortunately, the *Offensive Measures* rewrite helped keep his mind off the hovering clouds.

Matty, guessing that Jeremy might need the company of someone else who loved their house, took his dad out for dinner the next night to "celebrate" the end of an era—and the start of a new one, whatever that would turn out to be.

Over margaritas at Mercado, a hip, absurdly noisy, but festive Mexican restaurant located near the hectic West Hollywood intersection of Third and Fairfax—and around the corner from the Writers Guild, to which Jeremy's membership was thankfully revived by working for Monolith—father and son toasted to Jeremy's future.

"To your new chapter!" Matty cheered, clinking Jeremy's salt-rimmed glass. "It's gonna be great, Dad."

Jeremy took a swallow of the tangy cocktail and tried to buy into the kid's optimism. "I hope so," Jeremy said. "Though I'll feel better once I figure out where I'm going to live."

"I think there's a unit available in Mom's building," Matty tossed out with a mischievous grin.

Jeremy couldn't help but laugh. "Oh, she'd love that," he said, dipping a tortilla chip in guacamole. "It'd be worth it just to see the look on her face."

Matty sipped his drink. "I probably shouldn't say this, but I don't think Mom's doing so well."

"No? Why not?"

"She's been kind of low-key lately. Maybe just low energy, I don't know. She says she's fine but … who knows, maybe it's just in my head." Matty took a chip, considered the guacamole, and passed.

Jeremy was surprised, yet also felt a bit validated. Maybe she was feeling some of the same seller's remorse that he was. Or maybe it was something else. "Do you know if she's seeing anyone?" Jeremy gently asked, his ears finally acclimating to the noise level.

"I don't think anyone in particular, just, y'know, dates."

Sex dates thought Jeremy, as if he was being celibate. The margarita was going to his head. He watched as Matty, looking to get off the subject, returned to the chips bowl.

"Anyway, Dad," Matty said between crunches, "you can always crash at my place until you get settled. I stay at Gabe's half the time anyway, so."

"Thanks, honey, that's really sweet of you." Jeremy could feel himself tearing up, but didn't want to be a buzzkill. He lost himself in his margarita glass till he pulled it together. "So, sounds like things are still going great with you and Gabe?"

Matty, who'd been checking out the bustling room, turned back to Jeremy. "Yeah, great. Gabe's the best."

"But?" guessed Jeremy, hoping there was no but.

Matty took a serious slug of his cocktail and fixed his gaze on Jeremy. "But how do you ever really know?"

"Know what?"

"If someone is really right for you—and you for them? I mean, you and Mom thought you belonged together. Turns out that had an expiration date."

Of course, thought Jeremy, why wouldn't he and Cassie's split make their son think twice about his own relationships? He told Matty what he told himself: "There's no way to know anything. You just make the best decision you can at the time. Trust your gut and your history—and hope to succeed. It's really all you can do."

Matty absorbed that as he scarfed up the last tortilla chip. "Do you think someone can be too good? Too perfect?"

"Are we talking about Gabe?"

"Well, we're sure not talking about me," said Matty with more self-awareness than he often let on. "It's weird. He's only a few years older than me but, I don't know, he seems so much more ... together. He's really wise, y'know? It's like there's nothing he can't do."

"A Renaissance man."

Matty considered that, then opened his menu. "Let's order, okay? The margarita made me dizzy."

Join the club, thought Jeremy.

Matty looked at the offerings a moment and then put the menu down. "It's just that sometimes I feel like I have to work twice as hard to measure up. Like I don't want to disappoint him."

"Of course you don't. That's what people do in a relationship. You try to be better for the other person—you want them to make you better. And, hopefully, vice versa."

"Sometimes it's just hard to relax," admitted Matty, eyes darting around the restaurant. "God, just working out together can turn into, like, this battle of the gladiators or something. It's ridiculous."

"So don't try so hard. Be yourself. I've seen Gabe around you and believe me, he likes what he sees."

Matty stayed quiet and glanced at his menu again.

"And look, whether it's Gabe or whomever, eventually you'll

settle down with someone. And that'll mean enjoying their good qualities and learning to accept their less good qualities. And we all have them. Love is a package deal, kiddo."

Matty shut the menu and looked at his father. "Did you ever give Mom this pep talk?"

That struck Jeremy. He relaxed. "I didn't know I had to. Until it was too late." He broke into a smile. "So consider yourself lucky."

CHAPTER
30

JEREMY STOOD WITH Annabelle in the exact spot of his cherished grapefruit tree, which existed now in just a few old photographs. He'd decided that if anyone was going to have the tree cut down, it would be him and not the new owners who would have no emotional connection to the once majestic canopy of citrus and shade. In the end, all that was left was a massive load of firewood, which they could bring in and burn that winter. Jeremy fleetingly considered taking the stack with him as a fitting remembrance but realized there was little chance a wood-burning fireplace would be in his future.

It wasn't as if he didn't have enough on his plate, with his script rewrite mostly taking precedence over packing. Plus he hadn't even started to seriously look for a new place to live; he might have to crash at Matty's for a while after all.

But the dying tree had been gnawing at Jeremy—a neighborhood gardener pronounced it a goner due to some bizarrely named citrus disease—and he wanted to give it a proper send-off. It took an entire Saturday morning, but the gardener and his tree-trimmer cousin dismantled the thing limb by limb. They promised Jeremy what was left of the stump would decompose over time; he knew he wouldn't be there to see it.

Jeremy told Annabelle about the tree's place in Chez Lerner history: his and Cassie's once-upon-a-time respites in the Adirondack chairs beneath its branches; how one spring the tree bore such a bumper crop that they passed out dozens of bags of fruit to the homeless; the many strange grapefruit-centric recipes Cassie tried until the novelty wore off, after which they just used the tart orbs for breakfast juice (and how more than half a glass, to this day, gave Jeremy heartburn). It was small stuff that you might have had to be there to appreciate but, for Jeremy, symbolized happier, more hopeful times in Laurel Canyon.

"I didn't peg you for the sentimental type," Annabelle said later on as she helped Jeremy pack up a bunch of old clothes he planned to donate to Out of the Closet, a West Hollywood thrift store that benefited HIV/AIDS patients.

"Y'mean about the grapefruit tree or these ancient clothes I can't believe I ever wore?" Jeremy asked as he folded a pile of pleated pants and baggy button-up shirts that had 1990s written all over them.

"Oh, definitely the tree," she answered. "Your stories were really sweet." She looked wistful. "Reminds me of how I feel when I look at every other thing around my house. Always that damn flood of memories. Make that a flood of memories that could use a dam!"

Annabelle gave a rueful chuckle, though seemed contrite about bringing it up. The total honesty they swore in Cambria seemed less clear-cut now. She brightened again. "Look, honey lamb, however you slice it, it's going to be a transition. But you'll survive. I guarantee it."

He tied the drawstring on a bag of clothes. "Why, because I'm not the sentimental type?"

What, was he just another typical, middle-aged straight guy who buried his feelings and tossed out emotional bones strictly as needed? He liked to think, if he didn't exactly wear his heart on his sleeve, he was a pretty empathic, sensitive person. Right now, maybe too sensitive, which Annabelle, of course, picked up on.

"I like that you're not overly sentimental. You're watchful, clear-eyed about things," she said, packing a mound of loud, oversized sweaters into a carton.

Why did that ring a bell? Oh, right, thought Jeremy, recalling his first date with Cassie. The one where she dubbed him "reserved, but not in a geeky way," not "needy" or annoyingly transparent. Sure, it sounded good at the time—in a backhanded kind of way—but how did that ultimately work out for him? For them? Was he destined to repeat the same mistakes twice? Did he even fully know what they were?

Forget watchful, clear-eyed, reserved, sentimental, or whatever the hell he was or wasn't, a sudden tidal wave came over Jeremy and, without a safety net or an escape hatch, he blurted out, "Annabelle, what if we moved in together?"

She looked up from the box she was sealing. Jeremy wasn't sure he'd ever seen an expression on her face quite like the one she had that very second. It was a memorable crisscross of shock, wonder, and panic, as if she were being tested and didn't know the right answer. For Jeremy's part, his heart and head pounded out a neurotic duet; he wasn't sure what he'd done, but there was no turning back. And right then, it didn't seem like there was any going forward: Annabelle was speechless.

"You don't have to answer me now—or anytime soon, for that matter. Just putting it out there."

He disappeared back into his closet to bag up more old clothes, but they'd already packed them all. Now what? Jeremy pretended to be looking for something on an upper shelf; Annabelle's silence was deafening. Then again, he'd surprised even himself with his impromptu invitation. The few seconds that his head was buried in the closet passed like hours.

"Are you okay?" Jeremy had to ask.

"Yeah, I'm sorry, you just caught me a little off guard." She sat on his bed and smoothed out her wrinkled shorts.

"Anyway, as I said, it was just a thought. No worries," Jeremy plowed ahead, sounding more like a stranger than a lover. He picked up one of the knotted bags. "Help me bring this stuff out to the car?"

Annabelle grabbed the last carton she'd taped shut and followed him outside. As they loaded Jeremy's Prius, she broke the silence.

"Were you talking about moving in with me?" she asked, as if searching for a missing puzzle piece.

"Well, it's a little late for you to move in here," he said, indicating the Sold sign on Marjan's realty placard.

"Right," Annabelle said pensively. She started back inside. "I'll go get another carton."

"Annabelle, wait."

She stopped and Jeremy went to her.

"What's wrong? If you don't want to live with me, it's really okay. You wouldn't be the first," he said, hoping it would break the weirdness. It didn't.

"If I wanted you to move in, don't you think I would have asked you already? Don't you know me well enough by now? I mean, really, it's not like it hasn't been the elephant in the room lately."

It has? Sure, it had been on Jeremy's mind a lot recently. Hadn't he wondered if it was too soon to live with Annabelle, and if she'd even want to? And as much as he liked the idea of shared domesticity, wasn't he conflicted about it himself? Still, it startled him to realize the topic had been looming over their relationship in such an elephantine way. Had he been so wrapped up in his own frantic life that he'd missed the boat by a mile yet again? Twice in a matter of minutes, he was struck by the parallels to his emotional failure with Cassie.

"If I was a thoughtless idiot, I'm sorry," Jeremy said, thinking about Joyce's plea that he not hurt Annabelle. If he had, he certainly hadn't meant to. Just the opposite.

Annabelle walked back into the house. Jeremy trailed her. "Do you at least want to talk about this?" he asked as they entered the living room.

She faced Jeremy, a slight trembling around her mouth, her dark eyes moist. "You're not a thoughtless idiot. By a long shot."

"Then what is it?" He took Annabelle by her arms and tried to pull her into him, but she resisted. Jeremy let her go. She backed away and stood in front of a window as the late afternoon sun poured in, enveloping her in a light so bright she practically disappeared.

"It's not you, Jeremy, it's me." And just as quickly as that light had appeared it vanished, leaving a tearful Annabelle in its wake.

Jeremy wanted to go to her, hold her, tell her everything would be okay, that they could go back to exactly how it had been between them. Nothing would have to change, and they could live happily ever after, just not under the same roof, if that's what she wanted.

But the earth had just shifted on its axis and, it seemed, Jeremy had given it a push.

CHAPTER
31

DURING THE WEEKS that Jeremy rewrote *Offensive Measures*—which, sigh, had already been retitled by Monolith's crack marketing team as simply *Offense* (focus group testing revealed that the word "offense," all by itself, felt more "dangerous" and "exciting")—he received regular email missives of encouragement from Ian, such as "Hope you're knocking it out of the park, dude!" There was also the sporadic "What if?" brainstorm from Laz, proposing new or tweaked set pieces, locations, visuals, reveals, and twists ("Only if it doesn't fuck you up, mate." Translated: "Do it.").

Jeremy took the added notes as they came, sometimes working them in, other times letting them go, because there was just so much you could cram into any script without sinking the ship. As for his main character's gender switch, once Jeremy started to roll with the changes he found there weren't as many radical shifts to make as he first expected. It turned out that he'd created a strong, sufficiently dimensional protagonist to withstand the required tinkering. Cal Garfield became Val Garfield, erectile dysfunction was replaced with a good old-fashioned case of depression, the lobbyist wife was now a husband (Jeremy considered keeping her a wife and making Garfield gay but it would have meant all new focus-group testing—seriously), Val still smoked a pipe (why not?) and, not for nothing, relied on a more tuned-in emotional core than Cal did to best her enemies and stay alive. That Jeremy endowed Val with some of

Joyce, Cassie, and Annabelle's best attributes was no accident.

Speaking of Annabelle, she made herself scarce after the "let's move in together" fiasco, telling him she needed some time alone to get her act together and reiterating that he'd done nothing wrong. Jeremy was hard-pressed to believe that. He'd opened a trapdoor into an unreconciled part of Annabelle's psyche, the part where her late husband still lived and breathed and guided her from afar, let no man rend asunder—and it seemed Jeremy was that man. How could he have miscalculated so badly?

"I'm not sure you heard what I told you that day on the lanai," Joyce said when he called to tell her about Annabelle. He had woken her up from a midday nap, which was unusual for her; she rarely napped, said it screwed up her evening sleep.

"I heard exactly what you told me, Ma: not to hurt her," Jeremy answered defensively. "And that was my plan."

"You know what they say, darling: 'People plan and God laughs.'"

Jeremy wasn't sure what "they" said but he knew what Joyce said; it was her favorite expression. "Anyway, Annabelle still hasn't gotten past Gil's death, and the thought of another man living with her in the house that she and her husband basically rebuilt together was just a bridge too far."

"Is that what she said?"

"No, but I pieced it together." It didn't take Sherlock Holmes. "Also that maybe Annabelle doesn't want to sell *her* house and move into some all-new place with me. Not that I'd even offered that option."

"You may just be a victim of bad timing," Joyce considered. "Had you met her a year from now it might've all been different. Mourning is like a cloud that one day just lifts."

"Yours didn't. You said so yourself. What if five years from now, Annabelle's still in the same place?" He didn't mean to drag Joyce into the equation, but she obviously wanted to help—and it was a fair comparison. One that made him feel sad: for his mother, who chose to stay alone, and for Annabelle, who couldn't control her fear and grief—nor could Jeremy control it for her (so, yeah, maybe he was feeling sad for himself as well).

Joyce sighed through the phone. It wasn't a sound Jeremy often associated with his can-do, cheerleading mom. "Honey, I wish I had a crystal ball but I don't. All I know is if it's truly *bashert*, it'll work itself out. If not, well … just hang in there, okay, sweetie?"

Joyce didn't use a lot of Yiddish, just a few words left over from her parents' daily chatter. But bashert, or "meant to be," came up on special occasions for that extra dose of cosmic emphasis. Jeremy felt it best to leave it there.

IT WASN'T AS if Jeremy hadn't communicated at all with Annabelle since things went south, even if her few brief texts and emails were only in response to ones Jeremy had sent her. There apparently wasn't a whole lot to say at the moment. She repeatedly assured Jeremy that this was on her, not him, and Jeremy repeatedly felt like a heel.

Jeremy wanted to sit down and talk with her in person about it all, but she declined. Her bubbliness had burst. As much as he missed Annabelle and wanted them to figure out a plan B, he decided to back away until further notice—from her.

On the plus side, if there was any, Jeremy had more time to finish his script rewrite and to clear more old shit out of the closets, cabinets, and corners of his house (had they ever thrown anything out?). It also left him extra time to hunt for a new place to live (he was still moving slug-slow on that front and had to step it up) and, oh, yes, deal with his divorce. He'd been in almost daily touch with his lawyer to untwist the snags that kept cropping up in the negotiations with Cassie and her attorney, a surprisingly young guy named Clarke Campbell who, at least according to the Google images Jeremy found of him, looked like a taller, slicker version of Eddie Munster.

Most of the items, of course, involved money, the division of which wasn't quite as clear-cut as it might have been before the

Offensive Measures—er, *Offense*—sale. (Yes, Arvin Box had warned Jeremy about this but the devil was in the details.) And that temporary alimony thing Arvin first mentioned? Turned out to be a no-go for several reasons, not the least of which was that, unbeknownst to Jeremy, Cassie had just been laid off from the disability rights group where she had served as legal counsel the last seven years—the organization was having its own financial struggles—and was currently unemployed. (Jeremy was amazed Matty could keep that one a secret—unless he didn't know either.)

On top of it all, Jeremy's supposedly healed shoulder was giving him trouble, probably because he never finished his physical therapy and had started lifting heavy things again way too soon. What was he supposed to do, move the boxes he was packing around with his feet? The result was a throbbing ache up and down his right arm that rivaled the pain he felt before, and in the weeks after, his surgery. Lorena in Dr. Hockstein's office told Jeremy to take Advil or Aleve every day and lay off any serious lifting for two weeks. And that he was a bad boy.

By the end of that very long week, Jeremy put the finishing touches on his rewrite of *Offense*. (Couldn't they at least put a "The" in front of it? Jeremy wasn't a big fan of one-word titles, not that anybody asked.) He ultimately executed about 80 percent of Ian and Laz's notes, gaining more confidence as he hurtled forward.

"Just have some good bullshit ready when they ask: 'What happened to that hand-job-in-the-alley scene?'" Zoë advised him. Not that there was one but, you know, figuratively speaking.

Meanwhile, Juliana, who Jeremy checked in with that Friday afternoon right before he emailed the revised script to Ian and Laz, praised him for his fast work but told him to take more time if needed. "You don't get points for finishing early," she said. "They'll just think you rushed or forgot something."

It wasn't early. There was no specified deadline. "Maybe they'll just think I know what I'm doing," Jeremy maintained from his perch on planet Logic.

"They already think you know what you're doing. They bought

your script, didn't they?"

Jeremy shook his head, which was threatening to explode. "So should I not turn it in?"

"Are you kidding? They're desperate for your draft!"

Sometimes talking to Juliana was the verbal equivalent of a hall of mirrors.

"Okay, then," was all Jeremy could say as he stared out his kitchen window at the stump of his grapefruit tree. "What now?"

"You'll get more notes, you'll do your polish, and the rest will be up to the movie gods." Juliana was back to her usual keyboard clacking. "Meanwhile, I'm setting up meet-and-greets with a bunch of development execs I love who want to get to know you."

"They do?"

"They will. Once I get off the phone with you and on with them. How many new pitches do you have?" Clackety-clack.

"Three or four," Jeremy lied. He didn't want someone else telling him he was a bad boy.

Jeremy went to his office, attached *Offense* to an upbeat email to Ian and Laz, and pressed Send. He felt buoyant, accomplished, and a little like he'd jumped off a cliff.

Then he got the text from Cassie.

CHAPTER
32

"**WE SHOULD TALK.** Meet me Sunday?"

Just six simple words, but they felt awfully loaded to Jeremy, especially given how uncommunicative Cassie had been since the night of his fatal birthday bash. Then there was the teensy fact that they were enmeshed in pivotal legal wranglings, so maybe not the ideal time for a little coffee catch-up?

Jeremy's first impulse was to text back "What time and where?" because, well, morbid curiosity. And, look, he didn't exactly love having fuck-all to do with someone he'd known forever and who would always be part of his life, if only because of Matty. To nutshell it (yes, he used that phrase now), Jeremy wanted them to cut the crap and act like a pair of adults with a long and mostly decent history.

Yet, if he was stepping into some kind of trap by agreeing to see her, figured the guy who just spent six years writing a crime thriller about paranoia, he would only have himself to blame.

Jeremy waffled a few more minutes before texting back a terse "OK" before he could change his mind. At least he gave it slightly more thought than when he asked Annabelle to live with him—or rather, him with her. Also known as: the day of the lead balloon.

Cassie instantly responded: "Joan's on Third at 2?" It was one of those popular bakery-marketplace hybrids near the Beverly Center that was too busy and visible a spot to make a scene, so that was promising.

Jeremy: "See you then."

She texted back a thumbs-up, which Jeremy considered overkill and only further made him question her motives. It wasn't too late to back out.

It was something he thought about all that night and again the next day as he went residence shopping, which turned out to be as dispiriting an experience as he expected. That is, until about a quarter way in when Matty, who volunteered to accompany his un-nerved father, laid it out for him.

"Dad, I know this is a downer for you and all, but at least you can afford someplace decent and safe to live, which is a shit ton more than a lot of people in this city can say. It's not like, 'Hello—can I interest you in a nice tent?'"

Matty was right, of course. Jeremy didn't mean to be an asshat about the whole moving thing. He really thought he'd adjusted to the concept until he started looking. The first few apartments he'd found listed online were dreary and confining and overpriced, and they bummed him out. Maybe that was because he realized his monthly mortgage, locked in more than two decades ago, was less than the rent he'd have to pay for one of these generic, one-bedroom squares. In truth, they weren't that different from Matty's apart-ment, which Jeremy had always found to be a cute little place—for a twenty-three-year-old on his own in the city for the first time. Just like how Jeremy and Cassie's dinky Silver Lake apartment had seemed right for them back then. What would he think of it now?

On the other hand, Jeremy's glumness may have had less to do with aesthetics than with the perfect storm of anxiety he was feeling that morning over Annabelle's absence, Cassie's mysterious text, and the screenplay he'd shot off the day before. Did he ignore too many of Ian and Laz's notes? Should he have done one more pass? For once in his life had he been *too* confident?

Fortunately, Matty's frank words snapped Jeremy out of his

naval-gazing headspace, and he started to see the apartments—and the one guest house—as new adventures, a throwback to his youth and, perhaps, a simpler, more optimistic time. They looked at units on either end of Laurel Canyon: on the Valley side in Studio City, Valley Village, and Toluca Lake, and on the city side from Hollywood to West Hollywood and south to Carthay Circle. It was merely a start; L.A. went on forever. Still, Jeremy kept the search in the general vicinity of his current home and various stomping grounds. If it hasn't been made ridiculously clear, he was not exactly the king of change.

Though Jeremy's attitude had improved, his selectiveness had not, and he found reasons—some fair, some pushing it—to reject each apartment they visited. It ran the gamut from "too small" and "too dark" to "too old" and "sorta scary" (that one a result of a strange building manager who had a Freddie Krueger vibe going on; Matty didn't disagree). Some faced alleys and weedy vacant lots, others were right over the garage or smack next to the elevator.

"Egads!" Matty exclaimed in mock horror when Jeremy brought up that last infraction.

"Have you ever stayed in a hotel room that's next to the elevator? You can hear the damn thing going up and down all night!" Jeremy said defensively as they left the building just off Studio City's pleasant Moorpark Avenue.

"Okay, but don't let perfect be the enemy of good," said Matty with surprisingly brainy authority.

When they stopped for a quick lunch at a West Hollywood pizza joint called Vito's, Jeremy asked Matty how he was feeling about Gabe. Just a father making sure all was still copacetic with his capricious son.

"Dad, can I tell you something kind of personal?" Matty asked as he came up for air from a delectably sloppy slice of margarita pizza. "And please don't get judgy or anything, okay?"

"Whatever it is, it's fine. You know you can tell me anything." Jeremy's heart started hammering.

"Alright, so there's this guy, Roberto, who Gabe and I know from the gym. He's always hanging around when we work out, making small talk, acting flirty, that kinda thing. No biggie, right? Until one day Gabe tells me that Roberto asked him if we ever hooked up with other dudes. So I thought, 'Duh, no wonder this guy's so friendly to us.'" He stopped, eyeballed Jeremy. "Are you okay with this? Because if not I can stop."

"It's fine. Keep going," said Jeremy, even if he sensed this was edging into TMI territory.

"So the other night, without telling me, Gabe invites Roberto to his apartment to 'hang out with us and watch a movie.'" Matty's exaggerated finger quotes and dubious expression were classic.

"What movie?" asked the former film critic.

"A gay porn movie—starring the three of us!"

"Wait, he filmed you … having sex?" Jeremy noticed a couple a few patio tables over straining to hear Matty's lurid account.

"What? No, that was just …" Matty also spotted the guys listening in and lowered his voice. "Anyhow, we did what we did, and even though Roberto's quite the snack, I wasn't really into it. And y'know why?"

Jeremy formulated a reasonable guess but it was a rhetorical question.

"Because I didn't want to share Gabe with anyone. I know it sounds stupid but … I didn't want him to like anyone more than me."

"Then why did he invite this guy over to begin with? Or is this like … something you and Gabe do?" He didn't mean to sound judgy, but there it was.

"No—it was a total one-off. Gabe thought maybe I'd be into it. He said he did it for me: to surprise me, to make me happy." Before Jeremy could respond: "And look, don't go thinking all gay guys are sex monsters or whatever because I know plenty of straight people who—"

Jeremy put up a hand to stop him. "I don't think anything. It's cool, really. Though I assume you told me this story for an actual reason?"

Matty put up a "one minute" finger as he finished his Diet Coke. "Okay, so remember how you said I shouldn't try so hard with Gabe? Well, this three-way thing made me realize we were both trying too hard, we were maybe both afraid of disappointing each other—it wasn't just me being insecure."

"Honey, you're both finding your way. Relationships take time. They're a living, breathing thing." *And so fragile*, he thought. "But I think you're doing great, Matty," Jeremy said, because he truly did.

Matty smiled. "I guess sometimes you have to go through something really weird or unexpected to learn just how much you care about someone." He paused. "Not to get too bumper-stickery."

Jeremy admired his son's wisdom, for so many reasons. "Did you tell Gabe that?"

"Oh, he knows," Matty smiled as they rose to resume the apartment hunt.

It wasn't until their last stop of the day that Jeremy found a place he liked enough to consider renting: a spacious, well-kept unit on a quiet, tree-lined street near Beverly and La Cienega Boulevards. Or as Matty put it, someplace he "couldn't find enough wrong with to justify completely canceling its ass." The only issue: Jeremy was worried it was too close to Cassie's apartment.

"It's like eight blocks away," noted Matty. "There are people who live eight feet from me I never see. What are you worried about?"

It wasn't like Jeremy was never going to see Cassie. And who knew how long either of them would end up staying in these apartments? But he purposely hadn't been looking anywhere too far west in West Hollywood—Cassie lived on the westernmost edge—just so as not to complicate matters. He didn't want to run into her on his daily walks (okay, he'd been a bit lax about those lately, but he was busy!) or at the closest market or coffee house. She marked her territory; he'd have to mark his. If that seemed childish or neurotic or overreactive, maybe it was. But for right now, so be it. Matty sighed.

"I want to go on record as saying I think you're making a big mistake," said Matty.

"It wouldn't be the first," Jeremy answered, wondering if he was, in fact, making a big mistake.

CHAPTER
33

JEREMY AND ANNABELLE had an ambitious list of movies they were planning to watch together. But they had only gotten through a handful of titles, perhaps figuring they'd have all the time in the world together to see each one. *What does God do when people plan?*

Most of the films were old favorites they'd already seen; some not in a while, others they could watch over and over again (Jeremy: *Taxi Driver, The Breakfast Club, Chungking Express*; Annabelle: *Moonstruck, The Big Chill, Roman Holiday*). The rest were movies only one of them had seen and couldn't believe the other had missed (like the *Casablanca*-James Bond double bill they were supposed to watch the weekend after Cambria but somehow never got to). The point was to share the joy and experience the films through each other's eyes, as people who care about each other so often do.

Emotionally sapped from the day of apartment hunting and anxious about facing Cassie the next afternoon, Jeremy decided to skip dinner, make himself a vat of popcorn and chill out with one of the films on his and Annabelle's list. (He'd texted her when he returned home, but no response.) He chose one of her favorites, *Alice Doesn't Live Here Anymore*, an early Scorsese film about a New Mexico widow who takes to the road with her bratty son to rekindle her singing career. Jeremy hadn't seen it in ages and forgot how terrific it was in every way and how different it was from the great director's often violent, crime-centric, f-bomb-studded output.

The star, Ellen Burstyn, had long been one of Jeremy's favorite actresses.

But when the movie was over, he felt worse than when it started. Not because it was sad or depressing—it was incredibly funny and charming—but because of how much Jeremy wanted to cuddle up on the couch with Annabelle and talk about it. She always had such endearingly cockeyed takes on things, so in contrast with Jeremy's more pragmatic, straightforward reactions. And was it any coincidence that Jeremy's movie pick was about a plucky woman who finds love again soon after her husband dies only for the new guy to unexpectedly screw it up? Art, meet life.

At the end of the film, Alice's boyfriend, a sexy rancher played by Kris Kristofferson, shows up at the diner where she works and wins her back with a grand gesture, inviting her and her son to come live with him on his sprawling ranch. It's a wonderfully romantic scene that made Jeremy cry a little river, though it didn't occur to him until after that it was sort of the opposite of what he'd asked Annabelle. If only he owned a ranch.

He grabbed the phone to call her, even though she'd never answered his earlier text. Jeremy figured he must have a grand gesture up his sleeve somewhere that could make her come rushing back to him, but he came up blank and put down the phone. Life proved itself to be nothing like the movies at the most inconvenient times.

JOAN'S ON THIRD was its usual packed self when Jeremy arrived to meet the not-technically-former Mrs. Lerner. He scanned the front patio of privileged late lunchers for an empty table and was disappointed to see they were all occupied. He really wanted to sit outside; he thought he might need all the air he could get for whatever Cassie had in store. So it came as a relief when Cassie waved at him from a two-top at the far end of the seating area. He gave a small wave back and tentatively approached the table.

"You cut your hair." It was the first thing Jeremy noticed. For all the years he'd known her, there was never a time it couldn't have been pulled back in a ponytail of one length or another. She looked older, more serious somehow. It wasn't unflattering but it made Jeremy wistful. So much time had passed in their lives.

"Time to look like an adult, I suppose," Cassie answered with a noncommittal shrug. She studied Jeremy and gestured at the empty chair opposite her. "Have you had lunch?"

"Are you buying?"

"I invited you, so sure." Cassie shifted in her chair.

"Why did you invite me? If you don't mind me asking." Jeremy kept his eyes fixed on the still quite beautiful mother of his son, his cool defiance clearly catching her off guard.

"Why did you show up? If you don't mind me asking?" Cassie could always give as good as she got.

A smiling, impossibly beautiful couple passed on the adjacent sidewalk, walking a dog the size of a small pony as if they were all in some fancy magazine ad. No one looked twice; it was L.A.

"Given that you've barely spoken to me in four months, I thought we might have a few things to chat about," Jeremy said with a dry smile.

Cassie let that wash over her and shifted gears. "I'm going to get a salad. Can I order you one? Or a sandwich? I love their grilled cheese."

Jeremy's appetite was nil. He had too many questions. "Maybe in a bit. Talk to me, okay?"

Silence, then: "Matty seems to be doing great, don't you think?" Cassie said brightly. "That Gabe's a pretty special guy. They seem really good together."

"You do know how they met, don't you?" Jeremy asked, purposely stirring the pot, though he wasn't sure why. He wasn't sure of anything right now.

Cassie leveled a look at him. "How are things with you and … Annabella, is it?" She watched as a waitperson delivered a pair of eye-pleasing salads to a nearby table.

"Anna*belle*. No *a*."

"Oh, I must've been confusing it with that actress. The one from *The Sopranos*?"

"Annabella Sciorra," Jeremy answered impatiently. Cassie pointed a finger pistol at him. This was like the worst first—or last—date ever. Jeremy thought it best to skip past any talk of Annabelle and cut to the chase. "Cassie, you didn't call me here to talk about Matty or Gabe or Annabelle or … grilled cheese, did you?"

Cassie said nothing. This was not the Cassie Jeremy knew. She composed herself as the couple next to them vacated their table, metal chairs scraping against the patio's cement floor. "I think I made a mistake," she finally said, staring down at her hands folded in front of her.

"What kind of mistake?" Jeremy truly had no idea.

"Leaving you," she said to her hands. Her voice was small, pained.

You could've knocked Jeremy over with a Q-tip. He said nothing, didn't know what to say.

Cassie looked up and met his bemused stare. "I was just so angry."

"Over a stupid party?"

Two new customers grabbed the empty table next to them. Jeremy needed some space. His stomach was in knots. Was she fucking serious?

"I told you, that was just the icing on a badly baked cake. We weren't happy anymore." She glanced at the couple who'd sat adjacent, both engrossed in their phones. Cassie returned her gaze to Jeremy, awaiting a response he didn't yet have.

"I don't believe this," he eventually said, keeping his voice down. "You fucking left without so much as a goodbye."

"I was in a bad place. We were in a bad place."

"So why didn't you talk to me about it first?"

Cassie formulated her answer. "You may not have realized it, but for years you'd been checked out. You were tucked away in your own little world, in whatever interested you, not me. It was like once Matty wasn't around anymore, our marriage had no purpose. We didn't exist."

"Okay, I think that's an exaggeration," he said calmly. "And why are we talking about me? I thought you said you were the one who made a mistake." Jeremy eyed the pair next to them to see if they were listening in. They weren't.

"You're right," Cassie admitted. She sat up straighter, repositioned herself in her chair, composed her thoughts. "I'm sorry. You deserved better." Then, with a catch in her voice, she added, "The thing is … I miss you."

Jeremy was at a loss. He hadn't known what to expect from this meet-up but it sure wasn't this. He swallowed hard. "What are you saying?"

She paused. "I heard you and Anna*belle* hit a rough patch." Before he could ask the obvious, Cassie answered, "Matty may have told me."

A Range Rover pulled up in front and dropped off a trio of giggly teenage girls in shorts and crop tops who barreled past the outdoor tables and into the restaurant. Jeremy hoped they stayed inside to eat.

"Cassie, this beating-around-the-bush thing isn't you. What are you doing?"

She sighed, twirling a twisted silver bangle bracelet on her right wrist that Jeremy didn't recognize. "I wanted to talk to you about getting back together. About trying again."

Jeremy sat stunned. "You do know that we already sold our house."

"Yes, I'm aware," she said. "A new place to live could be part of our starting-over plan."

This was making less than no sense. "You already have a new place to live," he reminded her.

"I'm sure we could figure something out."

"We have lawyers working on our case."

"So they'll stop and we'll pay them for their time. It's just money," she reasoned, unreasonably.

If someone approached Jeremy that very second and said, "Sir, this is all a dream," he wouldn't have been anywhere nearly as surprised as he was by this crazy turn of events. There was so much to say, so much to ask.

He then realized he was forgetting a little something. He wasn't in love with Cassie anymore—he was in love with someone else, "rough patch" aside.

But before he could mention that, his phone rang. He was about to let it go to voicemail until he glanced at the caller ID: Encino Hospital. Jeremy gave Cassie a "one second" finger as he answered. Unless it was a wrong number, this wasn't going to be good. Especially given who lived just a few blocks from that hospital.

CHAPTER
34

UNLIKE LARRY'S FATAL heart attack, Joyce's was relatively mild. But a heart attack is a heart attack, at least in Jeremy's medical book. He should have seen it coming. Or maybe he did and just didn't want to face it. Or maybe he'd been too caught up in his own shit to pay proper attention. Didn't he wonder if she was okay when she mentioned taking that afternoon nap? Why didn't he follow up on that? And hadn't he found his mother more low-key, the lilt in her voice fainter during their last few phone calls? Joyce rarely complained, always said she was fine, even if you asked her outright. Still, Jeremy felt tremendous guilt as he barreled over Coldwater Canyon en route to Encino Hospital.

"You're a fantastic son, Jeremy, please don't beat yourself up over this," said Cassie, who offered to accompany Jeremy. He was too wigged out to say yes or no so she just hopped in his car and off they went.

They were largely silent on the ride over. When they did talk, it was idle chatter about Jeremy's script rewrite, Cassie's job loss and new work prospects, their son (Jeremy had left him an urgent voice-mail). Jeremy's head was swimming. Would Joyce be okay? Did Cassie really say she wanted "to try again?" What the actual fuck?

Joyce was in a room resting comfortably when Jeremy arrived. Cassie had the good sense to wait in the floor lounge for the moment; no need to give Joyce another heart attack.

"Boy, some people will do anything for a little attention," Jeremy joked, with a lump in his throat. He leaned down to hug his mother, who felt thin and fragile beneath her hospital gown. A beeping monitor stood guard behind her.

"That's me, a real attention hound," Joyce said, smiling up at her son. "You didn't need to come all this way, darling, I'm doing fine."

She actually looked pretty good, all things considered. Jeremy felt heartened, his waves of guilt subsiding. "You obviously weren't doing so fine when you called the paramedics."

"A little indigestion, I didn't think much of it," she said. Jeremy shot her an impatient look. "You're a nudge, you know that?" she smiled. "Okay, so I also had some chest pain and my jaw felt like someone socked it. Happy?"

"Ecstatic," answered Jeremy, "that you're okay. You are okay, aren't you?"

"If you don't believe me, ask her," Joyce said, with a nod to a young woman with a clipboard standing behind Jeremy. "Say hello to Dr. Chang. Isn't she lovely?"

Jeremy turned to Dr. Chang, who was indeed lovely and looked not much older than Matty. They shook hands and she updated Jeremy on Joyce's condition. A small artery blockage brought on the attack, though it likely caused little if any damage to the heart. (Yes, Joyce had already gone chapter and verse with Dr. Chang about Larry's killer heart attack; Jeremy hated that she had to relive that just now, but how could she not?) They administered oxygen therapy, treated her with nitroglycerin to boost blood flow and put her on several heart meds including blood thinners and beta-blockers. Standard stuff, if it's someone else's mother.

Jeremy was far more unnerved than Joyce—or Dr. Chang, for that matter, who confirmed that Joyce should be just fine, though they'd be keeping her in the hospital another forty-eight hours for monitoring.

"Not exactly my idea of a vacation, but at least I won't have to do dishes for a few days," Joyce quipped.

When Dr. Chang left, Jeremy told Joyce that Cassie was outside.

That got quite the eyebrow raise from his mother. Jeremy said it was a long story that he'd explain later, even if he hoped he wouldn't have to.

"Well, I'd love to see Cassie," Joyce decided. "I miss her, you know."

Jeremy wondered if that was the drugs talking. Either way, Jeremy left to get Cassie and ran into Matty as he exited the elevator onto Joyce's floor. They hugged, and Jeremy assured him that everything was okay. He also told Matty that Cassie was there, though, from his non-reaction, Cassie had clearly gotten to him first.

They collected Cassie and, doing their best to resemble a family, spent about twenty minutes with Joyce until she started to yawn and said, "Don't take it personally, but I need to sleep a little."

Cassie had been mostly quiet, letting Jeremy and Matty carry the conversation, though she piped in now and then like someone who'd never walked out on Joyce's son. Jeremy was thankful that nothing came up about his and Cassie's split or her sudden backtracking. Joyce kept to herself whatever she was really thinking, and just seemed appreciative that her ex-daughter-in-law had shown up.

Outside the hospital, Matty, perceptive boy that he was, offered to drive Cassie back to West Hollywood on the pretense that he lived closer to her—which he did—but also because, as he later told Jeremy, he was getting the vibe that his dad wasn't buying whatever it was his mother was selling. If Cassie was disappointed that they couldn't pick up their conversation where they'd left off back at Joan's on Third, she didn't let on. Instead, she gave Jeremy a quick hug goodbye and left with a simple "We'll talk," though there was nothing simple about it.

THAT NIGHT, JEREMY tried hatching a few new screenplay ideas he could pitch to the phantom development execs Juliana had promised he'd meet. But aside from a remake of *The Honeymoon Killers*, a lurid old crime-thriller he was obsessed with about the famed Lonely Hearts Killers, he was drawing blanks. His mind ping-ponged instead between thoughts of Cassie and Annabelle.

If there were no Annabelle, would he take Cassie up on her bombshell bid for a do-over? Could Annabelle ever get past Jeremy's misguided offer of shared domesticity and return to what they once had? And if she could—and did—was there a chance they could ever live together and, if so, where? If Cassie wanted Jeremy back in her life did that mean he wasn't really the detached, unfeeling clod she'd made him believe he was—and which the episode with Annabelle sort of reconfirmed?

Good questions all, he felt, though he came up short on definite answers. He returned to his laptop to pound out the pitch for his *Honeymoon Killers* redo when he received a text, as if on cue, from Annabelle: "Heard about your mom from Gabe. So sorry, but glad she's OK. She is, isn't she? Are you OK?"

Jeremy gazed at the message, so happy to hear from her, so sad that she wasn't there to share the feelings he was feeling. She'd know just what to say and just how Jeremy should handle it.

He immediately texted Annabelle back with an update, thanked her for checking in, and said he hoped they could talk soon. He knew if she wanted to talk, she would have called and not texted. Out of respect—and maybe a bit of fear that she'd end their relationship for good (if it wasn't over already; it was hard to tell)—Jeremy held back phoning Annabelle and let the text speak for itself.

THE NEXT AFTERNOON, as Jeremy was driving along Mulholland en route to visit Joyce, Juliana appeared on his caller ID. Cell service was spotty on that hilly stretch of winding road, so he considered letting the call go to voicemail; talking to his agent could be disjointed enough without bad reception making it worse. Then again, agents didn't just call to shoot the shit, so he'd better pick up. It could be important. Turned out it was. Very. He shouldn't have answered.

"I'm just gonna rip off the Band-Aid here, dude, because I find that's best," Juliana said, not even preceded by a hello. She wasn't fucking around.

Jeremy's mouth went dry and his belly did a quick flip. He knew: his rewrite. "What is it?"

"Monolith is bringing in a new writer." She flung the words out like the seven little knives they were.

"Say again?" Jeremy asked, as if that would change what she had just said.

"They thought you did a great job, but they want to bring in someone to do a tone pass."

"How 'great' a job could I have done if they want to replace me so quickly? And what the fuck is a 'tone pass?'"

"Honestly, it means different things to different people," non-explained Juliana. "The good news is they're paying off your next step, and you don't even have to do the work."

Jeremy pictured Laz cursing his fookin' head off while he read the rewrite.

"How is that good news? I want to do the work. I want to take the script as far as I can. That was the whole point!"

Jeremy turned into a scenic overlook and pulled up next to a tour bus: "Hollywood Sights," presumably a play on the Bob Seger classic, "Hollywood Nights," or maybe not. Not everyone thought like Jeremy did.

"Jeremy, if you want to have a career in this business you've got to put on your big boy pants, be grateful that you sold your first screenplay in forever, and move on to something even bigger and better. It's out there, I promise you." She left out "Plus you're fifty years old, for fuck's sake!" but he was pretty sure that was implicit.

As he took in Juliana's pep talk, Jeremy eyed the dozen or so tourists taking pictures of the sprawling San Fernando Valley that rolled out beneath them like a vast, sun-kissed carpet. If Jeremy hadn't seen the view a million times, he would be as taken as these goggling out-of-towners; like so much in L.A., it was truly impressive.

"I hear what you're saying, but it makes no sense. They had the script for, like, two days and they make that kind of move? Without even talking to me? I know writers are dispensable, but don't you think that's kinda pushing it? And where's Ian in all this?"

Jeremy got out of his car. He needed air.

"Ian thinks you're really talented and says he'll keep you in mind for another project."

"I won't hold my breath." Jeremy didn't mean to overreact but somebody had to.

Juliana stopped typing, sighed. "If you're looking for logic or fairness or basic human decency you're in the wrong business, my friend." She continued her reality check: "And not to say I told you so, because I'd never do that, but you could have taken a much bigger payday, skipped the rewrite, and jumped right into banging out a whole new script we could be out selling this very minute."

Jeremy wasn't sure what world his agent lived in where he could "bang out" a saleable screenplay that fast, but it sure wasn't his.

He felt his pulse calm as he watched the tourists gazing out at the knockout view. Was he really that surprised at what happened? He did good work, he got paid, they moved on. With luck, the movie would get made, and he'd at the very least share credit. If he was really honest with himself, the whole thing was a fluke anyway, hardly part of some master plan. Without Cassie's exit—and the chain of events that followed—Jeremy never would have unearthed his old script and found himself chasing a dream he'd forgotten he had.

Besides, his mother had just survived a serious health scare. Let's prioritize, folks.

"You're right, it's all good," Jeremy told the agent he realized he wanted to keep. A family of three that could have passed for Jeremy, Cassie, and Matty a dozen or more years ago took a selfie in front of the brightly painted tour bus as the other sightseers filed back on. It made Jeremy smile as he said goodbye to Juliana, but not before asking her to please set up those pitch meetings she'd mentioned.

For a fleeting moment, he wished he were just a tourist.

CHAPTER
35

JEREMY STOPPED AT a Ralph's supermarket near the hospital and picked up a giant vase of sunflowers for Joyce. He was playfully hiding behind the festive blooms when he entered her room, only to be shocked at who he saw when he moved the flowers away from his face. It was Annabelle, sitting in a padded metal chair next to his mother's bed.

"Jeremy, look who came to see me!" Joyce squealed, pointing to her visitor. "It's Annabelle!" she added, in case her son had come down with a bout of hysterical blindness.

Jeremy put the vase on a small table, then leaned down and kissed his mother.

Annabelle was a vision in red: coral tunic blouse, crimson stretchy jeans, maroon canvas slip-ons, scarlet lipstick. She smiled back sweetly, evasively.

"This is a surprise," Jeremy told her, as if it wasn't ridiculously obvious.

"I hope it's okay. I've been really concerned."

"Why wouldn't it be okay?" Joyce asked before Jeremy could formulate an answer. "You're an angel for coming all this way."

Annabelle blushed, adding yet another shade of red to her ensemble. "I had a client in Studio City, so I was kind of halfway here," she explained. "Another guy who had rotator cuff surgery." She turned to Jeremy. "Though it was nowhere near as bad as yours."

"Happy to hear I still hold some distinction," he said. Annabelle visibly flinched. Jeremy didn't mean to sound rude but, happy as he was to see her, he didn't know where they stood and it was kind of breaking his heart. He also felt powerless to do anything about it; their fate was in Annabelle's delicate hands, or so it seemed.

Joyce, who could read a room like nobody else, sat up. "So how do I look for an old lady who was just at death's door?" Joyce playfully lifted her face and struck a pose, batting her eyelashes for added effect.

"Like a *young* lady with a full life ahead of her," Jeremy answered with more optimism than accuracy. She looked a bit thin and pale but on the mend.

"Honey, I love you like my own son," his mother said, amused by her little joke, "but you're full of shit."

"Oh, I don't know if I'd say full," Jeremy grinned.

"Joyce, you look absolutely fine," said Annabelle, studying her, "though a little makeup wouldn't hurt." She eyed Joyce's big purse sitting on the bedside cabinet. "Got any in there?" Joyce gestured and Annabelle found lipstick, a compact, and a small nylon hairbrush.

"Oh, goodie, a makeover!" said Joyce, already looking better. Jeremy watched as Annabelle dusted his mom's cheeks with highlighting powder and then carefully applied the lipstick to Joyce's thin, dry lips. Annabelle stepped back, assessed her handiwork, then ran the brush through Joyce's short, silvery hair. It puffed up nicely.

"Take a look," said Annabelle, holding out the compact's mirror. Joyce studied her face in it and beamed.

"You're an absolute magician, darling." She looked up at her son. "Isn't she a magician, Jeremy?"

He didn't answer, just gazed at Annabelle as she smiled at Joyce.

"Oh, where's my head, I completely forgot!" Joyce clutched Jeremy's hand. "Whatever happened with your script? Did you finish the rewrite? Did they totally love it?"

Annabelle glanced at Jeremy, looking curious as well.

He simply didn't have the heart—or the energy—to tell the truth right then, and channeled his agent. "It's in the hands of the movie gods."

Jeremy and Annabelle rode the elevator down together in silence. Once they entered the hospital's buzzing, pastel-painted lobby, she pointed to a pair of empty chairs in the waiting area. "Wanna sit for a minute?"

"Why, do you want to talk to me or something?" Jeremy knew that came out wrong—again.

"Look, I know you must be pissed at me or offended or annoyed and I don't blame you," Annabelle said, not yet moving toward the bank of seats.

"I'm not pissed or offended but I *am* confused and I miss what we had and there's a lot going on and to top it off Cassie wants us to get back together," he said in a torrent of syllables.

"Why would she want us to get back together?"

"Not you and me. Her and me." Jeremy searched Annabelle's face for surprise or worry or betrayal but there was none. Just a sort of calm neutrality.

"Interesting," was all she said. "Let's sit, okay?" But as they started to cross the lobby an elderly couple took the last free chairs. Jeremy stopped.

"Let's just take a walk," he said. "Or there must be a Starbucks around here."

Annabelle mulled their choices. It seemed like a big decision. She had a thought. "Where are you parked?"

They ended up sitting in Jeremy's Prius, which was parked at a meter on Ventura Boulevard across from, whaddya know, a Starbucks. He was just glad to be with her. It was hard to tell if the feeling was mutual.

Annabelle did most of the talking as she tried to explain the wellspring of emotion let loose by Jeremy's move-in request. (He had wanted to explain the Cassie thing first, but Annabelle was already on a roll.) Jeremy had been right that it upset her to think about living with him in the same house that she and Gil created together. He'd also correctly guessed that she wasn't prepared to leave her house to move elsewhere with him.

"Still, if you asking me to live together took me by surprise, it really shouldn't have," admitted Annabelle, "at least not in such a bewildering, immobilizing way." She paused. "That's what Melinda says anyhow."

"Melinda?"

"She's this psychotherapist I've been working with."

"Oh, after we stopped seeing each other?"

"Actually, about a month after we *started* seeing each other." Annabelle turned away shyly, maybe embarrassed.

"Why didn't you tell me about therapy to begin with?" Jeremy finally asked. "What were you hiding?"

"Nothing. I just didn't want any more input than I was already getting from Melinda. I didn't want to jeopardize what you and I had. Which was so good."

"Not that good if you had to go to therapy." A car parallel parked behind Jeremy, its radio blaring classical music as if it were death metal.

Annabelle waited till the driver shut off his engine. "I knew you'd take it personally," she said. "That's why I didn't tell you."

"You could have trusted me." It wasn't an accusation; it was a fact. Jeremy stared at Annabelle for emphasis. She met his gaze head-on.

They were silent a few more moments.

"After just a few weeks of dating, I knew we were headed some-where special," Annabelle said. "And even if I seemed all chipper and enthusiastic on the outside, inside I was worried I'd screw it all up. I was still in love with Gil and, despite falling for you, I didn't know if I could handle a future with you. I mean, if there was going to be one."

"I don't get it. You seemed, like, all in with me. You were so open and present and ... amazing. Especially on the trip to Cambria. Was it all bullshit? Because if it was, I have to say, you were a terrific ac-tress." It was getting warm in the car. Jeremy turned on the engine and opened the sunroof. The early autumn air wafted in.

Annabelle shifted in her seat. "Maybe we should have taken a walk after all."

"We still can. I need to get back into my walks anyway. I've been kind of delinquent lately."

"Oh, that's too bad. You were really liking those." She paused. "Actually, no, here's fine. I don't have a lot more to say."

"What if I do?"

"Is it about Cassie?" Annabelle asked with a concern she hadn't previously shown.

"No, that's … that's all just kinda crazy. I'll tell you about it after. No, I want to talk more about you. Why did you shut down so fast after I floated moving in? I told you, it was just a passing thought. It was supposed to be a good thing."

"Of course, and any woman would've been flattered. *I* should have been flattered. Instead, I was flattened. And, believe me, Melinda and I are deep into trying to figure out why."

"Why don't you and I try to figure out why?"

Annabelle looked moved, conflicted. "That's a sweet offer, but all due respect, I'd better leave this one to the pros."

"Well, if you ever need a film critic or a screenwriter, you know who to call." It sounded huffy, but he was going for funny, and it somehow worked: Annabelle laughed and then looked out the window as a couple of Valley kids banged past on skateboards.

"Speaking of which," she said, turning back to Jeremy, serious again, "what did happen with your script rewrite? You kind of sidestepped your mother when she asked." Annabelle, as usual, was nothing if not perceptive.

Jeremy related the recent turn of events regarding *Offense* in colorful detail. And, though Annabelle was sympathetic, even indignant about his unceremonious dismissal, Jeremy was surprised to find himself feeling pretty sanguine about the whole thing. Who knows, maybe it'd come back to kick the shit out of him later. Meanwhile, the segue had effectively diverted them from the issue at hand, and it seemed like there wasn't much more to say for now about the state of their relationship—or lack thereof.

Jeremy just had one final question.

"So where does this leave us?" he asked, wanting to feel as if he left their meeting with more certitude than when it had started.

"I wish I could say, but I don't exactly know," Annabelle answered. Her expressive eyes looked especially dark just then, though they remained inscrutable. Maybe she really didn't know. "Melinda wants me to take it one day at a time right now."

Jeremy was sitting two feet from Annabelle but felt a million miles away. He flashed on that last talk he'd had with Matty about relationships: how they take time; how they were easily breakable; but how something totally unexpected could strengthen them, make you realize what you had. Perhaps for Annabelle, it would be Jeremy's proposal to live with her. It was a ray of hope. But he'd have to be patient—and believe.

Seeing her again also reconfirmed what Jeremy was pretty sure he already knew: that he was done with Cassie. He couldn't go backward, only forward. That Melinda had better be a fucking great shrink.

But for now, maybe less was more. He snapped on his seatbelt. "Okay, then," he said. "Well, thanks for coming to see my mom. I know it meant a lot to her. And to me."

"I hope she'll be okay. I'm sure she will." She gave his hand a quick squeeze and let go.

Jeremy watched her leave the car and cross the street. He sighed, cranked up his Pandora, and Night Ranger's "Sister Christian" poured out. He was reminded of his middle school days when anything still seemed possible, and drove off into the late afternoon sun.

CHAPTER
36

ON HIS WAY home battling Ventura Boulevard's rush-hour grid-lock, Jeremy received an unexpected trio of emails all at once: one from Ian, another from Lucien, and a third from, think of the devil, Cassie. He was itching to open the messages, of course, having no idea what any of them could possibly say, but didn't want to do so while driving (or crawling along, as was the case). So he made his way to the curb and parked in front of what had been, in his youth, a big old single-screen movie house called the La Reina. It was now the site of a cluttered retail complex which, for better or worse, had retained the theatre's spiffy, Art Deco-style marquee.

Jeremy steeled himself and started with Ian's, which Jeremy fantasized was an offer for another rewrite gig or something equally exciting, but quickly realized was probably some thank-you bullshit. Which it was, but without the thank you:

> Hey Jeremy, Hope all's good with you! So I know you talked to Juliana but just wanted to tell you Laz and I thought you brought a ton to the rewrite but he and a writer buddy (do you know Ty McDougal? He's awesome!) are going to jump on it from here. Laz has an amazing vision for the film—which we all love!—and the great news is we're fast-tracking it to shoot right after January 1! How cool is that? Peace, Ian.

There was so much wrong about the message that Jeremy didn't know where to begin. Still, Ian didn't have to get in touch at all, so that was at least something. Talk about a low bar. And, yeah, Laz may have been kind of a piece of shit—Jeremy's ousting was probably all his doing—but he was *Offense*'s piece of shit, so he had to root for him and this Ty guy to succeed. Hollywood.

He flipped to the next email. What in the world could Lucien want? He hadn't talked with him since that night at Pace.

> J: I know you're a hot screenwriter now and barely have time to even read this email :) but some interesting news: Geneva's out (long story—ugly) and I'm the new boss (short story—happy)! So if you have the interest— and the bandwidth—to start reviewing again, the job is yours. Short-term, long-term, one-offs, whatever. Your choice. Miss you, man. LMK! – L

Well, that was interesting. What the heck could Geneva have done to get sacked? Jeremy hoped it was something sordid. But good for Lucien that he was promoted. And nice that he wanted Jeremy back after what happened. Maybe Lucien was more of a mensch than he gave him credit for. Much as Jeremy liked reviewing, he hadn't thought a lot about going back to it, given how busy he'd been with the script and his house.

Which isn't to say he didn't feel a little pang whenever he read a review by another *Times* freelancer of a film that might have been assigned to him. (No fewer than six Holocaust documentaries had been released since Jeremy's firing.) And he definitely missed exercising the corner of his brain that forced him to think critically, yet fairly and objectively—and put it into words that were both reasoned and entertaining. Fuck it, he'd say yes. Who knew if he'd ever get another script job? Might as well hedge his bets.

But first, he had to open Cassie's email with its mysteriously blank subject line. Jeremy hesitated, wondering why she hadn't just texted. He held his breath and opened her message. It contained a photo of a large, elaborately wrapped gift box. Beneath it were the words: "A surprise is waiting for you …"

Huh? He checked to see if Cassie had been hacked. But no, it was from her actual address.

Whatever it meant, it didn't seem like Cassie, certainly not the Cassie she'd become. Jeremy would hardly describe her as playful over the last few years.

A horn honked behind Jeremy. He turned around. A guy driving a funky old Jeep Wrangler (they had once been so popular in L.A.) raised his eyebrows and slashed his index finger back and forth: the international signal for "Are you getting out?" Jeremy nodded yes, put down his phone, and exited the space, glad for an excuse to stop trying to interpret Cassie's email. He'd call her later and claim his "surprise," though a bigger surprise than her plea to put the brakes on their divorce was hard to fathom.

Jeremy proved to have a stunning lack of imagination.

As Ventura Boulevard traffic lightened up at the Coldwater Canyon intersection, Jeremy's phone rang. It was his realtor, Marjan. She was in the vicinity with her clients—his home's soon-to-be owners, as she was representing both parties—who wondered if they could stop by and take some measurements. Jeremy said sure, he'd be there in about ten minutes and meet them in front. Jeremy was intrigued: he would finally get to meet the buyers.

They were waiting at the curb when Jeremy pulled up and parked in the garage. Marjan gave him an effusive hug. Introductions were made, and Jeremy was relieved to find that Corey and Tasha were not the monsters he'd imagined but rather a friendly, seemingly down-to-earth pair who couldn't stop talking about how much they adored the house. They had him at: "And that wood-beamed ceiling!"

As Jeremy unlocked the front door, he was struck by the absence of the shrill whine that would typically erupt until the alarm was disarmed. Could he have forgotten to set it before he left for the hospital? He'd been kind of dizzy these days, so it was possible. And it's not like he hadn't forgotten before. (How many times had Cassie scolded him about that?) He shrugged it off and stepped aside for the others to enter.

"Do you mind if we just scoot into the master bedroom?" Tasha asked, hesitating in the doorway. "We want to make sure our king-size bed will fit."

"Sure, go on in," Jeremy said, having to think twice if his own bed was a king or queen. "I'll be right there." He left to retrieve the mail from the birdhouse-style box at the curb and then made his way back up the brick path and into the house. That's when he heard the scream. Jeremy nearly hit the ceiling.

Marjan, Corey, and Tasha came flying out of the bedroom and down the hallway, landing in the living room to face a terrified Jeremy. "What is it? What happened?"

"It's okay, it's okay," answered Marjan, catching her breath. "We didn't know someone would be in there."

"What? Who's in there?" he shouted, heart pounding.

"We're really sorry, we're so embarrassed," said Tasha, who, like her husband, seemed to be suppressing a grin.

"We'll just come back another time, okay?" Corey said, smile broadening against his better efforts. He reached for Tasha's hand, and they made a hasty exit.

Marjan looked at the unnerved Jeremy, stifled her own grin, and scurried out after her clients.

As Marjan shut the door behind her, Jeremy steadied himself and started out for his bedroom. But not before stopping to grab a fireplace poker just in case. He moved warily down the hallway and opened the door to the bedroom, poker primed at his side.

The window blinds were lowered and a dozen little candles flickered seductively around the darkened room. Sitting up in the bed, covers wrapped around her naked shoulders, was a woman sobbing profusely, dabbing at her eyes with a corner of the duvet. Jeremy could not believe what he was seeing.

"Cassie? What in the hell are you doing here?"

"I wanted to surprise you," she answered between teary heaves.

"Well, mission accomplished," Jeremy said. He had to admit, she looked rather beautiful: her short hair framing her radiant, candlelit face, her noisy weeping lending her a lovely vulnerability. She had never been much of a crier, more cool customer than emotional puddle. But now? Who knows? It was topsy-turvy time.

Cassie quieted, working to compose herself. Jeremy watched her, frozen in that spot at the foot of their bed. "Did you get my email?" she asked glumly.

He nodded, realized, pointed at her. "Oh, you're the fancy gift box …" He knew she still had a house key, but he didn't think she'd actually use it—at least not like this.

"Not so fancy," Cassie said, residual tears trickling down her cheeks. "How was I supposed to know those people were going to show up?"

"How did you know I was even going to show up?" His breathing had steadied again. He was pretty sure by then that he wasn't hallucinating.

"Matty told me he spoke to you this morning. That you mentioned you were going to the hospital this afternoon. I took the chance you'd come right home after."

"Because I couldn't possibly have anywhere else to go?" He didn't, but she didn't have to know that.

"I said I took a chance." Cassie scrunched further under the covers as if to disappear completely.

"What were you expecting? That I'd walk in, see you lying there naked, leap into bed and we'd re-consummate our marriage? Live happily ever after?"

"Is 're-consummate' even a word?" she asked, voice muffled by the duvet.

"I don't know. But if it is I doubt I've ever had occasion to use it." Jeremy dislodged himself from where he'd been standing and plopped down on the edge of the bed. He was facing away from Cassie and into the full-length mirror across; her reflection hovered behind his own. He watched as she disentangled herself from the covers and reached for her bra and panties strewn on the floor beside her.

"Look, I was hoping you were going to call me after our talk at Joan's yesterday. I mean, I know you had a lot on your mind with your mother and all, but …"

"But you thought I'd jump at the chance?"

She slipped on her bra—a sexy, black floral mesh deal that had "special occasion" written all over it—and swiftly fastened the hooks. "Actually, no," she answered. "But I know you, and I knew I'd probably have to be the one to make the next move. So I did."

Cassie shimmied into her matching bikini briefs and stood, her reflection disappearing from Jeremy's view. He turned away from the mirror.

"Cassie, I'm not really sure what you want me to say." It sounded lame but the whole surreal episode felt like being with some total stranger who'd stumbled into the wrong house, not one she'd lived in for twenty-two years and still half owned.

"Who was it who said, 'When people show you who they are, believe them?'" she asked evenly as she buttoned a familiar, sapphire-blue satin blouse. Jeremy had always liked her in it; it brought out the color of her eyes, made them glisten.

"Maya Angelou," he answered, embarrassed that he was getting turned on watching her dress. More than a little. He took a few steps back from her.

"Right. Smart lady," Cassie said, stepping into a short, pleated skirt that showed off her toned legs. Had she been walking every day as well?

Jeremy focused. The angrier he felt, the hornier he got.

"You really don't want to get back together, do you?" she asked.

"Do *you*?"

"I'm not entirely sure what I want. But I guess that's obvious."

"This is so unlike you, Cassie."

"Maybe it's not, and I just never let you see this side of me." She slowly, almost imperceptibly, moved toward him. They were maybe a foot apart.

"I don't think that's true. But if it is, well, that's a shame now, isn't it?" he noted as she inched even closer. He didn't budge.

He was suddenly, officially hard. He hated himself. He could also tell that Cassie knew just what she was doing. The question was still: Why?

She slowly moved her hand toward Jeremy's groin and placed her lips on his. They could both feel his resolve weakening and hers intensifying. It had been so very long—eons, it seemed—since they'd been this close, this tempted, this aware of each other's presence. Cassie parted her lips, let her tongue escape, forcing Jeremy's mouth to grant entry. His pulse raced, prickles of sweat forming on his forehead. He was swept back twenty-seven years to when they first met, when everything was new and thrilling and promising. When there was no history, only future. When life, love, and lust formed one single, inextricable force. When they felt invincible.

But that was then and this was now. There was truth and there were consequences. They had become separate, self-protective units in the last years of their marriage for a reason they didn't entirely identify until the damage was done. Meanwhile, that reason became everything to Jeremy: the source of a new self-awareness, his learning curve, the fence he continually struggled to leap. A desire to attach, to connect, to reveal. But not like this.

As Cassie guided him onto the bed, their mouths still playing memory lane, Jeremy grabbed his will by the horns and freed himself from Cassie's roaming hands and his own misguided instincts. He tried to be gentle yet purposeful, conscious of both her dignity and his integrity (not to sound too high-minded about, er, pulling out of a common sex act).

Cassie gazed up at Jeremy now standing above her, his heartbeat audible, eyes wide. She didn't look as much hurt as frustrated by their thwarted reunion, her momentary power vanquished by Jeremy's better angels. The tables between them had turned, perhaps for the first and final time. Cassie sat up and sighed.

"Well, isn't this a fine how-do-you-do." Cassie bent over, picked up a pair of simple black flats from the floor, and slid them on with finality.

"I think it's for the best," said Jeremy, tucking his shirt back into his jeans.

Cassie rose from the bed and locked eyes with him. "That's what people say when someone dies after a long and painful illness." She crossed to the full-length mirror to check her makeup.

"For the record, I don't think death is better than having sex with you," Jeremy shot back, hoping for some levity.

"Could have fooled me," Cassie answered. She shook out her hair and finger-combed a few stray strands. "I thought it would have been nice, that's all. Just forget I was ever here."

She was about to leave when she stopped and picked up their wedding picture that sat in an antique gold frame on the dresser.

"That was a good day," Jeremy recalled.

"Yes, it was," Cassie said. "Just a couple of crazy kids." She turned to him with a wistful look. "Do you mind if I take this? I've always loved the frame."

Jeremy considered her request. He silently held out his hand for the picture, which she passed to him. He unclipped the frame's velvet cardboard backing, slid the wedding photo out, and handed back the empty frame. "It's all yours," he said.

As Cassie took the ornate picture holder, she glanced at the photo in Jeremy's hand and seemed about to ask for it as well. For whatever reason, she thought better of it. There was something to be said for compromise.

"Thanks, Jeremy. And good luck with Annabelle, I hope it all works out. I hear she's pretty great."

"She is," he confirmed. And, although it seemed like there was much more to say, Cassie exited the bedroom.

"I just have to ask," Jeremy said as they reached the front door. "Yesterday, at the restaurant, you said that leaving me was a mistake. Why, exactly? I mean, after all this time, what made you decide that?"

Cassie studied her ex-husband, and looked for a second as if she might well up again. "There was a part of me that thought maybe there was something better out there. Or at least better for me," she began. "I met a lot of men these last few months. Went on my share of dates, had some nice dinners, the occasional stayover, even a weekend away. But after a while, you know what I discovered?"

Jeremy shook his head, couldn't begin to guess.

"That these guys were okay—funny, smart, hot, whatever—but, in the end, despite our problems, none of them could hold a candle to you. I'd come home and think, "This is what I left Jeremy for?""

Jeremy was astounded. "Maybe you just didn't meet the right guy," he offered. He had to admit, that sounded strange coming from one's ex-husband.

Cassie gave him an odd look. "Anyway," she said, moving on, "that's why I thought we should try again."

"Better the devil you know than the devil you don't?" There, now that sounded like an ex-husband.

"I think that's my cue to leave." Cassie gave him a quick kiss on the cheek. "Let's just leave it up to the lawyers from here on. Deal?"

"Deal."

Jeremy watched as she opened the front door and, without a glance back, walked off into the twilight.

CHAPTER
37

JEREMY LIKED TO say that you never knew what was going to happen when you woke up every morning. Hardly the most profound thought, but it pretty much always proved true.

Astonishment was the case that particularly bright and breezy late September day.

Jeremy spent the morning finishing up a review for the *Times* on a powerful documentary about a hundred-year-old Holocaust survivor who, until just a few years before, was a tour guide at the concentration camp where she was imprisoned during World War II. (You couldn't make that one up and, yes, he was back on the Judaic film beat.) With Lucien's okay, Jeremy had decided to limit his reviews to one or two a week instead of the three or four he used to do. That way he'd stay active with the paper and keep his journalism muscles limber, while leaving the majority of his work time free to focus on his screenwriting career. He'd been given a second chance at success, and he wasn't going to blow it the way he did so many years ago.

To that end, Juliana kept her promise and set a string of meetings for Jeremy with several upper-level film and TV development execs. While he was brainstorming stories to pitch, he asked Juliana if she had any particular advice. She told him to "Think out of the box but don't try to reinvent the wheel," which was a lucky thing because he thought it was a damn near perfect invention (the wheel, not the box).

"And can I tell you why?" she asked, as if anyone could stop her. "Because with most pitches, you're either too far ahead of the curve or too far behind the curve, so you might as well avoid the whole fucking curve altogether."

Jeremy wasn't sure what she meant, so took her word for it and used his own common sense. (Actually, he relied on Zoë's. She told him to just have fun and expect nothing.)

Something must have worked, because Jeremy already had two solid pitch sessions that week: one at Amazon Studios where the VP he met, a straight-shooter in her thirties named Priyanka, admitted they should have made a bid for *Offensive Measures* when they heard Monolith was into it (sure, they say that now!) and asked for something new from him just like it; and a second at a new mini-major studio, Paradise Pictures, where they sparked to his *Honeymoon Killers* remake idea and were "running it up the flagpole."

Two more meetings were scheduled for next week, and he was working on a romantic comedy pitch (think: a gay-straight version of *My Best Friend's Wedding*) as well as a workplace sitcom about a Mumbai office drone sent to small-town Ohio to run a call center. Have fun, expect nothing: so far, so good.

In the meantime, Joyce was happily back at home after her three days in Encino Hospital. Doctor's orders: three full weeks of rest, stricter diet (adios, red meat; put down that salt shaker, lady!), mild daily exercise (after said three weeks), daily doses of blood pressure and cholesterol meds, and for God's sake—start meditating! Joyce said, without irony, that she'd rather die than meditate; Jeremy told her if it was good enough for Oprah and Deepak Chopra, it was good enough for her. She sighed and agreed to download the app.

Jeremy had visited his mom almost every day since she returned to the condo. He offered to have her stay with him for a while, but she emphatically declined. As much as Jeremy hesitated asking for help, Joyce had an even deeper independent streak (apple, meet tree). "The day I can't take care of myself, start digging the hole," she had said in jest more than once.

She made Jeremy tell her everything that had happened with

Cassie and Annabelle since their unexpected visits to see her in the hospital. He got Joyce up to speed about both women, though fudged a few of the racier details about Cassie's desperate measure because, really, why put that embarrassing image in his little old mom's head? (Okay, it would have been weirder for Jeremy than Joyce, who would have lapped it up. Maybe he'd save the story for another day.)

"And, sweetheart, you're positively sure you have no desire to get back with Cassie?" Joyce asked.

That seemed like a strange question coming from his protective mother. And the word *desire*? Uh, not random. "Why?" he asked back, eyes narrowed as if she knew something he didn't. "Would you actually want me to?"

"Darling, this is not about what I want, it's about what you want. I'm just asking a question," she reasoned from her cozy perch in the old La-Z-Boy.

"Playing devil's advocate?" wondered Jeremy.

"No—a mother," Joyce volleyed back. Damn, she was good.

Jeremy confirmed for her what he'd come to learn with increasing certainty those last few months. "No, I have no desire to get back together with Cassie. Not anymore. Our relationship has been over for a long time now."

"Okay, now what about Annabelle?" Joyce asked, getting down to brass tacks. "Do you think you want to marry her?" She took a sip of iced tea and peered at Jeremy over her acrylic tumbler.

"*Marry* her? Mom, I told you, I don't even know if we're going to keep seeing each other."

"Well, let's say you do. Then what?"

"Ma, really. Don't you think I should finish getting out of one marriage before I contemplate another?" Jeremy's armpits went damp. He'd been having such a relaxing visit until then.

She placed her tea glass on a side table and eyeballed her son. "You men. You're all so damn practical. I'm not talking about getting married tomorrow. When you're ready!" Joyce paused, thought for a moment. "Say, six months from now."

He had to laugh. "Wow, you really want to go to a wedding, don't you?"

"I'm not getting any younger, you know." She shot him a wry look. "And neither are you."

"Thanks for the reminder," he grinned, "on both counts."

But Joyce wasn't letting him off the hook that easily. "Honey, listen to me. You have to decide if you want something badly enough. And if you do, you have to move heaven and earth to get it. Otherwise, one day, you'll be sitting in a La-Z-Boy drinking iced tea and wondering why you didn't make your life as happy as humanly possible when you had the chance."

His mother's words resonated with him, but the simple fact remained that Annabelle was working her way through her issues, and there didn't seem like anything Jeremy could do right then to get them to a mutually happy place. And that included moving heaven and earth. It still shocked him how they could have been so close to something so great and yet, at the same time, so far apart.

He had picked up the phone to call Annabelle a few times since their in-car talk the week before but never got as far as dialing her complete number. She did, however, send him a quick text that simply read "How's Joyce?" Jeremy had answered, "Getting better every day. How are you?" Annabelle's lack of response *was* her response, and Jeremy decided to respect the space she still seemed to need. He missed her so much but hoped good things would come to those who wait—even if that was one maxim with a patchy history.

Matty wondered if Annabelle would come around now that she knew for sure that Cassie was definitely, permanently, out of the romantic picture. Jeremy asked his son why Annabelle would know that. Matty shrugged and called it a "hunch," as he and his dad took an hour walk around the scenic Hollywood reservoir, home to one of the city's best views of the iconic Hollywood sign.

Shrug or not, Jeremy guessed that Cassie mentioned her and Jeremy's failed tryst to Matty, who then told a little birdie named Gabe who likely whispered it to Aunt Annabelle. Though he didn't press Matty about it, it made Jeremy rethink if he'd ever given Annabelle any lingering reason to believe he still carried a torch for his ex-wife. He could now easily extinguish that thought for her once and for all.

More instantly newsworthy was that Matty and Gabe were talking about getting a place together. Maybe someone in the family could make a go of it. Jeremy should be taking notes.

"Maybe it's easier between two guys," Matty conjectured. "I mean men and women: Whoever thought that one up?" He may have been joking and it made them both laugh, but sometimes Jeremy wondered the exact same thing. In the end, how any two people made it work was a goddamn miracle.

All of which leads back to that bright and breezy September day and Jeremy's amazement over a single turn of events, one that had never crossed his mind as a possibility yet would make all the difference in the rest of his life. If that sounds like a big fucking deal, it was.

Jeremy had just emailed his film review to Lucien when his phone rang. It was Marjan, who Jeremy hadn't spoken to since she and the buyers had hightailed it out of the house after walking in on the naked Cassie. He'd never forget the looks on their faces.

"Are you sitting down?" asked Marjan with an ominous tone.

"As a matter of fact, I am," said Jeremy from the comfort of his desk chair. Now what?

"A bit of bad news, I'm afraid."

He took a breath and listened for more. Her pause was hyper-dramatic.

"The house fell out of escrow," Marjan said with the gravity of a death notice.

There was only one reasonable response to that. "Are you fucking kidding me?" yelled Jeremy, leaping out of his chair.

"Oh, I know! Corey and Tasha are absolutely beside themselves," Marjan reported. "You have no idea."

"Yeah? Well, I'm 'absolutely' right beside them!" Jeremy took a breath, counted to five. "Marjan, what happened?"

Unbeknownst to Jeremy, because he hadn't read the fine print (Who does?), the buyers had to sell their Denver home before they could close on Chez Lerner. They'd left Colorado with their valuable old house on the market; their realtor said it would go quickly. But a buyer's inspection revealed major structural damage that tanked the deal and, well, the place wouldn't be selling any time soon.

"Now what?" asked Jeremy. He gazed out his office window at a pair of squirrels racing around an old black walnut tree. Imagine your entire life's work was to gather nuts and fuck other squirrels. It seemed pretty cushy right then.

"We find another buyer!" Marjan said merrily, like it was the easiest thing ever. "Could you just do me one tiny favor?"

Jeremy sighed. "What's that?"

"Remove the little 'Sold' sign from out front? It'll save me a trip."

"Anything for you, Marjan," Jeremy said with faux sweetness, knowing it would go right over her head.

"Aw, thank you, Jeremy," she answered on cue. See?

Jeremy hung up, shocked and defeated. He was supposed to be moving out in less than a month. And now, who knows? Despite continued searching, he still hadn't found a new place to live, so it may not hurt to have more time to look around. (That apartment he liked in Cassie's vicinity? Gone. He snoozed, he lost.) On the downside, he'd seen houses in the neighborhood sit on the market for a year or more, driving down prices, patience, and personal momentum. For as beautiful and peaceful as Laurel Canyon could be, it wasn't everyone's cup of tea.

"Maybe now's your chance to stay after all," said a hopeful Crash, who walked by as Jeremy was removing the Sold sign.

"I wish, but I still can't afford to." Jeremy reminded him about his deal with Cassie: either he bought out her half or they sold and shared the proceeds.

"People buy shit they can't afford all the time," Crash reasoned. "Especially in this city. You think Katie and I could afford our house when we bought it? We still can't—we're totally house poor. It's a miracle we got the loan altogether."

Jeremy posed the question he and Cassie had wanted to ask since their young neighbors moved in: "How did you swing it?"

"Borrowed the down from our parents, which we're paying back a little at a time, and our jobs cover the mortgage. Everything else, we figure it out as we go. Long as we have enough to keep Lola in kibble, we're good." Crash looked resigned. "But hey, don't listen to me, you've gotta do what you've gotta do. We'll miss you, dude, that's all."

It got Jeremy thinking: What if there was a way to keep the house and he'd just been taking the easy way out?

CHAPTER
38

JEREMY JUMPED ON the phone with his lawyer to update him on the escrow fallout. "So let's say I did want to stay here and buy out Cassie," Jeremy began with a renewed sense of wonder and vigor. He was already picturing some upgrades he might make: A new paint job? New garage door? Whoa, slow down! "I know you didn't recommend me doing it," Jeremy added, "but you also said it wasn't impossible."

"Have your personal finances dramatically changed these last weeks?" asked Arvin Box.

"No. I mean, well, not exactly. But I made that nice chunk of money for my script and there are some rewrite payments still due. Oh, and a production bonus if it gets made, which, fingers crossed, it's going to ..." Jeremy was on his second half hour walking the backyard. The Santa Ana winds were whipping up the sycamore leaves.

"And how would you say your future beyond that is looking? Money-wise, that is."

It was hard to say, so that's what Jeremy told him: "It's hard to say." He paused, considered the possibilities. "But it could be bright." Because really it could. And he could work his ass off to make it happen.

"Look, generally, I like to play these things safe. I've seen too many house negotiations get ridiculously ugly and protracted.

And the only ones who really make out are the lawyers because of all the extra billable hours."

Jeremy took that in. "Is there an 'on the other hand?'" He gazed at the walls of the house. He was thinking a nice sage green for the stucco with maybe a forest green for the trim. When was the last time the place was painted?

"Now and then, the couple works out a deal on the side, then they come back to the lawyers to make it official. Compromises are made on the amount and frequency of payments, sometimes even on the total price. I've had clients take out a second mortgage to pay for the buyout, but I can tell ya, guy: that's a slippery motherfucking slope." Arvin sounded pretty Bronx-y just then. "It comes down to this: Are you a betting man, Jeremy?"

That was easy—he was not, not really. And wasn't that kind of his problem? But most problems could be solved if you tried hard enough, and this one was no different. He passed the grapefruit tree stump, noticed new green buds springing from it. Was there life again in his beloved tree or was it just a cruel trick of nature?

"Yeah," Jeremy finally answered Arvin, "I'm a betting man."

"Okay, then roll the dice. Talk to your ex, make her an offer she can't refuse—or let her make you one. And don't say I didn't warn you."

Jeremy hung up, feeling like a dope for taking his lawyer's initial advice about letting the house go and for not trying to crack this financial puzzle sooner—like, say, before they hired a realtor and almost sold the place. Okay, enough self-flagellation; time to crunch some numbers. He cut his walk short and went to work.

It took a grand total of an hour for Jeremy to do the following: study the house mortgage; calculate how much they'd paid off versus the outstanding balance (still stupidly high after twenty-two years of payments); comb through their remaining savings, investment, and retirement accounts (more impressive in theory—it was shocking how little they'd accumulated); study the six-month sales contract they'd signed with Marjan (there was wiggle room for early cancellation); and then add, subtract, multiply, and divide to make

Cassie an offer that he could even slightly manage, and that she might possibly agree to.

His house in order, as it were, Jeremy steeled himself and called Cassie. He decided to make a sandwich as he talked to keep his anxiety in check. As usual, the more he wanted something, the more uneasy he felt; a diversion helped.

She answered on the first ring. "Jeremy, hi!" she chirped in a voice so unusually buoyant you'd think she'd just won the lottery. It turned out, she kind of did.

"What are you so happy about?" he had to ask as he sliced an avocado.

"You are talking to the new in-house counsel for Moka Java!"

"You got a new job? Already? Cassie, that's fantastic! What's Moka Java?"

"Oh—it's this new chain of coffeehouses coming to L.A. It's a division of this larger corporation called Tiger Industries, which is based in—" She stopped to catch her breath. "Anyway, it's an amazing opportunity, and I can't believe it. I just found out, so you're literally the first person I've told!"

"Well, I'm honored," Jeremy said. "And really happy for you. I know what a smart and capable lawyer you are—you deserve this." He meant every word, even if it may have felt like he was buttering her up.

"Wow, thank you, Jeremy. That's really kind of you to say."

He folded a stack of turkey slices onto a piece of rye bread and topped it with the avocado. "So I guess it's 'So long, nonprofit?'"

"Yep. I'm all about profit now—especially for me!" She laughed. "You do know I'm kidding, right?"

"If you say so," he joked back, but couldn't fault her for wanting to make a better living. As Jeremy spread mustard over the avocado he wondered how much Cassie would be making and if it would affect their as-yet-undetermined question of who would pay whom alimony.

"Anyway, I start next Monday. Offices are downtown so a bit of a hike, but I'll figure it out. Maybe I'll take the Metro."

Cassie was flying, so Jeremy had to bring her down to earth.

"So, Cassie, the reason I called was because I've changed my mind about the house." The sandwich making wasn't slowing his speeding pulse. There was silence at the other end. Cassie was clearly formulating a response.

Then: "Oh, I see," she said, a bit deflated. "Okay, well, shouldn't we just let the lawyers handle it?"

"We can save a lot of time and money if we work it out ourselves. But honestly, I'm going to need your help." He took a shot and added, "For old time's sake."

He could swear that Cassie snorted at that, but maybe not. "I'm listening," she finally said.

As Jeremy finished assembling his sandwich (romaine, tomato, a smear of lentil hummus), he evenly recapped the financial state of Chez Lerner and what he felt was a fair installment plan to pay Cassie her share of its current worth. He hit her with an impressive array of facts, figures, and logic that included small monetary incentives for her long-term cooperation. Sure, his proposal was kind of seat-of-his-pants, but it felt earnest and workable, and he assumed the lawyers could clean up any messy parts. Jeremy took a deep breath as he finished his speech and awaited Cassie's reply.

"Let me think about it, okay?" She sounded neither sold nor dismissive, and that might have been about the best Jeremy could hope for to start.

"Of course! Thanks, Cassie," Jeremy answered as he carved his teetering sandwich into halves, stood back and admired its stature. "And I'll let Marjan know we may be discussing a B plan."

"Let's not jump the gun, okay, partner?" The lawyer had spoken. Fair enough.

After they hung up, Jeremy sat at the dining table savoring his late lunch and thinking about refacing the kitchen cabinets: the wood was looking tired.

He needed to quit thinking about renovations; he'd be lucky to afford his house payments to Cassie—if she even agreed to his offer. Meanwhile, he shuddered to think what kind of bill Arvin Box would eventually stick him with. He and Cassie needed to wrap up this divorce pronto.

JEREMY FINISHED WATCHING a docudrama he was reviewing (nutshelling it: a young transgender Jewish woman harrowingly escapes the Nazis a day before they invade her native Poland) when Juliana called.

"Are you sitting down?" she asked breathlessly. What, did she and Marjan go to the same school of bad-news delivery?

"What's wrong?"

"What? Nothing's wrong. You should be asking what's right," his agent said without giving him time to ask. "Paradise wants to talk to you again about your *Wedding Crashers* pitch."

"My what?" And wasn't that already a movie?

"Y'know, the remake you wanted to do. Of that old crime movie."

Oh. "*The Honeymoon Killers*?"

"Isn't that what I said?" Juliana was already clacking away on her keyboard; there was no point in correcting her.

"So the flagpole spoke?" Silence. Clacking. Didn't Juliana once say he was funny? "They said they were running it up the flagpole ..."

"Ah, right, okay. Well, they did, and you're going back in to pitch to Tremaine."

Tremaine Taylor was the studio's production head. He was a star player, hired away from HBO for big bucks and extra stripes when Paradise was formed. Wait till Jeremy told Zoë.

"But they want two takes," Juliana told him, "one as a film, one as a limited series. Can you do that?"

Jeremy said of course he could, though wasn't sure he had any real idea how to put together a series. But he'd figure it out. He was jumping into the deep end, and he was going to fucking swim.

"And by the way, it's tomorrow at 11," Juliana casually informed him, "so better get to work." That was an understatement.

Jeremy pulled the better part of an all-nighter to prepare. He expanded his outline for a feature redo of the strange tale of Martha Beck and Raymond Fernandez's 1940s murder spree, and reconfigured the sensational story for a potential six-part limited series: a two-hour pilot followed by five one-hour episodes. Working off the original movie, a copy of which he had on DVD (thank you, Criterion Collection), it broke down fairly naturally into those half-dozen chapters. But would it be as persuasive in the morning when sitting across from golden boy Tremaine Taylor? Jeremy fell asleep at his laptop before he could fully consider the answer.

He awoke with a jolt four hours later: the time on his open laptop screen read 7:57 a.m. His mouth felt cottony and his neck ached from dozing on the hard desktop. Brushing his teeth, it occurred to Jeremy that he had never finished that film review. Never finished? More like never started. He'd jumped right into working on the Paradise pitch after Juliana called and forgotten all about his *Times* deadline. He now had just a few hours to prep for his meeting, make himself presentable, and get to Paradise headquarters in Culver City (thirty minutes without traffic—and when does that happen in L.A.?) with enough breathing space to feel—or at least seem—relaxed by the time he was in the room pitching his heart out.

There was no possible way he could dash off a critique of that docudrama before he left home. He was getting a sinking sense of déjà vu about this blown deadline but, this time, decided to confront it head-on. Jeremy shot his editor a quick and confident email:

> Hi, Lucien—Hit with a surprise pitch meeting for this morning, had to cram last night, couldn't get to the review. Can write when I return, file by 4. Cool? Thanks for understanding.

He reread the note after he sent it and thought it sounded arrogant and dismissive—like throwing over your trusty old best friend for your shiny new one. It didn't sit well. But it was too late now; he needed to prioritize and hope for the best on all fronts.

Jeremy made a pot of coffee, then spent an hour at the kitchen table studying his notes for the pitch. He realized he officially knew way too much about a depraved pair of serial killers. As he was about to jump into the shower, he got a text from Cassie: "Call me when you can." Had she decided about his offer? He was desperate to know, but the answer would have to wait until after the meeting: he couldn't chance any more distractions. And that included thoughts about screwing up again with Lucien, who had yet to respond to Jeremy's email.

Tremaine was a warm, ebullient guy, way more charming than the coolly guarded underlings Jeremy had previously pitched to. He got a kick out of watching them kowtow to their boss in the same way he'd sucked up to them at the last meeting. It was the nature of the beast. He also liked that Tremaine was in his late forties, closer to Jeremy's age and, maybe, his worldview, than the others he'd met. It guaranteed nothing, but couldn't hurt.

Jeremy blocked out the rest of his life for the half hour he took to recount the gory details of the Lonely Hearts Killers: the obese Martha and smooth Raymond's ill-fated encounter via a classified ad, their unlikely romance, dastardly scheme to bilk money out of lonely widows, string of murders, arrest and circus-like trial, and back-to-back executions at New York's Sing Sing prison. Jeremy enjoyably embellished his account for Tremaine's benefit, mindful to highlight all the gripping real-life bits absent from the original movie that could easily flesh out a bigger film or deeper-dive TV series.

Jeremy had the group in the palm of his hand with a level of enthusiasm and strength he summoned from a place he barely knew existed. Despite the barrage of visceral and visual gold he spun out in Tremaine's sleek, sizable office, one obscure factoid brought the pitch home: none other than the iconic Martin Scorsese was the original director of the low-budget *The Honeymoon Killers* (it was his second feature film) until he was fired after a week or so for working too slowly. It left the quartet of Paradise execs, including Tremaine, slack-jawed, and gave the more than fifty-year-old movie—and its stranger-than-fiction story—instant cred. Jeremy laughed to himself: he may not be the world's greatest writer but he knew his movie trivia, and it was serving him astoundingly well.

Tremaine applauded when Jeremy finished, and his team instantly hopped to and copied their boss's response. (He came off lively and sincere, the others like eager sock puppets, but it was a hugely memorable moment.) The pitch, as they say, sold in the room—the holy grail of screenwriter experiences—with Tremaine pronouncing "Let's make a movie!" mere seconds after the applause died down. The stars aligned for Jeremy. He couldn't fucking believe it.

Neither could Juliana when he called her from his car after the meeting. She still mangled the project's title, but less so than the last time. (She somehow landed on "The Wedding Killers.") She could call it "Meatballs" for all Jeremy cared, as long as she cut him a great deal, which she assured him she would. He could have flown home without a car.

It was 12:30 by the time Jeremy arrived at the house; there was a voicemail waiting on his cell that he'd missed in all the excitement. It was from Lucien: luckily for Jeremy, the opening date of the film he'd been assigned had just been pushed back a week, so he had plenty of time to file his review. But it would have to be his last.

Lucien was making a decision for Jeremy: "I know you enjoy reviewing for us, and you're a fine critic," he said in his message. "But you have a bigger career now, and you have to focus on that. Neither of us needs to be stressed by your workload. This is your shot, friend, please take it. I'll be rooting for you."

Jeremy realized he was holding on to his past, and he needed to let go. As Lucien said, it wasn't fair to either of them. Maybe he never should have gone back to reviewing, but it had been such a part of Jeremy's identity for so many years that he hadn't been ready to give it up. Perhaps the same way that part of him hadn't been ready to give up Cassie—until he finally was. And Annabelle hadn't been ready to give up Gil or their house.

Sometimes you have to be pushed to make the right decision and move yourself forward. Other times it happens naturally. But occasionally, the two things happen at once. That day, it all made more sense to Jeremy than ever.

He wrote Lucien back, agreeing and thanking him for the second chance. He said he'd send in his last piece shortly and hoped they could stay in touch. It was confirmed: Lucien was more of a mensch than Jeremy gave him credit for. Maybe one day someone would say the same about him. He could do worse.

CHAPTER
39

JEREMY CALLED CASSIE back, buoyed by the morning's victory yet also bracing for her response. But it turned out to be a day of unexpected pleasures. She accepted his terms to pay off her half of Chez Lerner; her lawyer would share the details with Arvin Box, and they could finalize their divorce settlement. The only caveat: the house would remain in both their names until she was entirely reimbursed—just in case.

"I can't thank you enough, Cassie," Jeremy said as he stared out the kitchen window at the overgrown backyard. He imagined trimming everything back, planting a row of citrus trees, maybe a vegetable garden. So many new possibilities.

"If it makes your life better or easier, I owe you at least that," she answered. "Consider it my personal mea culpa."

"It wasn't all your fault, you know." It came out like a joke, but he meant it. If there was some responsibility to be taken, he would finally take it. The truth might hurt, but it also did set you free. It wasn't just a cliché, not in this case.

"We rose together—we fell together. I just took action," said Cassie.

Jeremy turned from the window and looked around the sunny kitchen that he and Cassie once shared. "You know what? I'm glad you did. And I mean that in a good way."

"Me, too," agreed the pretty girl with the ponytail who'd once stolen Jeremy's heart.

Jeremy hung up feeling elated yet wistful. All he wanted to do was find Annabelle and tell her the good news. To see her beautiful dark eyes and sweet smile and hold her so close that he would feel her heartbeat—and she feel his. The more he tried not to think about her, the more he missed her. Keeping his emotions in check was not the answer. It never was.

He showered, shaved, put on his nice pitch-meeting Levis, a pressed button-down shirt, and a new pair of navy suede Pumas he impulse-bought when a Zappos ad popped up on his laptop. Jeremy then got in his car and sped off, mapping out in his head the stops he'd need to make before reaching his final destination.

JEREMY PULLED UP in front of Annabelle's house around 6:00 p.m. as the autumn sky began to darken. He didn't know if she was even home. Her car wasn't in the driveway; maybe it was in the garage. But it didn't matter. He could wait. He could wait forever if he had to.

Holding a bouquet of red, white, and yellow roses the size of a mini-fridge, Jeremy walked up to her front door and rang the bell. There was no answer. He tried again in case she was in the shower or the backyard. Still no response. He sat on the front stoop, gazing out into the twilight as the occasional car drove past, none of which contained Annabelle. Until about twenty minutes later, when one did.

Jeremy stood as she turned into the driveway and parked. Annabelle stared at him through the passenger side window. For a moment, it didn't look as if she would leave the car, but she finally did. Jeremy went to meet her. She looked tentative, nervous, as she crossed onto her front lawn.

"These are for you," Jeremy said, handing her the flowers. She didn't take them at first, so Jeremy pressed them further toward her until she had no choice but to accept the mammoth bouquet. She said nothing, just looked curiously at Jeremy and inhaled the roses' heady scent.

"I need to talk to you about something," he told her, wishing he could have summoned grander or more poetic words. But his facility with dialogue escaped him, and he wanted to get to the point. He felt as anxious as a teenager on his first date.

"Oh, Jeremy," Annabelle said with a melancholy sigh as she smelled the bouquet again. She studied her eager, handsome suitor with his neat outfit, carefully combed hair, and earnest smile.

"Can we go inside?" he asked with a head tilt toward the house.

Annabelle considered him, considered the moment. Jeremy could see her resolve receding in front of his eyes. She turned and walked to the front door as she clutched the flowers. Jeremy followed, his heart thumping in time with his steps.

He sat on Annabelle's living room couch—more loveseat than sofa to accommodate the tightish space—as she hunted about for something large enough to contain the explosion of roses. She came back with two ceramic vases and split the bouquet between them, placing one on a copper and glass coffee table, the other on a birch accent table next to the loveseat, though it meant removing a lamp to make space. She stood there, lamp in hand, unsure where to put it.

"Sorry to make you redecorate your living room on such short notice," joked Jeremy, trying to cut the increasing tension. Annabelle crossed into the adjacent dining room, stuck the lamp on the antique farmhouse-style table, and returned to the living room. She eyed the open cushion next to Jeremy and sat in the bentwood rocker across from him instead.

"Thank you for the flowers, they're beautiful," she said stiffly, her customary sparkle in hiding. "You didn't need to do that."

Jeremy observed her as she rocked lightly in the chair, hands tightly gripping its narrow arms. She wore the same coral tunic blouse as the last time he had seen her, but the red ended there. White cotton sailor pants, low-heeled black strappy sandals, and a silver-and-turquoise amulet with matching bracelet rounded out her outfit. Her hair looked longer and wavier than usual; she was as adorably sexy to Jeremy as ever.

"How have you been?" he asked, realizing he should probably ease into the discussion.

She mulled his question, weighed her answer. "Better, I think." There was the faint hint of a smile. Jeremy could feel his shoulders relax. "Melinda and I have been doing some good work."

"Good. That's good," Jeremy said brightly. He waited to see if she was going to elaborate. She wasn't. "So—some exciting news: I sold a movie pitch to Paradise Pictures."

"You did? Oh, Jeremy, that's fantastic!" Her smile broadened. She looked more alive, more genuine.

"Yeah, it was kind of a long shot, but they went for it. Did we ever talk about the movie *The Honeymoon Killers*?"

"No, but it sounds familiar." She thought a minute. "Or maybe I'm confusing it with *Wedding Crashers*."

Jeremy burst into a grin. What were the chances?

"What?" Annabelle wanted to know. "Why is that so funny?"

"Just that one is about serial killers and one is about serial *crashers*." He didn't want to mention Juliana also mixed up the two; Annabelle always thought his agent sounded a little flaky.

"Well, whatever, I'm really happy for you." She was still smiling as she shifted in her seat, sensing a bigger agenda at work. "You deserve it."

"Anyway," he said, turning the three syllables into five, "I have something else for you."

Annabelle looked wary.

"No more flowers, I promise," Jeremy kidded. He dug into his jeans pocket, took out a koala bear keychain (a lucky find at a Hollywood Boulevard gift shop), and handed it to her.

Annabelle examined the keyring and the triangular brass key dangling from it. She seemed perplexed.

"Remember? You were wearing that koala bear T-shirt the day we met?" Jeremy sat up straighter in the loveseat. She gave a faraway nod. He gestured at the keychain, smiled. "I thought it'd be … appropriate."

Annabelle gazed at the key again, looked back up at Jeremy. "I don't understand."

He went to her and knelt by the rocker. He took a deep breath, reached for her hand, and held it in his. She didn't pull away, just watched him as if in a trance.

"This is the key to my house," Jeremy began. "I want you to have it. I want you to live there with me. I made a deal with Cassie, and I'm staying there. And I know you're still working things out, and I'm sorry if all the good between us became complicated and over-whelming. And even though I can't pretend to fully understand what you've been feeling, I know how I've been feeling, which is that I think of you all the time and miss you every minute, and I can't imagine what my life would be like without you. So please come be with me, and I swear to everything I know to be real and true that I will make you the happiest woman ever. And if you need time to decide, take as much as you need because I'm not going anywhere. And not to be presumptuous, but I have a kind of cool idea of what you can do with *this* house to preserve its place in your life *and* hon-or Gil's memory but only if you do decide you can leave it, which I realize may not be possible, but I'm hoping and praying it will. And I never pray so you have to know how incredibly important I think this is."

For a fleeting moment Jeremy thought he'd pass out. Instead, he gulped some air and, for some reason, sneezed. He also had a crick in his knee from bending like that and wasn't sure he could immediately stand. But he could, and the few cracking sounds were masked by the sound of Annabelle's noisy weeping as she rose from the chair and into his arms.

"I never thought you were crazy," Annabelle finally said when the tears stopped, "but now I'm thinking maybe you kind of are." She gazed at him and added, "You know, just a little. Just enough to be interesting."

Now Jeremy thought he'd start to cry, but he held it together. "I'll take that as a compliment then," he said with a hopeful smile.

"So … is that a yes?"

Annabelle clutched the koala keychain. "It's not a no," she said, which Jeremy took as a win for the time being and a definite sign of progress. As he said, he could wait.

EPILOGUE

IT WAS A year to the day of Jeremy's fiftieth birthday debacle, which also meant that he and Cassie had been separated for 364 days—though officially divorced since the day before Thanksgiving, which had made for a kind of strange if cathartic family holiday at Jeremy and Annabelle's house with Joyce, Matty and Gabe, and Cassie and her new boyfriend, the exceedingly tall and agreeable veterinarian Peter Piper. (Yep, the Piper parents picked that one for poor Peter; the pickled pepper jokes abound.)

Today, however, at the site of Jeremy's last birthday party, a different sort of gathering of family and friends was underway on a picture-perfect spring afternoon. The backyard, which Jeremy and Annabelle had replanted together (yes, a new grapefruit tree!) in the months since she rented her house to Matty and Gabe, now held dozens of padded white folding chairs split by a lane of red carpet and bounded by strands of yellow and white carnations. A floral canopy or, as at least half in attendance would have it, a chuppah, fronted the seating area that had slowly filled with well-dressed well-wishers as a string trio played gentle versions of familiar pop hits.

Jeremy stood tall and proud in a new royal blue suit and purple and gray tie; Annabelle wore a subdued ecru lace midi dress with silvery slingback heels. She looked like a million bucks; Jeremy maybe four hundred grand. Either way, they looked like they belonged together, which, luckily, seemed to be the prevailing wisdom.

Joyce, who turned eighty-five years young in March, stood near-by. She was fit and healthy again after months of careful eating and exercise, full of her usual high spirits and puckish charm. She was blissful to be among her loved ones on this special day, one that she would tell you she saw coming as early as last summer. She was leaving on a cruise to the Greek Islands the next week. Jeremy wasn't thrilled, but her doctor approved it, so what's a concerned son to say? "Opa!" seemed best.

Cassie and Peter Piper (Jeremy always called him by his full name) were standing with the others, holding hands and whispering sweet nothings—or maybe criticizing the outfits. Even if Peter towered over Cassie, they seemed to make sense together, and Jeremy was happy if she was happy because, really, what would the point of their breakup have been if she were still miserable?

Matty and Gabe made a dashing couple that day, to no one's surprise. They wore hip blazers—Matty's was a deep burgundy, Gabe's a shimmery gray paisley—with skinny black pants and Italian black leather sneakers. They were loving living in Annabelle's old house, keeping it as intact as possible while finding ways to make it their own. Matty went off and opened his own special events company (staff of one), while Gabe was starting chiropractic school in the fall. As Joyce exclaimed when she heard, "Finally, a doctor in the family!"

Jeremy cried like a baby when Rabbi Lynn Rosenberg rattled off the whole "in sickness and in health, till death do you part" bit because it always sounded so damn eternal when, really, whoever knew what the future had in store for any couple? Annabelle cried seeing Jeremy cry but maybe also because those words cut a little too close. And even though she'd made great strides in moving on from Gil (she and Melinda had called it quits the month before), he'd always be there—as he should be.

But everyone wept or sniffled or applauded when Rabbi Rosenberg said: "I now pronounce you husband and husband." Matty and Gabe stomped on the glass, kissed like they were on their third date, and got more than a little teary-eyed themselves but managed to keep beaming. That's what you call happiness.

Later, the string trio added a feisty bass guitar player and jammed out some foolproof party anthems that packed the makeshift dance floor. Jeremy, tipsy father of the groom that he was, merrily rotated among dance partners, but saved the last dance for his best girl, who had earlier dispensed with her silvery heels, let down her pinned-up waves, and was having such a joyful time you'd think it was her own wedding. Speaking of which:

"So when are we going to say 'I do' and file a joint tax return?" Jeremy asked with a sly smile, holding Annabelle close as the quartet played a lovely version of Eric Clapton's "Wonderful Tonight."

She raised an eyebrow. "Is that your idea of a romantic proposal?"

"The mushy ones haven't worked on you so far so I thought I'd cut to the chase." He surprised her with a dip and she whooped with delight.

Annabelle straightened up, landing eye to eye with Jeremy. "All I'll say is if I decide to marry anyone, I promise it'll be you." She smiled in that loopy way that melted Jeremy's heart every time.

"I'm going to keep asking, you know," he said as the song ended. "If you haven't noticed, I've become a very persistent person." He was joking, but they both knew there was a kernel of truth there. And that Jeremy would be the first to credit Annabelle for its existence.

As the other couples drifted off the dance floor, Jeremy and Annabelle stayed in their spot and shared a spectacular kiss beneath the canyon's burgeoning ceiling of stars.

It was the best birthday he'd had in a long, long time.

ACKNOWLEDGMENTS

IT MAY NOT seem so when you're in your head, sitting and writing a book alone day after day, but it really does take a village to help bring a novel to life and find its way out into the world. My joyous journey creating *The Last Birthday Party* is no exception and I have many people to thank for their love, support, generosity, insight, and inspiration along the way.

So let's name names—starting at the beginning.

My mother, Natalie, who instilled in me a love of books and movies and theatre and always fostered my creativity and individuality. I would not be who am I today without her integrity, guidance, friendship, and deep, abiding love. Mom, I think of you every day.

My father, Leonard, who, as a self-made man, taught me that if you don't do something yourself, it may never get done. He didn't realize he was talking about the life of a writer. Miss you, dad. Thanks for giving me so much good "material."

My sister, Lynn: cheerleader, ready ear, co-witness to family history, and dear friend. I've been so lucky to have you and am thankful for all we've shared over a lifetime, now including writing. Even if, when we were kids, you told me "they could send me back" until I was ten.

Bill: My life-mate, soul-mate, laugh-mate, and best friend. Thank you to the moon for all your love, kindness, patience, and unwavering belief in me every day—and through each step of my creative endeavors. Your input on this book, as always, was invaluable. You're my hero.

To my extended family members, including my nephews, nieces, cousins, and in-laws: I am so grateful to have you all in my life. You mean more to me than you can know.

To my Aunt Eppie, whose warmth, optimism, and lovely, lilting voice lives on in Joyce. You said "don't forget me" and I didn't.

I've been blessed with so many wonderful, longtime friends: you know who you are. You have provided me with so much love, care, camaraderie, fun, and great memories over the years. I'm beyond happy to share this achievement with you.

My many friends and compatriots at the Writers Guild of America West who bring sanity, perspective, humor, and a shared sense of purpose to this wild ride we've all undertaken—and could not live without. It's been an honor to be on the trip with each of you. Special thanks to Bruce, Cathryn, Susan, and Ken for sharing your unique wisdom about the book world.

To the terrific trio at Hadleigh House: Allison, Alisha, and Anna. It's an understatement to say that I couldn't have done this without you, but I will anyway. I thank you from the bottom of my heart for your amazing collaboration and support and I wish you endless success.

To my editor, Kate: I am in awe of how you helped trim and shape the book with such elegance, intuition, and precision. I know so much more now because of you and greatly appreciate your efforts.

To Amanda, who swept through the manuscript with her crack editing skills before it ever went out to the world and helped make me look like I actually knew what I was doing.

Kevin, my editor at the *L.A. Times*, who is the anti-Lucien, a dream to work with, and has an uncanny sense of which films to assign me. Keep those Holocaust docs coming, dude. And to the rest of the folks at the *Times* (Hi, Elena!) who've been such smart, encouraging, and considerate colleagues.

Thank you to David Dean Bottrell, Jennifer Dorr-Moon, Barbara Graustark, J. Todd Harris, Beverly Kopf, Mark Sarvas, Barbara

Speiser, and Mark Temple for your generous assistance. Did I say it takes a village?

And finally to the readers, without whom none of this would make much sense. I hope you've enjoyed Jeremy's twisty journey and have seen a bit of yourself in his life and those around him. And don't forget: you never know what's going to happen when you wake up every morning. Who knows? You might decide to write a book.

ABOUT GARY GOLDSTEIN

Gary Goldstein is an award-winning writer for film, TV, and the theatre with more than 30 produced screen and stage credits. The New York native and longtime L.A. resident has also been a contributing film reviewer and feature writer for the *Los Angeles Times* since 2007. *The Last Birthday Party* is Gary's first novel.

Visit him at GaryGoldsteinLA.com or follow Gary on Instagram and Twitter @GaryGoldsteinLA